BETTY BITES BACK

BETTY BITES BACK

STORIES TO SCARE THE PATRIARCHY

Edited by MINDY MCGINNIS
Edited by DEMITRIA LUNETTA
Edited by KATE KARYUS QUINN

Betty Bites Back

edited by Mindy McGinnis, Demitria Lunetta, and Kate Karyus Quinn

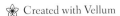

For the quiet, bookish, and rebellious types—this one's for you.

INTRODUCTION

The news in the past few years has been full of women—nasty women, angry women, persistent women, women in pink knitted hats. There's been pushback, but there's also been overwhelming support. This collection of sixteen tales comes from writers who picked up their pens to add their words to the resistance.

You're helping, too. By buying this book—and reading it—you're allowing our words to find a space inside your head, to plant a seed, and to offer a different perspective. We hope you enjoy these tales, but more importantly, we hope they make you think about the position of women in the world, how our everyday lives are different from a man's—and even different from each other's experiences.

We all have our own tale. A cat-call. An unwanted touch. A joke at the water cooler... . Other stories make the news. But we're making our own headlines now, with marches, demonstrations and—in our own small way—this book.

Thank you for joining us as we bite back.

Mindy McGinnis, Demitria Lunetta, and Kate Karyus Quinn

ACKNOWLEDGMENTS

Thank you to all our Kickstarter backers who have made Betty Bites Back possible, especially Teri Comber. Your support is greatly appreciated!

Thank you Lori Goldstein for your keen eye on copy edits.

Thank you to Alex Lunetta for all of your hard work on the cover and many revisions.

VAGINA DENTATA

MINDY MCGINNIS

W hen asked why she scheduled an appointment with a plastic surgeon, Taylor says that she would like to have a ring of teeth implanted in her vagina.

"They need to be retractable," she goes on, pulling a rough sketch from her purse.

The physician's assistant's eyes linger on the purse a second before going to the drawing. She's accustomed to shiny hand-bags with tight stitches in this office, designer brand names boldly displayed. The shapeless denim thing at this girl's side seems handmade.

Her glance slides from the purse to Taylor's sketch, then quickly away. Her face remains pleasant, but her fingers stumble for a moment on the keyboard of the tablet she holds frozen in place, inadvertently adding a line of lowercase r's to the patient notes.

"And the reason for this change?" Her tone is still perfectly in line with her controlled, professional face as she swiftly deletes the string of r's.

"Evolution has failed me," Taylor says. "Mollusks have shells. Blowfish expand. There's no stinger in my honey pot."

The PA has no option to tick in her list of boxes that fits this response. She chooses "other" and watches the cursor blink as it waits for her to elaborate.

"The last place turned me away," Taylor says.

"The last place?"

"Up on Central. They requested a psychological evaluation." She folds and refolds her drawing to create a sharp corner, then uses it to clean under her fingernails. "I didn't ask them for the teeth, though."

"What did you request?" the PA asks, tablet now resting on her lap.

"I asked if they could make my vagina detachable, like a prosthetic arm or a leg. I'd only have it on me when I needed it."

"Oh," the PA said, her usual stock phrases for intake meetings falling short at this one. She settles for, "I'm afraid that's not possible."

Taylor winces, having pushed the edge of the sketch too far under her nail. A bright dot of blood forms. "That's what they told me," she says, words slipping out from around her thumb as she sucks at the wound. "So I came up with the teeth."

The PA sets aside her tablet, screen now black from inactivity. She asks to see Taylor's drawing again and opens it, better prepared now.

"Retractable," the PA repeats, almost to herself.

"Like a cat's claws," Taylor says. "Claws for my pussy."

The PA's eyebrows come together at the girl's crassness. The dirty corner Taylor had used to clean under her fingernails rests at the top, a warning flag that she should shuffle this girl along, like the office on Central had.

"Can't we have one feline analogy on our side?" Taylor asks. "Pussy. Cathouse. Catcalls. Sex kitten."

"Cougar," the PA adds, eyes still on the sketch, mind following the possibilities as well as Taylor's words.

"Nice one."

The PA rests with the drawing a moment, still thinking. "Assuming you did get . . . vagina teeth, how would you use them?"

"I'd wear whatever I want. Go where I please. Stay out late. Get drunk. Anybody fucks with me, I do a Kegel." Taylor squeezes her fist tight to illustrate and makes a *scrich* noise that sends spit across the drawing.

The PA does not wipe it away. "You do realize you could be charged with assault. What would you do then?"

"I'd say he was asking for it."

A snort escapes the PA, and she considers the pencil drawing, smudged from Taylor's anxious fingers, the spray from her spit magnifying a sharpened canine.

"Are you going to recommend a psych eval, too?" Taylor asks.

The PA's tongue plays at the edge of her mouth, touching a small white scar, put there by another's incisor. "I'm not."

MINDY MCGINNIS is an Edgar Award-winning author who writes across multiple genres including post-apocalyptic, mystery, thriller, historical, fantasy, and contemporary. HERO-INE, a story of the opioid epidemic in the heartland and how far one female athlete will go for her team, releases in March of 2019 from Katherine Tegen Books.

One last bite from Mindy McGinnis...

The idea of a woman's vagina being ringed with teeth is one that occurs throughout folklore and myth in various cultures. In 2005, Sonnet Ehlers, a South African medical technician, invented an anti-rape device she called Rapex: a female condom lined with teeth. Although the device never made it to market, it got a lot of attention online - including mine - bringing me to consider what an implant version of this would look like, and who would want one.

My favorite piece of feminist literature is the poem NO IMME-DIATE CAUSE by Ntozake Shange.

YOU WAKE WITH HIM BESIDE YOU

CORI MCCARTHY

you wake with Him beside you
murder on your mind, cold pressing,
He's stolen the blankets, rolled them over
    Himself
even the fitted sheets are ripped from the
    corners
like a light, quick, slap to the face

asleep, He's a monster of inactivity,
a monstrous wall of a back, taking up most of
    the bed
and the room, and the house, and your life
and the truly monstrous part is that He never
    notices

no one ever taught Him to notice

you elbow His stiff snores,
creak the floorboards,
enter the stale air of the kitchen

the house is your shell, and it's too small
you tap the hermit crab tank once, twice,
but no one is skittering around, and if they die
you won't know until you smell the aftermath
they've been hiding for so long

your towel is gone in the bathroom,
He left your shampoo open, now full of water
you ask the cruel gods how this is better than
    your parents' house

you find your towel on the bathroom floor
behind the door
covered in the hair He shucked from His face
without a mind of where it would go, stick to,
    muck up

and back in the kitchen, well, it is clean,
because you woke in the night
to His whiskey snores and loaded the
    dishwasher
and ran it with a daydream of running away
to anywhere, nowhere,

you wonder about lee, at school, with the flirting
    smile
you wonder about moving back home
you wonder about the Titanic, was it so bad?

you're drunk on melancholy, and it's not even
    eight AM.

He's up as you're off for school,

He still thinks His smile works wonders
when all it works is the breakup clock inside,
    churning, whirling,

striking

no more, you say, no more

He swears and acts like He's not awake enough
    for this
you point out that it's a reoccurring problem

He calls you sad
He calls you menstrual
He doesn't use that word
no one taught cis boys the real words

so He tries emotional, crazy, and the coup de
    grâce, your mother
He switches channels to half-cracked apologies
He calls you all the girls in the world, wanting
    attention

you don't call him all the boys in the world, half-
    finished humans
you slip up your hood and leave, into the
    vacancy of a snowstorm

that shades into the white of bleached sheets

you wake with Him beside you
leaving on your mind, nothing new
He's left your alarm running,

you have to get up; He gets to sleep
you have to get up; you have to be pretty
He gets to sleep; His pretty is you

was it a nightmare then?
a handsome daydream that you escaped?
a sign, maybe?

you shake Him up and ask if you left yesterday
sleepily He says He loves you, because that
    worked
once upon a time
and He's never thought to change his tactics

the toilet seat is up in the bathroom, and two of
    the three
vanity bulbs have blown, the glass a charred
    look to them
which seems to whisper fire,
fire,
fire

burn this whole home down
you remember your mom's parting jab of
now you're His problem

married at eighteen, love wasn't on the list

escape was. still is.
the water is cold, cold in the shower
leaving a raw smell to your skin like being
    outside too long
as a child, in the winter storms, never wanting

to go in the house to the other kinds of cold

you look in the mirror and find that you are
        ancient
in feelings these days

you are wronged by yourself
and no one knows

how hard is it to leave

in the kitchen, He is making eggs, three pans
        dirtied,
the sink so full nothing can be rinsed
which will be your job because He deigned
        to cook
even though all the other times you cook and
        clean

is this the fifties? you yelled just last week
and He laughed

He gives you eggs and you give Him an
        ultimatum
You leave or me. And He points to the door, and
        says,
it's His house, even though the lease is in both of
        your names
and it's not a house so much as an apartment
        straight from hell

and then He's mad, mad enough to glare
and He'd never hit you, but His words

volley curses and insults that remind you
    of mom
and tune you out, so far out that all you hear is
    static

when you come to, you're watching his favorite
    movie
for the seventieth time with whiskey in the air
and you partake because it means
something less than anything else

you wake with him beside you
fear on your mind, nothing new,
your alarm hasn't even chimed and you're out
    of bed
you pray to the less cruel gods that he sleeps
    sleeps sleeps
that your day can be yours before he takes it
like all the air
and the words
and the food

you clean the bathroom instead of yourself
it feels a little better to rub the tile shiny,
breathing bleach
you shower in the heat, too hot,
rubbing off whatever clung to you
in the night

you make the eggs this morning,
washing each utensil
after it's used, washed, dried, put away
the kitchen is spotless,

although the sink reeks of discarded whiskey
and he burps his way in shirtless and smiles to
    rub his chest
he still thinks you think he's handsome. no, he
    assumes it.
like everything else.

you give him a small smile. let him believe
    anything he wants.
you're not here anymore. you left so long ago,
    you're a shell

you're having a bad week, he says. you'll get
    over it.
and even though love wasn't ever on the list,
you wonder if it was ever in his mind at all
you say okay. and he says let's get out tonight
and you say yes

outside the door, a snowstorm nearly stops
    everything
but you clear the car and the drive, and he gives
    you a peck of appreciation
he's never so creepy as when he wears a mask of
    caring
and combs his hair

at the movies, the little-kid-toy-turned-adult
    movie,
the ones that make him feel like
a king of the world little white boy
the same ones he doesn't like because they're
    not "the original"

and the only thing he's king of anymore is you
but then you're not alone

there in the dark cinema audience,
the unblinking eyes of
a hundred boyfriends turned ruler of a hellish
    apartment
a hundred girlfriends turned into secret, failed
    murderers
and if you leave him, you'll just be set up with
    the next one

they are endless

brand new shells for overgrown hermit crabs
a generation of love interests fat with privilege
charmingly incompetent

scuttling over to your life,
climbing inside
pushing at your body
taking your space
air
words
life

and when you get home
there's a smell in the living room like a few
million hermit crabs have started to die

you wake with him beside you
a hundred thousand hermit crabs
have escaped their shells in the night

searching you out
falling from the ceiling,
the lights,
crawling out
of all the spaces in your mind, your goddamn
    mouth,
your eyes pierced by a few thousand small claws
scurrying inside

taking, stealing, ripping pieces of you with a
    thousand
tiny, insignificant motions

the towel
the eggs
the past
the future
the day
its misery
the night
and you
taken
over

and over

at first you're killing them with your fists
your feet
your rage
an explosion
of
no
more

he doesn't wake up so snug as a bug
the crabs fall off him; they only want you
they want all of you
everything
every minute

and you light the entire house on fire
and accidentally burn down
the world

you wake with him beside You
something new

You jump over him to shut off Your alarm,
wake him with a grunt and groan
pack Your bag
write a goodbye note
flush all the dead crabs
and leave through a sunrise so white
it feels like snow

CORI MCCARTHY studied poetry and screenwriting before earning an MFA in Writing at Vermont College of Fine Arts. They are the author of four acclaimed young adult novels, including BREAKING SKY, YOU WERE HERE, and the feminist romcom, NOW A MAJOR MOTION PICTURE. Their forthcoming space fantasy, ONCE & FUTURE is a gender bent retelling of the Arthurian canon, co-written with their soulmate, YA author Amy Rose Capetta. Like many of their characters, Cori is a member of the LGBTQ+ community. They live in Vermont. CoriMcCarthy.com

One last bite from Cori McCarthy...

My niece came home from preschool with a bag of beautiful shells she collected during recess. It was a gift for her mom, but when her mom pulled the bag out of her backpack, the plastic was a teaming mess of harsh, sharp legs and angry kidnapped hermit crabs. And this, well, reminded me of my ex. And how cis men too often crawl into their partner's lives as if they own it...

For further reads, check out the Amelia Bloomer Project, an annual booklist of recommended feminist literature for birth through eighteen, affiliated with the American Library Association.

THE WEIGHT OF IRON

AMANDA SUN

Dusk is falling, and the silver cuffs are slick with blood, but Galen's wrist is nearly free.

She struggled at the beginning, the sharp pain when she'd tugged against the chains deterring her from breaking free. But as the sky stained crimson and orange, as the cold and the wind swirled around her, as the decaying forest in front of her lay silent, hungry, waiting, she had grown numb to the fear of pain.

With pins and needles stinging her fingers as the blood drained from her arms, shackled from above, she began to tug once more. Desperate to escape, if only for a moment of relief.

Lysander hasn't come. She wondered if he would. But it's too dark now. The chilling breeze feels like the very gasp of the forest's own maw, as though it opens to unleash what is waiting inside to consume her.

Behind her, shallow hills rise and fall like breaths of green, leading back toward the village. They'll be lighting candles now, singing songs in the temple while they huddle in a circle, the doors and windows barred, their voices drowning out the screams. Her screams. If she cannot escape, Galen is determined to die silently, but looking into the mist of the black forest, she isn't sure how long her resolve will hold.

The hilt of the iron sword driven into the ground beside her gleams as it catches the falling light. She tugs against the slippery warmth of her own blood, moans through the wave of pain like a woman in labor. The agony shoots through her arms, her shoulders, her back. She understands now how wolves can chew through their own legs to free themselves from winter traps.

She should've been safe from the Penance for another year. No one's names are drawn under the age of eighteen unless they commit an act of corruption. But Galen has.

She's guilty of witchcraft, and condemned to die.

Her parents died years ago. She lives alone on the hill, about half an hour walk from the temple. Her mother was a governess, her father a professor before he fell too ill to continue and they moved to the village for his health to recover. Then a plague swept through, taking half the village and all of Galen's world. Galen had loved life in their little house, filled with books and discussions and ideas.

She sleeps in the attic now, with her telescope and star charts and thick woolen blankets. She loves the large windows that flood with moonlight and face away from the village, away from the forest where the Arbiter creeps in to feast on Penitents. She keeps geese and dogs, and a garden full of herbs and spices from faraway lands. She reads every book she can afford from the merchants who stop on their way through to the bigger cities.

Just a few months ago she was in the tavern, a new tome in hand, when it started. The leering. The drunken men calling out to her from the back of the inn. She looked up at the tavern keeper's wife, who shrugged as she dried the inside of a pitcher with a towel. "They're just being lads," she said. "Ignore them. It's harmless."

But Galen went home and let down the hems of her dresses by candlelight, pricking her finger so many times the threads turned crimson with blood. She unpacked her mother's old-fashioned shawls that felt scratchy and heavy on her bare shoulders. She wore her hair up in a tight bun like an old governess, and when the pretty floral fabrics came in at the weaver's, she instead favored burgundy and navy, wrapping every hint of femininity in cloaks as black as midnight.

"You're wasting your youth and beauty," the weaver said, shaking her head. "I'd give anything to look like that again." But Galen felt safe veiled in darkness. She could vanish like a crow in the night, and her problems would dissipate like mist scattered amongst the grassy hills.

The last of the light winks out from the blade of the iron sword plunged into the earth beside her. A sapphire jewel on the end of the hilt dims to a deathly gray. The chains rattle as she pulls against the cuffs, the warm blood and stabs of pain trailing down her arm.

She'd been selling goose meat and eggs to Acton, the butcher. He'd bent down to inspect them, and when he stood up, he'd slid his hand right up her leg and into her skirts. She'd frozen like a deer, as if the world were sliding sideways. No darkness would hide her; no shawls would envelop her. She didn't know what to say after; she needed him to buy her wares.

She asked Lysander to walk her home after that, but whenever he was working late at the blacksmith's she had to walk alone, every raven caw and breeze sending her heart fluttering against the bars of her rib cage. One day she swore Acton followed her halfway home. She didn't dare look behind her, and she walked so quickly that she tripped and hurt her ankle. She thought she heard a laugh. When her home was in sight, she sprinted for the door, shoving the bolt hard into place. But her once beloved little house turned into a prison on the hill. She couldn't sleep at night, listening, waiting.

In the end, it was the innkeeper who locked her in the stable, holding a hand over her muffled screams. His wife walked in to fill the milk pitcher. Galen still remembers the sound of the pitcher shattering on the stable floor, blue-and-white porcelain shards scattering in feathery straw. She clutched her loose bodice to her skin, burning with shame. And although she shook with fear, she cried tears of relief, because he had been stopped. His wife knew. Galen was safe now.

But safety was the mist that swirled away, gusted by the breeze from the Arbiter's dark forest. Galen was accused of witchcraft, of cursing and charming the men of the village. The wife appeared as a witness, her cheeks flushed scarlet as she insisted Galen had bewitched her husband. The husband and wife sat together, clutching hands, two halves of a beating heart, as a village elder listed the evidence. *She has a garden full of strange herbs that she grows for her potions. She has a room full of candles and star charts, a window that floods with moonlight for her spells. She wears black, scorns other women, lives alone and unmarried when she should be wearing florals and engaging in sweet, innocent flirtation. She tried the same thing on Acton in the square. Don't you think it's strange that the plague took both of her parents and not her? If we ignore this corruption, she will condemn our village to burn under the Arbiter's judgement. The time for Penance is near. It's a blessing; her penitence will save our righteous ones.*

She waited for Lysander to save her, to speak up. He tried— once. They patted him on the shoulder, assured him of his bewitchment, and said that now he was free of her curse. After that, he disappeared into the shadows, his eyes filled with fear and doubt.

He feared the Arbiter, of being chained alongside her.

Now the moon rises, but its light barely touches the forest, as if it too is afraid to tread there. The wind is a stale breath, the forest silent as death. She wonders if Lysander will be at the temple while they light the candles and drown out her screams.

She pulls again, and the skin on her wrist peels away, her hand slipping finally, horribly, through the silver cuff. She stares at her palm, strange and bloody, as if it's not hers at all. The relief instantly floods down her arm, warm and aching. But her other hand is still caught, and the darkness has fallen around her.

She hears a sound. A whisper? A footstep?

She looks at the iron sword. Its holy blade is said to burn the Arbiter. If the one chosen for the annual Penance is truly innocent, the sword will save her.

It has never been unsheathed from the earth by any who have been sacrificed. The village elders say it's because none were worthy, none innocent of corruption.

Lysander isn't coming. But death is.

Galen strains against the remaining silver cuff, reaching her free bloodied hand for the sword. It's just out of reach. She tries again, her slippery fingers nearly touching the sapphire jewel on the end of the hilt. Her chains creak as she fights for just a hair's breadth more, just enough for her fingertips to slide across the jewel. Her blood drips down the hilt; the sapphire jewel slices her finger open.

She cries out, tears spilling down her face as she struggles toward the blade.

She hears the sound again, like a heavy rasping from the woods. She isn't imagining it. She's almost certain.

They say the Arbiter is as big as a barn, that he is shadow and corruption made flesh. He is condemned to writhe upon the earth like a maggot, and he is hollow like a tunnel, filled with razor-sharp teeth of every size. He feasts on corruption, devouring the Penitents and carving their immorality up into his newly shed skin.

How long does it take to be digested? How many days wandering in agony as he grinds her into his stomach? Will she live on as part of the Arbiter, her soul forever bound to his, devouring living souls over and over until she forgets what it was to be one?

She hears a long, heavy noise, like a sled piled with metal blades dragged across broken branches and moldering ferns. She can see its pulsing outer skin, hear the blades dangling inside the shadowy jaws like a brutal razor labyrinth, sharpening against each other with every heave forward. Teeth scraping together, awaiting their meal.

He's coming.

She strains for the sword again. Her fingertips encircle the hilt, but they slip under the stream of blood running upward from her wrist. She can barely see through her tears in the darkness. "Please," she whispers, tugging hard at the restraint on her other wrist.

Her footing slips, and she swings backward in an arc. The motion yanks her shoulder sideways, and she cries out. The breathing is louder, the sliding sound whistling through the forest.

She looks again.

The bare trees reach their dead branches up to the sky. She thinks she sees a glint of light in the forest—and another. She can see the shape of him now, the wriggling of an enormous larva coming to devour her. She weeps openly with fear.

A pale blue light glows in the forest, pulsing larger with each movement. Moonlight on razor teeth? No. A light as if the moon itself was inside the forest, emanating out. The colossal tunnel of pulsing blades dissipates, as if it had never been there.

A figure steps out from the woods. It's not a giant maggot lined with jagged teeth. It's . . . almost human.

Darkness swirls around him as if he's half shadow, made of lines of charcoal that trail into nothing. He moves slowly, the sketched shadows swirling around him like a cape of black mist. His eyes have no whites to them but are flooded black as night. He has two horns of twigs and leaves, twisting and entangling in his long black hair, but Galen can't tell whether they are truly horns or some sort of invasive plant life that has grown from a too long stillness. Two large wings droop over his shoulders, as if the weight is more than he can bear. They, like the rest of him, are sharp and angular, but she can see right through them like dragonfly wings, the world distorted and swirling in their windows. The edges are thick black and dripping, as if with ink or blood. The black liquid curls down his wings and onto his shoulders, his jerkin and his arms, leaving trails that pool into the cloudy shadows around him.

As he steps closer, she sees that the outlines of the wings and the rest of him aren't black at all but . . . void. They gleam every now and then with pinpricks of white and blue and yellow. It's . . . it's like her star charts. Her fear is briefly set aside by fascination. If she reached into the blackness, it's as though her fingertips would roam the galaxies above.

She sees the glint of a pair of swords, one dangling on either side of his hips. There is another pair of blades, crossed in sheaths on his back like an X. Each is a different shape, jagged or curved, straight and plain, or broad and bejeweled in black and silver.

His alien black eyes stare unblinking as he approaches. The hem of his shadows ebbs against her bare foot like a wave; it's cold as ice.

At first, Galen cannot speak. Her throat is parched from a

day of struggling. But she finds her words, and they come out in a hoarse whisper. "Are . . . are you the Arbiter?"

He makes no reply, shows no emotion. There is a sort of silence that she has never heard before. Not a quietness, but as if sound itself is being sucked away. His outline dances with planets and stars, but devours even the faint breeze that curls around it.

He reaches his angular fingers for the jagged sword at his left hip. He draws it slowly, the metal singing against the sheath. The blade is black, its surface alive with swirling stars. The edge is metal teeth, ready to take her life as painfully as it can.

Fear rears up within her. She looks away from the figure, again reaching for the holy sword embedded in the earth. She pulls with every ounce she has left. She forgets her promise; she screams as the skin on her wrist peels under the sharp edge of the cuff, as her free fingers clench as tight as they can around the jagged sapphire on the hilt of the sword.

The Arbiter lowers his blade back into its sheath, instead reaching easily for the sword Galen strains for in desperation. He curls his fingers around the hilt and pulls it from the earth; soil crumbles along its iron blade as it rises up.

The sacred sword does not burn him. It does not destroy him. It is lifeless in his grip, an empty promise of salvation.

He raises it high above his head as Galen cries out. She wants to be brave, but every ounce of her life longs to be lived. She will not die like this. She will not let her soul, the one broken thing she has left, be taken by this man.

Pain shoots through her shoulder as he cuts through the chains and she drops to the ground. Warm blood rushes through her veins as she pulls her arm toward herself and cradles her bloody wrist, the silver cuff sliding to her palm.

The Arbiter stands above her, holy sword in hand. He

plunges it slowly back into the earth, reaching an open palm to her as she shakes.

When he speaks, she hears his deep voice, but also multiple voices at once—female, male, accents she can't recognize, and one in another, curling language—all in different tones. But the result is not chaotic. It's overwhelming, larger than she can imagine. It's boundless, transcendent.

"I understand you're a witch," the Arbiter says in his chorus of voices. "We need your help."

IT TAKES GALEN SEVERAL MINUTES TO STOP SHAKING, AND even then she shivers in the cool nighttime breeze. If he's going to take her life, he isn't making the motions now. Is it some kind of trick? A test, perhaps. If a witch is useful to him, denying it will be her death. But if he's looking for a pledge of innocence, admitting to corruption will doom her as well.

He stands silently as she tears strips from her Penitent robe and wraps them around her bloodied wrists, holding the end in her teeth as she pulls the fabric tight. If he feels sympathy, scorn, hunger, patience, he doesn't show it. She almost wonders if time has stopped, if she's gone mad and created this entire fantasy out of thin air. Perhaps she is already in the Arbiter's jaw, half carved up by the jagged blades of his razor teeth.

She pushes the silver cuff, now free from its chain, up her left arm to secure the fabric bandage around the wound. At last the Arbiter moves, and the motion sends panic tingling up Galen's spine. She's not sure how far she can run on her wobbly legs, aching from being chained in one position all day. But he shakes his head slightly, shadows rippling through the air. Shooting stars and pinprick planets spin across the void of the dripping liquid down his arms. She thinks, senses, hopes, he isn't going to hurt her.

He reaches for the sword on his right hip. The blade is blinding, as though the sword was made from the sun itself. Even with her arm raised, it sears through her closed eyelids.

She feels a cold touch on her arm and tries to open her eyes to look.

The Arbiter's slender fingers pull the cuff away from her skin. He touches the shining blade to the silver, and its edge melts instantly, pooling on the earth below in a shimmering puddle. He sheaths the sword, and the burning edges of the silver cool as his shadow laps against them. He releases her, and Galen takes the broken cuff off her arm, her eyes wide. She is full of awe, of fascination, of terror.

"Who are you?" she whispers.

He does not reply.

She looks at the sacred sword, plunged at an angle into the earth. "I don't understand. It didn't burn you."

"Why should iron burn me? It is life. Survival."

"But the sword is holy," she says. "It's pure."

"It is a lump of ore, melted and beaten to a point."

She doesn't know what to say. There are stories, beliefs, legends whispered throughout her childhood of iron burning the ones like him. The temple doors are set in iron as protection. The village has iron gates.

Looking at him now, in all his power and glory, in his shadow and star systems swirling, she can't imagine anything hurting him at all.

"There is little time," he says. "If you are a witch, let us depart."

She can't remember standing, but she must have, because suddenly she is at the edge of the dead forest with him, the long dry branches scratching against her bare arms. A soft blue light is still glowing in the forest, filling it with strange shadows.

"I can't," she says. "It's . . . it's in there. The demon belly filled with teeth."

The Arbiter does not answer. He only reaches out his cold, slender fingers. "You must hold onto me. So you are not lost."

"You don't understand. He's coming for me."

"There is nothing more fearful in there than that what you have already lived." His black eyes look down at his outstretched hand. "He will not appear. I have already come for you."

"Is he one of you? The monster of corruption that eats the Penitents?"

The Arbiter tilts his head to the side. Galen thinks she glances Mercury as it slides across the width of his arm. "It was created from the corruption of the village. You may consider it a reflection, a facet. One of our names. One of our voices."

Galen goes ice cold. "Is it . . . is it you?"

"We are given many facets. Arbiter. Unseelie. Auditor. Transients."

Unseelie. She's heard this one before. "You're a fairy?"

But she can't imagine him dancing to a merry fiddle, playing tricks on wandering merchants and braiding flowers into a sleeping maiden's hair. He's more like a demon, but grander, more terrifying, with the cosmos dancing on his skin.

He lifts his hand toward her again.

Behind her lies death. If she returns, the villagers will call her ghost or witch or worse. No one has ever returned, ever been spared. Would they believe her claim of innocence?

The wind gusts gently from inside the forest, and her hair slips about her shoulders in the cool of night. She takes his hand.

He reaches for one of the swords on his back. "No matter what you see or hear, you must not let go."

The goose pimples rise on Galen's neck and down her arms. The black of the Arbiter's wings trails down his arms and onto her fingers. It's cool and wispy, the way she imagines starlight might feel.

The Arbiter slowly pulls the sword from its sheath. She expects the sound of metal scraping metal, but instead she hears a whisper, as if the sword is speaking. It takes a moment to realize it isn't a whisper at all but a tearing sound, like paper being ripped from top to bottom. Along the edge of the blade, the forest seems to pucker and ripple. Then there is a sound like the plucking of strings, and the world comes undone at the seams. The forest flutters open like a split sail, stardust and endless sky opening between them. The Arbiter cuts careful and straight, like a surgeon, through the fabric of reality. And then, holding Galen's hand, he steps in.

At once she feels the cool of night slip away, and the air around her feels like nothing at all: no warmth, no chill, no breeze. Galaxies drift above her and stars below, strange lights and shadows swirling like clouds in every direction until she isn't quite sure what's up and what's down. Behind them, the last vision of forest seals shut, the two halves snapping together. She holds on tightly to the Arbiter's hand, the only constant she has.

The clusters of stars and shadows and light soon shape into a pulsing tunnel that she and the Arbiter walk through. There is no absence of sound here; her ears flood with the cacophony. Voices—some like the Arbiter's—animal cries, sounds she can't interpret or recognize, they all echo in the swirling passageway around her. She hears someone crying for her mother, another singing a tribal chant. When she hears shouts for help, she hesitates, but the Arbiter coaxes her forward.

"There are many doors," he says. "If you let go of my hand, I may lose you."

An arm thrusts through the tunnel, reaching. Its fingers curl into Galen's hair and pull.

"Please," a woman's voice says. "Help me. Don't leave me!"

The fingers pull until Galen's scalp aches. She starts to lose her grip on the Arbiter's hand. He feels her hand coming loose, whirls around to grab the alien hand by its wrist and force it back into the swirling stardust.

"She needs help," Galen says, alarmed.

"A siren," Arbiter says. "There are many creatures that scuttle between universes in search of sustenance. You were her prey; nothing more."

A siren, Galen thinks. Did she want to drown her in starlight? She holds onto the Arbiter's hand like a sailor tied to the mast.

"The voice she mimicked shouted out five thousand years ago, in another universe," he says. "Reality is not bound by your laws here."

A tunnel through worlds. "Where are we?"

"Nowhere. And everywhere."

She sees flowers in the shapes of stars, in colors she has never imagined. She sees people and animals and creatures unlike any she has ever seen. She sees stars that burst eons ago and those that will form when she is long dead. "Are we inside the whole universe?" she asks.

"Many versions of them," the Arbiter says.

And she looks at the vastness of the worlds and thinks of her tiny house in her village, and wonders how she can be of use to this powerful being who has saved her.

The churning tunnel of stars empties suddenly, and they are in a world of darkness and shadow, a silhouette of a place against a dark maroon sky. The silence is startling after the noise of the passageway. The Arbiter's wings pull closer around him as he treads on the dark cobblestones. They swirl with the blackness and the pinprick lights of space, and she wonders if the feathers catch on the fabric of the worlds as he walks through them. Perhaps that is the source of his strange outline; he is painted with universes.

The earth here is the gray of a tired old blade, but the dirt is as soft as goose feathers. High above them, on a cliff that juts forth from the earth, a large castle looms, raven black and still. It's not quite like the ancient castles of Galen's world. The turrets are strangely shaped, like the sapphire on the end of the sword hilt; it's architecture she can't place, and the whole building looks ill-conceived, without any defensive features. No candles glow in the windows, no guards stand at the gates. It feels like a place outside of time itself. She's frightened, but the Arbiter is already looking back to make sure she is following.

"We are outside," he says, as if everything is as simple as that.

Outside of what? But Galen feels childish to ask. They have traveled through space and time and many realities. What else *could* they be outside of?

"But it's a castle," she says, as the cobblestones lead them up, winding round and round the cliff as they near the top.

"It is another facet. You see as your mind comprehends."

She supposes she imagined the Unseelie to live in some sort of dark medieval court, but she never could have imagined a castle on so still a plain with no trees, no life, no sound. The sky has no stars at all, just lit faintly through fog by a maroon light.

Inside, the halls are empty, but she can feel eyes crawling all over her. It's stifling, and she is deeply aware that they are not alone.

In the top of the tallest tower, they enter a dark chamber with a simple bed. The blanket upon it is made of the same void as the Arbiter's outline, the stars and galaxies swirling across its fabric and disappearing into lapping shadows at the foot of the bed. Under the coverlet lies a woman, her face etched with age. Her long white hair spirals around her face and onto the blanket, where the ends of it sway as they're pulled back and forth by the orbits of the stars. She is beautiful, her skin like an iridescent shell, but she is still and too thin. A simple circlet of crystals rests on her head, entangled with white vines and twigs like the Arbiter's horns.

"My queen," says the Arbiter, and the other voices chorus *Empress, Sovereign, Ahani, K'lar* and others Galen does not understand. He falls to one knee and folds his wings over himself, like a cloak dripping black galaxies, the shadows ebbing around him like he's a rock in the ocean waves.

The woman looks at her. Her eyes are large white pearls, searing into Galen's soul.

"A witch." She speaks in only one voice, small but daunting. "At last. I have been waiting for you."

"I don't understand," Galen says.

The Arbiter stands, the light from the swirling blanket catching on the jewels and scabbards of his swords. "You must help us, Penitent. She is dying."

THE ARBITER QUEEN LIES IN THE BED IN FRONT OF HER, AS pale as though she were already a ghost. The shouts of Galen's trial still ring in her ears, the shivers still shaking her from her wait for the Arbiter to devour her. And now she is on the other side of the universe, of many universes, and this Unseelie monarch wants her help.

"Leave us," the queen says, and the Arbiter puts his hand to his heart in obedience. He looks at Galen with his deep black eyes, and she finds herself unwilling for him to abandon her in this strange place with this woman who is made of stars.

"Have I died?" Galen asks. "Am I dreaming, or gone mad?"

"With regret, this is not the way of things."

"Who are you? You and the Arbiter?"

The queen's skin glistens with sweat from her weary breathing. "We are scavengers who live in the seams between universes. We feed off the living and castoff elements from many worlds. Carbon, hydrogen. Iron. We only live through the life we have devoured."

"Is that what has happened to the other Penitents? Did you . . . devour them?"

"We did not *eat* them, child. We unknit them, back into stardust."

The room is cold, suddenly, a pit opening in Galen's stomach. "Is that why I'm here?"

The queen tilts her head to the side, her pillow drenched with sweat. The crystals on her circlet clink against each other like death knells. "You are here because I need your craft. If you have studied your old tomes, you know what I ask of you."

Galen cannot put it off any longer. Watching this queen dying in a foreign world, seeing the belief in her eyes of salvation. She isn't sure whether the Arbiters mean her harm, but she can feel the fear and the loss. She pities this scavenger, starving to death.

"I'm sorry," she says. "I'm not a witch. I tried to hide from unwanted attention under my thick cloaks and shawls. I did study the stars, but I cast no spells nor studied any craft at all."

"I know all this," the queen says, as Galen hangs her head.

"I am nothing but a girl unfairly judged. I am innocent and powerless."

The queen laughs, and it is like the spark of the creation of stars. "If you are truly powerless, then why do they fear you so?" Her eyes gleam like constellations as she presses a cool finger against Galen's inner wrist.

It is like a kiss of frost on Galen's wound that spreads into her veins, filling her arm with sharp swirls of ice. The queen's face isn't so pale now, nor so helpless. She looks strong, resilient, her eyes blinding as the sun. She licks her lips with a split tongue like a snake as the fear and the cold spread through Galen faster than she can think of a way to escape. She's trapped in this other world with no way back. Why did she think she was safe and among friends?

The queen's grip tightens, the crystals on her head filling the silence with their strange chimes. "Would you return to your silver chains, to your sentence of corruption and the slow drag of flesh and blades from a dead forest?" Her fingernails cut into Galen's veins like knives. "It is in here that your true chains are, your true power. Do you know what makes your blood crimson and heavy as old stars? What gives you life and strength?" The queen's eyes gleam as she presses on Galen's wrist. The pressure pushes Galen's arm into the blanket, into the galaxies swirling around the queen's icy fingers. "Iron," she hisses. "Iron that can burn and melt, that can be forged into chains or into blades. Here are your chains, witch. And it is here where you need to break them."

Galen's cheeks glitter with ice crystals as the cold spreads through her. Her voice comes out as a faint whisper. "What do you want?"

"Your innocence," the queen says. "Your featherlight innocence."

Galen wants to say, *I cannot give it to you*. It's gone, murdered by the innkeeper and Acton and Lysander's betrayal. It was cut down under the wife's disbelief, under the cry of the ravens that shook her as she tried to walk home in the terror of solitary night.

Instead she says, "Take whatever is left."

The Arbiter steps into the room, pulling the last sword from his back. It is curved like a scythe, the blade gleaming with the void of space.

I'm going to die. I'll be unknit into stardust.

The Arbiter Queen loosens her grip on Galen's wrist so that it no longer stings with the burn of frost. She reaches her other hand to hold Galen's other wrist, and then she closes her pearl eyes.

Galen's world floods and spins with galaxies, like the tunnel she walked through with the Arbiter. She sees time and space and realities. She sees women reaching their hands through the portals, although she thinks now they are real and not snares nor sirens. She sees them cloak themselves in black and walk quickly as she does. She sees them avert their eyes, laugh in fear, dread to say no. She sees them tremble under the iron chains of living, of surviving. She sees the unbearable, the unliveable, things that cannot be forgotten but only endured. They are like her, these sisters from all universes, the links of each chain binding her heart tighter and tighter. Penitents, she thinks, but not of corruption.

She feels her body turn cold under the Arbiter Queen's icy stream of visions. How long do they sit there and watch? Time itself drifts away under abuse and atrocity until she cannot sense minutes or hours or years. And when she feels she can bear no more, when she blinks the frost from the corners of her eyes, something happens.

She feels a warmth start in her fingertips, spreading like a thaw over a barren, flattened plain.

It stirs slowly, building with each vision she sees, with each tear and each scream and each disbelief, with each reaching hand scraped through soft earth for the pommel of a sword. She warms; she ignites.

The warmth turns searing hot until sweat pools on her forehead and drips into the void of the queen's blanket. As soon as they hit the surface they float up and sideways, droplets of rain drifting through nothingness.

This is not the innocence she thought the queen would take. That no longer exists to her, such a juvenile and learned notion. This is the innocence of isolation, of solitude. She thought she was alone in what she'd endured. Now the voices echo in a chorus of fury, and she fills with the blood and rage of others.

When she feels as though she will burst like a forming star, the queen's eyes open, flooded with blinding light. She releases Galen's hands, and the Arbiter steps forward out of the shadows, where he's been watching.

He holds his curved blade in his hand. But he does not swing it. He turns the hilt to Galen.

The metal sizzles and steams under her grip.

She swings it herself.

At once she comes undone, into stardust, into carbon and iron and fire. She is molten with the weight of truth; she is ore ready to be forged to a point.

The queen rises from the bed; her dress is made of stars. She is no longer frail, no longer old. Her eyes gleam with anticipation.

With a multitude of voices, she knits Galen together again, out of stardust and will and fire.

It looks so small, Galen thinks, that tiny village. From her upstairs window, she used to think the rooftops looked like long, flat pill bugs. They curl now under the heat of the flames, as the village folds in on itself.

The fire started in the temple and spread across the floor, melting the iron on the doors into silver puddles on the cobblestones. The inn and stable caught fire next, then the butcher's.

Once the flames touched Lysander's house, they spread like the flap of phoenix wings to the rest of the village.

She walks down the green hills leisurely, humming the old songs over the screams, toward the dead forest where the large gaping mouth of gnarled branches leads to a too silent mist.

She thinks she can hear the scraping of flesh against the ground, the clatter of mismatched blades clanking against one another.

The girl is there, in a pure white Penitent's robe, her wrists soaked in blood. Galen doesn't know her, but she isn't sure how many years passed in the castle outside. She could be anyone; she could be Galen. The girl watches her approach with wide-eyed terror.

The heat of the flames wafts through the air. Embers caught on the wind land on the dry, dead branches where they glow with deadly potential.

Galen reaches her hand toward the iron blade plunged into the earth. She pulls it free slowly, the dirt crumbling over the soft grass. The weight of it is heavy in her hand, but not as heavy as the truth that rushes through her like a river of molten fire.

She raises it high as the girl squeezes her eyes shut, as she squirms against the silver chains.

Galen swings, the sparks flying like the birth of stars. She drops the sword with a clatter to the ground and pulls back the thick black of her hood.

"Who are you?" the girl whispers, collapsed in a broken heap on the ground.

"A witch," Galen replies, and holds out her hand.

———

Amanda Sun is the author of the Paper Gods series, INK, RAIN, and STORM, a YA Fantasy set in Japan about dangerous drawings coming to life. She also wrote HEIR TO THE SKY, about floating continents and monster hunters, and has contributed to several award-winning anthologies, including TESSERACTS FIFTEEN, and STRANGERS AMONG US. Many of her novels and short fiction have been Aurora Award nominees and Junior Library Guild selections, as well as Indigo Top Teen Picks and USA Today features. When not reading or writing, Sun is an avid cosplayer, gamer, and geeky crafter. Get free Paper Gods novellas and other goodies at AmandaSunBooks.com.

One last bite from Amanda Sun...

There is an innocence in our lives that is broken when we begin to see what the world around us can be--unequal, unfair, unsafe. But I think there is a second time this happens in our lives, the innocence shattered when we see the suffering that other women have faced. There is a weight to understanding it is not us alone, but every woman, who has experienced the fears and sometimes horrors of the world. But there is also a sisterhood in this realization, from which we can draw courage.

This is THE WEIGHT OF IRON--the weight of what is it to be human, to be female, to exist in this world—and that together we can break the chains of the past and forge a new and collective strength to move forward.

WHAT SHE LEFT BEHIND

E.R. GRIFFIN

1976

All Erin Wilcox left behind was an earring.

Well.

Left behind may be a bit generous.

The grass was disturbed. A bush crumpled as though by a great weight. The gate was closed but unlocked. And her father never forgot the lock.

That night, as every night, he walked the house, checking and rechecking each door. His last stop was the sliding glass door leading onto the small cement slab that counted as a porch in these cramped Florida subdivisions. He walked outside, eyed the gate, tested its resistance with a mighty pull. Satisfied, he went to bed.

Erin was supposed to be asleep. But she had a flashlight beneath the blankets. She held it in her teeth while she scribbled in her diary, holding it against her lap, pressing her pen too hard.

The last thing she wrote was, *I will never forgive that stupid motherfucker.*

The house was entirely dark but for the flashlight, which Erin had left on after she fell asleep beneath the blanket, the diary splayed across her stomach.

What followed is a matter of debate.

Perhaps Erin let him in. Her window was unlocked and there was no sign of forced entry.

But then there was the flashlight, still on by the next morning. The diary, bird-winged with a broken spine and crumpled pages, lying open on the floor.

All the police knew for certain was that it didn't happen in her bedroom. He took her to the backyard, through her widow, which overlooked that sad cement slab.

The grass was disturbed. The bush crushed. A single faux-diamond earring was half-buried in the dirt by the hibiscuses.

No blood. No body.

But Erin Wilcox was gone.

2018

My first impression of 1138 Rhododendron Way is that something is missing. It's too neat, maybe, packed beside its nearly identical neighbors. It's washed of personality.

Or maybe it's the lack of plant life. Some of our neighbors have invested in landscaping, palm trees brushing the too-blue sky. Our yard has a stump, a place where a tree once grew. The little garden patch by the front door grows only weeds, but the ground is lumpy with the left-behind roots of bushes.

It could be just a feeling. This place isn't home yet, so it feels like nowhere. It looks like the third house up the road, and the fourth away from that, down to the peach paint.

"We can afford this?" I ask, resting a box on my hip. It's not like it's even a great place. An old neighborhood people are probably trying to climb their way out of.

Mom gives me an amused look over a tower of cardboard boxes stacked in the driveway. "It's cute, right?"

"Sure. Not what I asked."

Her face tightens, just a bit. "We got a good price."

"Oh, Jesus." I drag my hand down my face. "Indian burial ground?"

"*No.* The original owner died without leaving it to anyone. It's been empty for a while." She winces. "It's a bit of a fixer-upper."

I check the neighboring houses and realize our house *isn't* the same. Not exactly. Same design, but 1138 needs a fresh coat of paint. The windows need a good scrubbing. The grass grows long against the side of the house. This place must have sat here, vacant and decaying, for a long time.

Still. Mom told me how much she got in the divorce. Enough for a down payment on an old, empty house, sure. Enough to pay the mortgage on a cashier's wage at Publix? Probably not.

I glance at the house and suddenly, the heavy beat of sunshine and bright paintjob fade. I'm wondering how long we have before the place is foreclosed on when Mom's voice breaks into my spiral, pleading.

"Please don't worry, Mel," Her voice is the one she uses when she thinks I'm about to reach for my pills or a knife.

So I drag my lips into a smile and say, "I'm sure it'll be great."

———

THE HOUSE IS SMALL, OPEN. THE FRONT DOOR LEADS RIGHT into the kitchen, with a door to the right leading to the laundry room. The living room extends behind the kitchen, and a sliding glass door with yellowed blinds lets narrow bands of sunlight across the floor. A hallway splits the other side of the house in half, Mom's bedroom to one side, mine opposite. I take an armful of boxes and head toward it.

My bedroom feels too tight. Humidity is trapped in the small space. Dust lines the walls and floor. Despite the damp heat outside, I'm eager for fresh air.

My window overlooks the backyard, a small thing of thick, overgrown grass and weeds. A cement slab extends from the sliding glass door and reaches beneath my window. Somebody left a grill sitting there, but its old, crusty with the browned and crumbling juices of barbeques gone by. I flick the blinds aside to get a better look at the pathetic excuse for land-owning, then seek the latch.

Before I can reach for it, a small, misty handprint flares in the corner of the window.

I pause my mind before it can formulate a panic attack. It's my handprint. I touched the window and don't remember doing it.

I place my palm above the print. My fingers extend a half-inch beyond it. Before I can pull my hand back, the print beneath my skin smears down, the spectral fingertips dragging into a claw and then vanishing beneath the sill.

Mom? I try to call, but my voice sinks back into myself. *You're just freaking out. You're losing it, like you always do.*

I stop the tirade before it goes down its familiar route, the one that starts with the stale memory of the hospital and ends with, *You're why Dad left.* Dr. Jannis told me to map my thoughts and see how they always take the same path toward blaming myself.

Mom wanted a new life for me, away from the emptiness and blame and questions.

I tug down my sleeve and wipe away the handprint's path.

MOM ORDERS CHINESE, AND WE SETTLE ONTO THE LUMPY couch we brought from Miami. The cable hasn't been installed —probably never will—so we put in a DVD and watch an old rendition of *Wuthering Heights*.

"Laurence Olivier was almost hot," I say.

"Almost?" She gestures to the screen with a forkful of General Tso's. "He's gorgeous."

"Eh." I stuff a steaming mass of chicken and broccoli into my mouth and relish the thin, tangy sauce rushing the back of my tongue. Things might suck financially, socially, and fifteen ways in between. But as long as there is Mom and Chinese food and old movies, things seem all right.

We doze into half-viewing the movie, talking through some of it, but pausing in reverence for our favorite lines. Olivier's delivery during Catherine's death scene is perfect in that over-acted mid-century way: *Do not leave me in this abyss where I cannot find you.*

"They never found *me*."

I sit up from my slouch, upsetting the leftover sauce in my tray. A grease stain sinks into my jeans, blooming brown and hot against my thigh. I set the tray on the coffee table, turn to Mom. "Did you say something?"

"Hm? No. Why?"

"I swear I heard…"

Mom waits, her face blank. She does that well. Keeping her worry and judgment out of her expression, so I can't see her thinking, *God, my kid's cracked.*

I shrug. "Must've been the movie. I think I'm falling asleep." I force a yawn, crack my neck for effect. "Long day."

"Too true." Mom sips from her stemless wine glass and her

eyes drift back to the movie. Despite her exhaustion, I see how much better she is. Hopeful, finally.

The movie ends, and I contain my jitters as I rise. "Well, 'night," I say over my shoulder.

"Goodnight, Mel. And...thanks. I know this was a lot—"

"We both needed it," I say. "I'm happy we're here."

She smiles, and I try to carry her relief with me as I enter my new, cold room. Only my bed has been set up so far. The emptiness echoes at me from the bare corners; the window spits moonlight through the old, yellowing blinds. The handprint is gone, but I feel its presence, insistent.

There's something about these four plain walls. Like they're holding the pressure of something dark.

———

In my dream, a yellow-haired girl sits on the edge of my bed. She turns tired eyes caked with mascara and eye shadow toward me.

"I...will never..."

I sit up, curl the sheets in my fist.

"Forgive...that..."

I open my mouth; I want to say, *It's okay, you're safe*, but that's not true.

"Stupid motherfucker." She shuts her eyes, opens her mouth, and a scream builds around the room, filling the blank space and at last coming to a point in my head. An ache bleeds from the back of my eye into my brain and I scream too, until we're a symphony, making cracks in the glass.

The window shatters, and the girl rises, reaches for a hand waiting between the shards of broken glass.

"Never forgive," she whispers, and her smile flashes like a blade.

I nurse my migraine with a can of Coke and a bowl of Cocoa Puffs. Mom eyes me above a square of toast, cooling in her hand for the past five minutes.

"It's just a migraine," I tell her.

"You look pale."

"I'm fine." I force a spoonful of chocolate-dusted cereal into my mouth. My stomach clenches against the idea of swallowing, but I push the bite down. I guzzle half the soda can.

"You should have real food," Mom says.

"Sugar helps." I set my spoon down, give my curling stomach a break. "Really, I'm totally fine."

"Have you been taking your—"

"Of course," I say, and realize how fake my voice sounds. High, cheery. Did I take my meds? In the chaos of moving, sleeping in hotels, I might have missed a dose or two. I took them this morning. Maybe.

"I could call out…"

"On your first day? Please, Mom, don't make a big deal. I'll take it easy. I'll eat real food."

"You're sure it's okay to leave you? What if it's—"

"Don't say 'something worse.' It's not." Besides, my brain does a fine job of conjuring the many possible ways I'll die horribly all on its own.

"You don't have to be brave," Mom says.

"I'm not. I'm being rational." I shove my cereal around the bowl. "Maybe if I'd started sooner, we wouldn't be in this mess."

"What does that mean?"

"That…" I gesture all around. "You're paying for all this working at a grocery store. And we're in a weird—a new house. And we don't have any of our friends around us anymore. And maybe if I'd just kept the crazy inside none of this would've—"

"Mel."

I sigh. "Yeah?"

"The divorce had nothing to do with you. We had problems. It wasn't your fault."

She's probably sick of saying this. But what else would I think, when the divorce papers started showing up in tandem with my doctor bills? I want to believe her. I just can't.

"Okay," I say. "I'm sorry."

She smiles sadly. "No hard feelings. I'm going to call on my lunch break. Answer the phone. Otherwise, I'm driving back here in a panic."

"Got it."

She demolishes her cold toast in three bites and pours herself a tumbler of off-brand coffee. "Wish me luck. Ringing up groceries will require all of my mental faculties."

I salute as she walks out the front door, lunch tote banging from her hip, and I miss her the second the door closes.

Okay. I'm alone. In a new, empty-ish house. And I feel that ticking in my brain, the warming-engine sound of my thoughts readying their cycle. Dr. Jannis's voice cuts in, *Stop the thoughts before you have them. You anticipate these cycles. Use that to your advantage.*

So I grab the first thought—*I'm alone*—and reframe it. I'm alone. I can work on something for me. A project. A distraction, at least.

When I got out of the hospital, it was crosswords. Every day. For hours. I have books and books of *Dell's Easy Crosswords* filled out and stacked in my boxes, tokens of my crazy trying to quiet itself. I've done them so many times, I even know the answers that only make sense to people born before television was invented. A four-letter word for fake butter? *Oleo.* I have no fucking idea what it is, but I know it's the answer, and I like that part.

I head for the boxes stacked inside my bedroom and open three of them before I come upon the one holding my crosswords. I flip through the books, desperate to find a single blank puzzle, but I've done them all, it seems. I'm tearing through the Fall 2017 edition when a finger digs in between my ribs.

I jolt, drop the book beside its siblings, all limp on the floor. The perfume of newsprint is heavy in my nose. My pulse ticks up my arms, driving hard into my heart. The dull roar in my mind quiets, alert.

And the house is empty. Nobody poked me. I'm just a crazy—

No. Dr. Jannis said it wasn't like that. *You're not crazy*, she said, a line psychiatrists must get tired of repeating. She kept the word psychosis out of our sessions. Said that wasn't what was wrong with me. *Trauma manifests itself in different ways.*

I prefer the word crazy to the word trauma. Crazy fits me. Trauma, I feel like I'm borrowing that word. Taking it from people who really deserve it. Traumas happen to people.

I didn't have to go to Geoff's house. I didn't have to call Mom, say, "I'm fine, just staying at a friend's place." I could have fought, screamed. Said *no*. Instead, I cried quietly until it was over. Vomited in the bathroom. Snuck out while he was snoring on his futon.

What happened after—the memories growing teeth and digging into my mind; the knife I dragged across my arm; seeing him in the bodies of strangers; hearing him in the voices of other men—that falls into the crazy category. It followed from what was already true about me, best summed up by Dad: *She's always been a little off.*

Mom calls at noon to say, "Honey, people suck."

Some lady in the return line screamed at her for the condition of a piece of fruit—bought with a coupon five days ago. She was surprised and infuriated by the progress of decay.

"I told her, 'Ma'am, you know a peach isn't going to last five days outside of the refrigerator. She reported me to the manager! Total whore."

I laugh along with Mom's story and let myself pretend I don't feel eyes on my back as I sit on my bedroom floor, hunched over my phone, counting my pills.

"So how's your day?" Mom asks. "How's the head?"

"Migraine's gone." Lie. "I'm good, though."

"What have you been doing?"

"Crosswords." Another lie. There wasn't a single blank crossword in my collection. I tried to make up my own, and then solve them, like I didn't know the answers already.

"Once we get some pictures of the new place, maybe you can start a new scrapbook," Mom suggests.

"Yeah, totally." I glance over my shoulder at a slight snapping sound. Did somebody move the blinds?

"Are you okay, Mel? You sound distracted."

"Just tired. Didn't sleep great."

"You should take a nap."

"Sounds great. I might do that."

"Okay, good. I gotta get back, but I'll call you on my way home. Be safe. Love you."

"Love you, too."

I let her hang up first, holding onto her almost-presence as long as I can. Then I return to the pile of circular yellow pills counted out on a napkin. I've sifted through them twice, and the result is the same. I haven't missed a dose.

I gather the pills and return them to the clear orange container they came in. They're not a cure-all. I know that. Like Dr. Jannis always said, they're a tool I can use to get better, but the work is my own. Self-care—god, I hate that word—is the most important factor. Affirmations, positive talk. Blame and guilt and shame will drown me. So I try out the words I've been told to say a thousand times, but never could.

"It's not my fault," I whisper to the bare room.

"That's what I always said."

I shoot to my feet and scan the room. The voice dangles in the air. I touch my ear, still ringing with the sound I couldn't have heard, and my fingertips come away red. My lips part, first in surprise, and then, without consciously knowing what I'm doing, I bring my fingers to my tongue. The iron tang of blood rushes my mouth.

I run to the bathroom and pull my hair away from my neck, expecting blood on my reflection in the mirror. But there's nothing. No wound, even. My fingers are clean. And the taste—was it ever there?

"Shit. Shit." I gather my hair at my temples and press, hard, against my skull. I stare into the mirror to see something concrete, my own reflection. But...

My hands drop to the counter and I lean close, shaking, upright by some desire to know that is stronger than my fear. My eyes are brown. I know this. But my reflection shows a pair of pale blue eyes, and they're not afraid. They're sharp and glittering with fury.

I RIFLE THROUGH MY PURSE FOR MY WALLET AND FLIP IT open to my ID. The information beside my unsmiling photo confirms that, yes, my eyes are brown. Always have been. With a shaking hand I dig for my compact mirror in the bottom of my purse. The tiny circle of my face shows a brown eye staring back, wide, pupils dilated.

I've never been crazy-crazy. The shit I saw, it was always linked to reality. Past things that came up at the worst times to haunt me. Dr. Jannis said it would get better over time.

But maybe I cracked. Maybe my *trauma* was a rift that only grew, and now I'm full-on schizophrenic. Is that how it works?

A sound above me breaks up my thoughts. A *rattle-thump* that sounds like something toppling over. My guts knot inside me.

Do we have an attic? I text Mom.

Her response is swift. *A crawlspace. Why?*

I could say no reason, but she won't believe me. *Might want to call an exterminator lol I heard something up there. Maybe we have raccoons?*

I shove my phone in my pocket and go in search of an entrance to the supposed crawlspace. It's easier than I thought it would be. A closed entrance is embedded in the hallway ceiling, right outside my room. A grimy pullcord dangles half a foot above my head. I tug against it. Nothing happens.

I blow out a frustrated breath, then try again, putting all my weight into the pull. At last, a groan emits from the ceiling and the crawlspace door gives with a bang. A narrow wooden stair-well unfolds with the door, and with it falls another object. It slams down before me and I jump back.

It's a box, dented and worn at the corners. Old, wrinkled packing tape peels from the flaps. I nudge it with my toe, half expecting a wild animal to leap out.

A weary sigh brushes my cheek. I swing my hand at the air, as though I could slap away the presence.

The box sits before me, wilted, pushing against the ancient tape. I shouldn't open it. It's not mine. And...something else. A nagging, prescient force tells me that I should just toss this box back into the crawlspace and forget it.

But curiosity is stronger than fear. I bend down and pry the box open. Inside are old clothes, badly folded and shoved in without care. I pick out a sweater, turtleneck, yellow. I set it aside and dig through a few other pieces of clothes. Beneath them lie the detritus of a teenager's life: A barrette, broken. A hand mirror. Scattered Polaroids. And...a book?

I lift it out. It smells like a teenage girl from days gone by. Chanel No. 5 and cigarettes, musty sheets and salty tears. It's a diary, red faux-leather and locked with a tiny padlock. A slender gold key, slightly bent, sticks from between the pages of the book.

I tug it out and consider the lock, the secrets and sayings it was sworn to protect. I should put it back.

But a diary is just as tantalizing as a box, if not dirtier. At least a box might be meant for you. A diary is intended for one mind, for the eyes of the writer.

Still. I stick the key into the lock and the already-broken spine swings wide, splaying pages.

I read the inscription inked into the back of the front cover: *My secrets and my shame. E.A.W.*

Page one is a diatribe against some bitch named Christy who sat at lunch with Ferris. I roll my eyes. She sounds just like some of the girls from my old school, always picking fights over boys. I check the date, curious.

May 5, 1976.

"Woah," I whisper.

"Get to the good stuff."

I throw the book to the floor and scream, "Leave me alone!"

A faint giggle fades from the hallway. Whoever whispered in my ear...

Nobody whispered in my ear. I'm freaking myself out. End of story. Full stop. That's all she wrote.

I pick the diary up. It's tiny, but suddenly imbued with

weight, with meaning. I expel a steady breath and flip to the end. The last entry is for July 12, 1976.

The handwriting, so neat and proud on page one, is nearly illegible here, hard and slanted and washed away in places by what might be tears. I can only read a few lines.

But I get the message.

I was only ever his toy... thought he could do things like that to me and I wouldn't... Jan says I should tell the cops but what will the fucking cops do? Blame me, that's what.

I am just a girl, just an item, flesh and blood in the fuckable sense only.

And then I see it. The thing I've heard before.

The thing she whispered in my dream.

I will never forgive that stupid motherfucker.

A KNOCK ON THE DOOR STARTLES ME FROM THE PAGES. I shove the book back into the box and creep toward the door. I shouldn't answer the door. I clutch my phone, ready to call Mom. *Somebody's here, I'm scared, I can't...*

I peer through the peephole. A man stands on the other side of the door, warped concave in the little glass. He's stiff, anxious looking. As I watch, he knocks again.

"Hello?" His voice comes thick through the wood. "Anyone home? Um. Are you okay in there?"

I keep my hand on my phone, ready to dial 911, and crack the door open.

"Yes?" I say.

"Oh! Hello. I'm sorry, but I heard a scream...I thought. Are you all right?"

"Oh, yeah, yeah. Just...crawlspace. It, um. I opened it and a box almost fell on my head."

"I see." He clears his throat. "I...didn't realize anybody had moved in. So, well, welcome to the neighborhood."

He's dressed in khaki shorts and a polo, total suburban-dad vibe. He's smiling, slightly uncomfortable, as he says, "Sorry to have bothered you. Glad you're all right."

"Hey," I say before he can back away, "who lived here before?"

"Mrs. Wilcox. Died last year, I believe." He nods. "Glad to see they finally sold the place. Turning into an eyesore." He glances around the yard, shorn of trees. "Your parents, they plan on investing in some landscaping?"

I ignore the question, most of all the word *parents*. The assumed plurality of my family unit. "This Mrs. Wilcox. Did she have a daughter?"

His mouth thins. He checks his watch, sighs.

"I don't know. She kept to herself. Sorry again to bother you." And with a small wave, he starts down the walkway without another word.

⸺

THE DIARY GOES BENEATH MY MATTRESS, THE BOX INTO MY closet, where it will blend in with other unpacked boxes.

I need to know what the hell happened here.

We don't have Internet set up yet, but my momentum demands action. I grab Mom's old laptop and stuff it into my backpack. I saw a shopping center with a Starbucks not far from the neighborhood the day we moved in. Mom would flip if she knew I was walking there, but she doesn't get off for two more hours. I'll go, do some quick googling, and be back before she knows.

I'm not opposed to the idea that I'm insane. It might be better than believing a dead girl lives here and wants to talk.

Either way, Dr. Jannis told me once that if finding answers to the answerable questions made me feel better, I should go for it. It was the things that didn't have a black-and-white solution she said I should give up on. The *why'd he leave*s and *what's wrong with me*s.

I sling my backpack over my shoulders, lock up the house, and head down the sidewalk. The streetlights flicker on as I go, passing carbon copies of my own home. A few neighbors are out, sitting in Adirondack chairs with glasses of sweet tea, giving me the *Who the hell are you?* eye. I nod politely but press on. I'm on a schedule.

I have to cross a highway to exit my subdivision and make it to the shopping center, a harrowing feat in Florida. Even though the logo of a busy little pedestrian flashes for me to cross, I am nearly run over no less than three times as I sprint across four lanes, backpack abusing my shoulder blades.

The Starbucks is nestled between a dentist's office and a boutique-y antique shop, and it's packed with hipsters and trendy moms with strollers and fussing toddlers. I spend my last five bucks on a caramel macchiato and, realizing there are no available seats or tables, plop onto the floor by the bathrooms.

I fire up Google and type *1138 Rhododendron Way Wilcox 1976*.

The hits are scarce, but it's enough. I click on the first link, an old PDF copy of a newspaper from the date. I squint at the grainy typeface, marred by pixilation. But I know it's what I've come for. Now, E.A.W. has a name.

Erin Abigail Wilcox vanished from her home late on the night of July 12. Her parents reported her missing at 7:40 July 13. Their back gate was unlocked, and the window leading into Erin's bedroom was found opened, authorities say.

Detective David Yeats of Pasco County PD says the case is being treated as a missing persons', though Wilcox may very well have run away.

"We're not going to raise any alarms or start rounding up suspects until we can determine we're dealing with a kidnapping. No sign of forced entry tells me she may have gone off on her own."

Wilcox's parents insist their daughter would not have gone away willingly.

"She was just getting back to her old self," Mrs. Wilcox told this reporter. "She was beginning to be happy. She's had a hard time lately, but we saw hope in her eyes again. She did not run away."

I sink against the Starbucks wall. The girl who owned the diary, the girl who lived in my house forty years before me...she disappeared.

I download the file of the newspaper, and any others I can find. Reading about a worried mother makes me more aware of my own. I need to get home, be there waiting when she gets back.

I return my laptop to my bag and brave the highway to make it home.

Mom dishes out heaped plates of baked alfredo and pours herself a hefty glass of wine.

"What a day," she says, lifting the glass to her lips.

Her job sucks. The customers are assholes, her manager is a watery-eyed creep, and she did the math: today, she earned sixty-four dollars.

"I was thinking, maybe I should work part-time," I say.

"Nuh-uh. You need to focus on school."

"It's summer. And when school starts, I can do homework after work. I'm only talking, like, four hours a day."

She sips her wine. Her alfredo cools before her, untouched. "We'll think about it."

After dinner, we head to the couch and pop in a DVD. *Citizen Kane.* I try to relax, sink into the grainy black-and-white world, but my mind wanders, fevered with questions. I'm grateful when the credits roll.

In my bed, I curl my back to the window and try not to think of the handprint, the diary, the girl who vanished. Erin Abigail Wilcox.

I'm sleeping in her room. Her breath mixed with this very air. My inhalations are her exhalations. We're blending even now.

I roll onto my back, stare at the window, the window that was opened. No forced entry.

I think of walking into Geoff's house, so sure it was a normal date. So sure I could trust this boy. How terrified I was when things kept going, when I pushed against him and he didn't care. When I wanted to say no, but my voice vanished in a whimper.

"I know exactly how you felt," I whisper.

There's no reply. The air conditioner kicks on, and I jolt, thinking its her, a growl in the darkness. But my mind adjusts, accepts the familiar sound. I'm going overboard, thinking too much about dark things.

I need my crossword. *Four-down, fake butter.* Oleo.

THE SCRAPE OF MOM'S TIRES VANISHES DOWN THE STREET, and then, I give myself to the diary. I sit on the living room floor, sunlight pouring in from the sliding glass door behind me. Light touches the old pages of the diary in my hands, waking them from secrecy.

I read her. What she said, what she was like, the nuances of her elevated style. She was dramatic, putting more weight on her simple life than need be. Unaware of stakes higher than claiming the seat next to Ferris and smirking at Christy as she took a seat across the cafeteria, mascara running black down her cheeks.

She seems semi-popular. Not a cheerleader or a prom queen or even valedictorian. But she's smart; I doubt she let people know how smart. She has a solid group of friends, but not too many. Aside from Ferris, her obvious romantic destination, she regularly brings into her narrative Jan, Doug, Laura, Hannah. Christy is her arch-nemesis, and though Erin doesn't seem to know it, Ferris loves the game he has them playing. The way, one day, he drools after Erin in the halls, but the next day he seems not to hear her, and he's sharing notes with Christy in the smoker's area.

Ferris is a dick.

DOUG SAYS I'M TOO GOOD FOR FERRIS, BUT DOUG'S ALWAYS *like that, puppy-ish, thumping his tail when I enter a room and hoping for a treat. My literal boy next door. He'd love it if I broke up with Ferris—but are we even together?—and went for him. Prom's coming up. It'd make his year.*

Ferris hasn't asked me to prom, by the way. And Christy was talking with Mandy yesterday; she's already bought her dress. Did he ask her and not tell me? I can't take much more of this.

I WANT TO REACH THROUGH THE YEARS AND TELL HER TO

dump him, but I've been there. When you think you're in love and take flickers of abuse as passion.

I leave the diary aside and open my laptop to the newspaper articles I downloaded. I scan through the first few, the pale assurances that Erin was simply on a teen-girl tantrum, living it up in Daytona. Her mother hired a private investigator and told the press, "If the police won't act, I will. This is my daughter's life."

The papers take a darker turn as the days become weeks. The police returned to Erin's house at the request of her father. He'd found a single faux-diamond earring embedded in the dirt of his yard.

I touch my ear, remembering the blood. My heart beats so hard I feel it in my throat.

At one point in the articles, "police are searching for a suspect in the disappearance," but they can't find him. I read and read, until I realize: They never do. They finally name who they're seeking, and I'm not surprised: *Police are seeking any information on the whereabouts of Ferris Black, last seen in the late afternoon of July 11.*

Ferris vanished. Nobody saw him since the day of Erin's disappearance. The pieces fit, and the case was apparently closed. Ferris killed her. Ran off. Got away with it.

I flip forward in the diary, scanning banal interactions and searching for hints of a darker side to Ferris. He's a jerk, obviously, but a murderer?

He and Erin get high one night. He doesn't talk to her the next day. He asks her to prom. She buys a dress. She's prepped to swipe her V-card that night.

And then he stands her up: *Here I am waiting, dressed up, nowhere to go. Such a goddamn cliché.*

The next day's entry:

. . .

I WENT TO PROM AFTER ALL. *D*OUG SHOWED UP. *I*T'S LIKE HE *knew Ferris would do this to me.*

I'm so over that loser. I'm not sure Doug and I will ever be more than friends, but I do know it's time I started dating guys who were more like him. I'm going to college in the fall. I decided on William and Mary after all. It's the best school to accept me. To think I almost turned them down because it would be too far from Ferris! I'm finally thinking clearly. Not to sound like everybody's yearbook quote, but the future is bright!

I PUSH THE DIARY AWAY. *H*OW DID SHE GO FROM THIS TO that scrawled final entry? *I will never forgive that stupid motherfucker.*

"What happened to you?" I say.

I hear a thump. My head whips up. A bird lays sprawled before the sliding glass door, bent and broken, wings like wrecked sails spread on the cement. Specks of blood and bits of feather stick to the glass. As I watch, a single, small handprint disturbs the blood.

———

"Y*OU SEEM...DISTRACTED.*"

Mom's voice is gentle, worried. I blink at my empty dinner plate and realize I can't remember what we ate tonight.

"You've barely said a word," she tries again.

"Yeah... Um, Mom? Did you...did you hear about... Mrs. Wilcox—"

Mom pales. "How do you know that name?"

I shrug. "She lived here before."

"I never told you her name."

I blow out a breath. "Yeah. I did some research."

Mom's lips scrunch to the side. "How?"

Crap. "The Internet?" Mom continues to stare, her mouth thinning the longer I drag this out. "At...Starbucks."

"Mel! It's across a major road. You could've—"

"I get it, okay? I shouldn't have gone." I sink back in my chair, barely daring to meet her eye. "Do you know? About Mrs. Wilcox's daughter?"

The only sound is Mom's fork scraping the last of her dinner around her plate. She's determining what to say. How to react. I see flickers of anger, disappointment, frustration. She won't let any of them out. Sometimes, I wish she would. Normal daughters can be yelled at by their moms. Mine is too scared that I'll break.

"I found out just before I signed the papers. God. I knew I should have backed out."

"What? Why?" But I know why. Because Erin's tragedy is too close to mine.

"I never wanted you to find out. Honey...be honest with me. Are you okay? Is this why you've been so distant?"

"No. I just... You should've told me."

"I didn't want to bring up—"

"Mom, Jesus Christ. This girl was kidnapped and probably murdered. I was date-raped. It was my own fucking—"

"No." Her voice is firmer, harder than I've heard it in a long time. "Don't say it's your fault."

I roll my eyes. "Maybe it was Erin's fault. She apparently opened the window for the creep who took her."

She tosses her hands. "How much have you researched? Mel, you can't do this to yourself."

"I'm not doing anything to myself. I'm trying to help her."

"Who?"

"Erin!"

Mom blinks. "How can you help her?" She must realize the

delicate tone of her own voice, the way she's talking to me like I'm skipping merrily toward the mental ward. She clears her throat. "Mel, honey, I know it sucks, but...that girl died. She's dead. It happened a long time ago."

"Maybe."

"You think she's still alive?" Mom bites her fork, though there's no food on it.

"No. She's dead."

"Mel. I'm trying to understand, but..."

"She's dead, but whoever killed her got away with it. That's not fair to her."

"I know. Of course, it's awful. But you can't change that."

"I can try."

"Mel. If the police, with all their resources, never found the man who hurt her, how could you possibly do anything more?"

"Maybe I can't," I say. "But I need to know."

Mom tells me to stop. Leave it alone. I'm grateful I didn't mention the diary, because she surely would have taken it from me. She only thinks I googled the house. She doesn't know I have Erin's own words to tell me the story.

I pick up where I left off. *The future is bright!* She doesn't write in the diary for a few days, and when she resumes, her life is back in chaos.

June 29. The story is rambling and furious, but I get the message. Ferris hit Erin not long after prom. They hadn't spoken since he stood her up. She saw him outside a bar one night, arm snaked around a new girl—not Christy, someone old enough to buy him beer. Erin walked up and called him out for being a pathetic, two-timing loser, and Ferris, drunk and stupid, punched her. Black eye. Two stitches above her eyebrow.

It seems too clear in hindsight. Ferris goes from violent drunk to sober killer. He couldn't stand that she had stood up for herself, or maybe that she was over him. He came for her when the fury grew too large.

But the open window. No sign of forced entry. Erin let her killer in. Had she reconciled with Ferris? After that? No. There's no way.

But I know that isn't true. I've travelled the dark corridors of a lonely, desperate mind. I know the bad decisions we make when we think nobody will care.

Maybe Erin believed nobody else would love her.

Maybe she let him back in.

I read on. Erin's next entry on July 3 details the fallout of the punch. Doug and some of his friends from the soccer team went to Ferris's house and beat the shit out of him.

IF ONLY DOUGIE KNEW THE HALF OF IT. I DIDN'T CONDONE *what he and the guys did. Just a little punch, I thought. When Ferris got out of the hospital, I went to his place, where he's staying with his cousin. And God, what else did I think would happen? I wanted to offer an olive branch. I'd practiced my line a dozen times: "Now we're even; let's stay out of each other's lives."*

Ferris was drunk. So was the cousin. But that's no excuse.

I can't even write it. It's trapped inside me, this evil, clawing pain. I feel so sick. Like the hurt just wants out.

But it's not inside me. No. The evil is out there, in a shitty apartment, thinking he got away with it.

I know exactly what needs to happen now.

HER PENULTIMATE ENTRY IS DATED JULY 11.

. . .

I have a scar, now. Newly pink and shining. Jan has one, too. A blood oath between best friends. How old school! She promised to tell no one. Crying and shaking her head, begging me to tell what happened. She said, "Everyone will understand. You don't have to live with this."

"It's too late, and I do," I said. "Promise me."

She held off for another second. She even said, "Doug deserves to know." It's so like her. Taking his side all the time. Like I owe him anything.

I said it again. "Promise me." And this time, she did.

After she left, I climbed out my window, went to the palm tree, and carved his initials. F.B.

I've buried what I did.

I touch my own scar, red and raised on my forearm. In a way, it was my own blood oath. My punishment for being stupid enough to trust a boy I thought could love me. After Geoff, I carved my skin. Dr. Jannis thought it was a way to release the pain. But what I never told her was that the scars were meant to be reminders. *This is when you were stupid. This is when you let him hurt you. This is what you get.* It was a self-hate so powerful I could only communicate it with blood.

My scar was shame. But hers was a secret. And I have to know what it was.

We both walked through a door, ignorant and whole, and came out broken and wiser.

I am Erin Wilcox now. I am breathing for her.

I WAKE WITH THE DIARY SPLAYED ACROSS MY STOMACH. The smell of coffee reaches into my room, and I rise to the promising scent. My head is thick with cobwebs and nightmares.

"There you are," Mom says when I reach the kitchen. She's already in her uniform, black pants and green button-down. "I was about to wake you."

I check the clock. Nearly 10. "I was up reading."

She gives me an exasperated look.

"Just a book," I say. "Not...not house stuff."

"Okay," she says, unsure. "I'm going to call on my breaks. Please, just, while I'm gone..."

"I'll be good," I say, and smile. It doesn't reassure her.

Once she's gone, I make good with my promise, at least for a while. I drink my coffee, flick through an old crossword, ignore the call of the sliding glass door. Is the palm tree still there? I want to see his initials myself, see something carved with the hand of this vengeful girl.

I down the last dregs of lukewarm coffee and head for the backyard. Through the sliding glass door, I see it immediately. A solitary palm tree reaching beyond the worn wooden fence. I slip outside and jog toward it, coming to my knees at its base.

I brush aside an overgrowth of scratchy grass and weeds, only to find nothing there. I guess it would be long gone by now, even if she had marked his initials in the tree. Whatever Erin left has faded with time, erasing her that much more.

I've buried what I did.

The line comes back to me like her voice in my ear. And I wonder...

I reach forward and dig my nails into the earth. It's hard, resisting any force, but I pull against the grass and dirt and begin displacing lumps of our yard. I dig at the base of the palm, the Florida summer wet and hot against my back. I'm focused, unaware even of time passing. The hum of cars and lawn-mowers fade, and I only hear the scrape of my nails against the ground.

At last, something wakes me from my task. Pain. I draw my hand from the hole I've dug in the ground to find a line of blood across the tips of my fingers. Below, in the hole, something reflects the merciless orb of the sun back at my eyes.

I move more dirt aside with my uncut hand, revealing the long, rusted blade of a knife. I reach for the hilt and pull it from the earth. It looks like an ordinary hunting knife, serrated and deadly.

Is this the murder weapon? But how? The articles said there was no blood. Had she been stabbed to death here, there would have been scores of evidence.

I've buried what I did.

No. Erin put this here. But, then…

"Excuse me?"

I drop the knife back into the hole and turn. The neighbor guy, the one who came to my door, is peeking over his fence.

"I'm sorry to bother you again. I tried the front door but there was no answer."

My heart twists in my chest and seems to push toward my throat. I swallow. "What do you want?"

His face darkens, annoyed. "Well, I was coming by to ask… look, I know you just moved in, and this neighborhood may not be what it used to be, but your lawn really needs to be mowed. Can you let your parents know, please?"

His request is so banal, so suburban, that it takes a moment for my murder-obsessed mind to register why this series of words even makes sense put together. But then I remember Dad, how angry he would get at the neighbors for letting their yards grown long and weedy.

"Um. My mom works all day."

"There's a great lawn service that works the neighborhood."

"I doubt we could afford it." I rub my hands against the grass, trying to clean them before rising. "Does it matter that much?"

He sighs. "Look, how about I do it for you this once? Until you get settled."

"Uh, okay?"

He suddenly seems to notice my grimy hands, the disturbed ground behind me. "What are you doing out here?"

"Digging."

His eyes widen. "For?"

Secrets. Answers. But I can't tell this man any of that. "Exercise? It's a great upper-body workout."

"Don't do it anymore," he says, as though he has any right. "It'll just be harder to mow."

"Okay... Sorry?"

He shakes his head and says, "I'll come over this afternoon," and disappears over the side of the fence.

I bring the knife inside, set it in the box where I first found the diary. I could call the police, but they wouldn't believe the story unfolding. Even I'm struggling with the pieces, now matter how clearly they align.

I shut my eyes, add the evidence together. The knife, buried by Erin. The secret she carved into her skin. Ferris, missing since July 11. An entire day before Erin's disappearance.

Ferris couldn't have killed Erin.

Because she'd already killed him.

I can almost conjure a happy ending: Erin skipped town. Ran off after killing the boy who abused her. She opened the window herself. Designed a struggle in the backyard to throw the cops off. I wouldn't blame her. She avenged herself, but nobody would see it that way.

But that can't be her story. She's dead. Trapped in this house. Talking to me.

The doorbell rings, but this time, I'm not afraid to answer. I'm expecting Mr. Next-Door and his lawn mower. So I'm surprised when a thin, fifty-something woman with mousy brown hair and a sharp little nose stands on my porch, holding a gallon of Arizona sweet tea and a plate of cookies.

"Hi, hon. I'm Mrs. Simmons."

I cock my head.

"Mr. Simmons's wife?" She nods to Mr. Next-Door, already astride a riding lawn mower at the edge of our yard. The engine revs, and he waves in passing as he starts on the overgrown grass.

"Oh. Sorry. He never said his name."

The woman smiles. "Just like him. I should apologize on his behalf. He can be a bit brief with people."

"He really likes neat yards, huh?"

She laughs, a shrill, forced sound. "He's lived in this neighborhood all his life. He remembers the glory days." She lets herself inside and heads into the kitchen, where she deposits the cookies and tea. "This neighborhood used to be the most desirable in the county. But that was forty years ago, of course."

I watch this woman make herself at home. She pulls out a chair at the kitchen table and tells me to sit, then goes for glasses in our cupboards. A flicker of disappointed judgment crosses her face when she realizes we only have plastic cups.

"Right. Well, tell him thank-you for this, by the way. It's really nice."

She barely glances at me. "Oh, sure, not at all. He's used to it by now, anyway. He helped out the poor old woman who used to live here. Mowed her lawn every week, brought her groceries. She didn't have anyone, it was so sad."

I sit at the kitchen table, eye the snacks warily. The lawn-mower's growl passes by the kitchen window, a muted sound that somehow fills the room. "Wow. That's a lot to do for a total stranger."

"Oh, well, he knew her all his life."

"Has he always lived in that same house?"

"Mm-hm. It was his parents'; they sold it to him to help us get started." She twists off the cap, aims to pour the tea.

"Did he know Erin Wilcox?"

Mrs. Simmons misses the plastic cups, splashing tea across the table. She sets the jug aside with shaking hands.

"Oh. Um. Who?" She giggles. "Silly me. Doug's always saying I'm so clumsy."

"Wait." I shoot from my chair. She's flitting around the counters, searching for paper towels. I almost feel bad for her. I go the cabinets under the sink and bring out a dish towel. "Did you say Doug? That's your husband's name?"

"Yes." She wipes her hands, her mouth pressed into a line. "Here, have some tea. The cookies are homemade."

Something warm and sharp fires off in my brain. A wrong-ness, simple and primal yet usually spot on. The sense that says some coincidences are just too big. And the diary, a throwaway line, but so potent now: *My literal boy next door*.

"Are you all right, hon?" Mrs. Simmons touches my shoulder, and I realize I'm sitting again, the kitchen blurred around me. I force myself to concentrate, to come back to the present, and when I do, I realize something is off. The silence of the room rattles me.

"Here, drink." Mrs. Simmons pushes a plastic cup toward me. I shake my head, rub my bare feet across one another. I never thought of how warm my skin was, how alive and hot with blood.

Erin was alive in this same house. Warm, complete, a heart-beat keeping the metronome of her life.

But somebody opened a window, crawled into that life. Ended it.

Something is missing. In the little kitchen there is silence, my breath locked in my chest, Mrs. Simmons silent as she stares at me. It's so quiet.

The lawnmower.

I leap from my seat and yank the blinds up, dumping hot light across the kitchen. Mrs. Simmons shields her eyes, and I scan the yard wildly, searching. He's not there.

Terror travels up my spine and shoots out, into my heart, my mind, the ends of my fingers. Doug. He stayed next door, all his life. Why? Grief, sympathy, those are reasonable answers. But there are others. Fear. Guilt.

I taste blood and realize I've bitten my tongue. I swallow the hot, soupy gulp of iron and salt.

"Are you...are you okay? Hon?"

Mrs. Simmons grabs my shoulders to guide me to the chair, but I tear away and bolt for the sliding glass door. There, by the palm tree, stands Mr. Simmons. Doug. Just watching the hole in the ground like it holds an answer for him.

I touch the door handle, and a scream fills the nearly empty room. I cover my ears and grit my teeth.

Something warm and thick runs from my ear, through the crevices of my fingers, down my neck. I pull my hand away to find it red. Fingers trembling, I reach for my ear. The lobe is split from the center, and my throat suddenly closes, the air cut off. I beat a fist into my chest, trying to force my lungs to respond.

The blood, the airlessness, Mrs. Simmons's voice sharp through the house. I bury my head in my hands, curl into a ball on the floor, and beat the floor with my fists.

Stop it! I think to her, hoping she can hear me. *Let me go!*

Air rushes my lungs. A final drop of blood dots my sleeve. I wait, distrusting of the quiet. I feel my heartbeat through my chest, pulsing in my skin. Just as it slows, I feel a hand on my shoulder.

"Should I call the hospital?"

I drag air into my lungs. "Mrs. Simmons—your husband —Erin—"

"You keep saying that name, but I don't—"

"He *killed* her."

"Oh. Oh, honey, no." She sighs, then extends her hand toward me me. I reach out to take it, but I freeze. My body seems to know what's wrong before my mind can register it. Her hand, extended to help. The palm, pale already, but whiter at the center, where a long cut was once made.

The sliding door opens, and Doug steps inside. "Jan?"

Mrs. Simmons sighs. "Yes, dear?"

"I think she knows."

She nods. "I was afraid of that." She retracts her hand, steps back. Doug takes her place before me, his face lined with a frown as he watches me.

"We need to figure this out," he says to Jan, and then his fist curls, winds back, and blackness shoots through my mind.

———

My head rings. My stomach lurches. I roll onto my stomach just in time to let a wave of vomit escape my throat. When I blink my surroundings into focus, I realize I'm in my bedroom, lying on the bed. Vomit coats my pillow. I scramble up, too quickly, and vertigo drops me to my back.

I stare around the room—my room? No. The pale walls seem suddenly dark. The scent, distinctly masculine. I'm on my back, on a bed. Geoff—he left for the bathroom, didn't he? After he was finished, he said, "You're the best, babe," and he went off to piss like he hadn't just—

A hand brushes my forehead.

I scream, thrash. Footsteps clatter back against the floor. Once my body tells me the danger is past, too distant to hurt me, I feel not relief, exactly, but emptiness. I am allowed to collapse, and then, the tears follow.

"You didn't have to hit her so hard," a female voice mutters.

"We needed time." A male voice, not Geoff's.

And then I remember. Doug. Jan. Erin's two best friends.

"Hey. *Hey*." Doug's voice is close, but not close enough that I could strike out at him. I peel my eyes open to see him standing a few feet from my bed, a red book in his hand. Erin's diary.

"You read this?" he says, waving it at me. "That's where you got all this, hm?"

I prop myself on my elbows. I'm nauseous and weak, but I force myself to sit up, then stand, my hand on the bed for support. Doug takes a cautious step back.

"You..." I take a breath. "You killed her, didn't you? That's why she opened the window. She trusted you."

Doug shakes his head. "No. Whatever you think you know, you don't. Erin was a master manipulator."

"Then why is she dead?" I say.

Jan's jaw locks, her eyes flare. She's angrier than Doug, I realize. He's calm, all business. But there's a buried passion somewhere in this mousy woman.

"Erin asked you to keep her secret..." I start.

Jan's mouth flicks into a dry, mean smile. "A secret? Is that what she called it? Oh, just a tiny little thing between friends, right? She *burdened* me." Jan's voice elevates to a scream. Doug shoots her a look, and Jan quiets.

She looks at the box, opened on my bedroom floor. The rusted hunting knife sits atop everything else. "I know what he did. But how *could* she?" She works her thumb against the scar on her palm as though she could erase it. "How could she give me such a terrible secret to carry? I begged her to admit it, to tell the police, claim self-defense. But she wouldn't. And...I had to tell someone." Her eyes dart to Doug. He drops his head, whether in shame or resignation, I don't know.

"We confronted her," Doug says. "Together, that night. And she attacked us."

"Oh, did I?"

I turn at the voice in my ear, and there she is. She's a flash of light and then a girl. I wait for Doug and Jan to see, but they don't. Their eyes stay on me, focused, afraid.

Erin turns and winks at me. "Give me a moment with my best friends, okay?"

"I—" My voice stops. *I* stop. I feel my body go cold, and when I look around, I no longer see Erin. But she's here. Close. I feel her anger and her pain as though it were my own. My heart pounds in fury. My fingers clench at my sides. I take a slow step forward.

"The knife was already buried," Erin says with my mouth, her deadly sweet voice foreign on my tongue. "I was furious, sure. My best friend gives up my big secret. And the boy who said he loved me...tell the girl what you did, Dougie."

"What are you...?" Doug's voice fades, flat with fear.

"She's crazy, Doug," Jan hisses. "Something's wrong with her head. You shouldn't have hit her so hard."

"You told me," Erin says, "that I was finally too damaged for you." I step closer, my feet unconsciously travelling toward them.

"Hey. Stay back." Doug lifts his hands toward me.

I'm not doing this, I try to say, but I'm no longer the one making choices for my body. I feel Erin's warped glee in my stomach, a blooming joy at her own power.

Doug lunges suddenly toward the box—the knife—and I do, too. I grab the hilt, he the blade. He bellows as the blade is torn from his hand, leaving a gruesome slice.

"Aw," Erin says with my mouth. "Now we all match."

I turn to Jan, and Erin says, "I told you what Ferris did. And you said it was my own fault." I take another light step. "And then you watched while good ol' Dougie strangled me. After that...well, looks like you finally got him, didn't you?"

Jan blinks, finally realizing. "This isn't possible."

My lips grin, manic and quick. "Jealousy never was pretty on you, Jan."

I know what Erin wants. I feel her intent as it builds pressure in my arm and lights a fire in my heart. *Erin,* I think. *Don't do this.*

And then my arm swipes across the air, the blade it my hand connects to thin flesh. Jan tries to gasp, but the open wound in her throat makes the sound a mere burble. She stands for a moment, then drops as a wave of crimson rushes her chest.

"Red is *so* your color," Erin says.

My screams hang in my throat, unable to rise above Erin's laughter. Jan's blood runs down my palm, tickles my wrist. I want to black out, but I'm hostage in my own body, watching a woman bleed out. Crying inside for what my hand has done.

Doug watches his wife die, but he doesn't scream. Doesn't cry. He looks up, hot fury sharpening on me.

"You're a crazy little bitch."

Erin tsks. "Doug. You know I don't like that word."

"Someone had to stop you."

"No. Someone needs to stop *you*." I kneel above him, the knife poised at his throat. "You know, Doug, I don't think you cared so much that I killed him. Why would you? You almost did it yourself." My hand dig the point of the blade into the hollow of his throat, just enough to draw a trickle of blood. "I think what really pissed you off was that I never loved you."

My arm tenses, drawing the knife back. *Don't,* I try to say, *please, please don't make me do this.* But Erin is too strong. Doug throws his hands up and cowers back.

"Wait, wait! Erin, please. I—I was always sorry. I took care of your mother. I tried to make it right. Me and Jan, we—we never got over it."

Erin is thoughtful a moment, the knife still in my hand. "You seemed to be doing pretty well."

"No. It was wrong. It was—you're right. I loved you, always did. And I just...I couldn't stand to see what you'd become. What he made you. I thought it was...merciful."

Erin's anger rushes through my body, so intense it hurts. "*Merciful?*"

"Yes. How—how could you *live* with yourself?"

"Oh, Doug." My hand reaches out, runs a finger down his chin. "How can you live with *your*self?"

My arm draws back and down before I can scream at Erin to stop, and a rush of blood pools around the knife sticking out of Doug's heart.

I fall back against the floor. I no longer feel Erin's anger, her vindication, her pain. I carefully pull my arm to my chest, testing. It's me. My mind controlling my limbs. My heart is wild, but not with fury.

"Erin?" I sit up, glance around. She's beside the window, faint, almost gone.

"Sorry to leave you with clean-up duty," she says. "Thanks, by the way. I needed that."

My mouth falls open. "No. No, no, no. You are not leaving me with—"

Her figure vanishes through the window, and I know she's gone for good.

I stare at the bodies on my bedroom floor. Doug. Jan. Erin has taken her final revenge.

I understand her, I do. How many times have I wished I'd been able to take a knife to Geoff's throat? Beaten his head in. Anything. I understand why Erin killed Ferris. Jan and Doug couldn't comprehend her pain. They thought she was insane. So they killed her.

And now, she's killed them.

But…god, what has she done to me?

I have the knife, the diary. But nothing to justify why the bodies of Doug and Jan Simmons, friendly next-door neighbors, are on my bedroom floor.

The only thing I have linking Erin to these murders is my own experience. And what is that worth? I know what they'll say: *She finally snapped.*

A key rattles in the front door. No. Not now. She can't…

"Mel? I'm home."

Mom.

"Erin," I whisper. "Come back. You have to tell her what you—"

"Mel?"

"Erin! *Erin!* Come back! You have to tell her—?"

"Mel?" Mom knocks on my bedroom door. "Mel!"

"Erin! Erin!"

I look back at the bodies on my floor. Mom pounds against the door, and my fists create a harmony against the window, begging her to come back.

"Erin! Erin! Erin…"

But she's gone.

She's not coming back.

E.R. GRIFFIN loves books, dogs, crosswords, and all things Legend of Zelda. She holds a BA in Creative Writing from Geneva College and graduated from the Publishing Institute in Denver, Colorado. She currently lives in northern Georgia with her dog, Hermione.

One last bite from E.R. Griffin...

I wanted to write a ghost story. But I wasn't sure I wanted there to be a ghost. A haunted house is scary enough, but a haunted mind is so much worse. Mel's struggle to untangle the strangeness of her new home with the trauma of her past comes from my curiosity about what would happen if a girl met a ghost with a past like hers, a ghost she can't prove exists but feels compelled to help anyway.

Considering my love of horror which takes place in the psyche, my favorite feminist author would have to be Shirley Jackson. Though she died before feminism became the movement that it is today, she wrote horror that also highlighted the constraints placed on women by society, their families, and sometimes their own minds.

AFTER THE FOXES HAVE THEIR SAY

TRACIE MARTIN

The Warden Takes a Wife

There once was a prison in the middle of a dusty state, not far from where the Devil sits at the crossroads, pointing the wrong way to hell. One day, the Warden of that prison found himself a pretty wife. Folks whispered that she was a little too pretty, at least for the likes of him. It just didn't make sense that someone with eyes so cornflower blue and a golden tumble of hair shining down her back would choose a jailhouse life in a town the ass-end of nowhere. But the Warden, he didn't care. He married her before she could change her mind and took her to what everyone called Stonesong Prison. Old Jebediah Pickmaster gave it that nickname when he started beating a rhythm to the ring of the prisoner's pickaxes on the quartz boulders *"Listen to 'em make them stones sing."*

But Jebediah's music was a terrible racket to the new Mrs. Warden. She called it the song of bestial barbarism, and despite all the Warden's efforts to explain how much devilry the convicts would get into without the labor to wear them out, she proclaimed that she'd not enter their marriage bed until the noise ceased. Now, the Warden, his salary, and his job depended on meeting the quota for his quarry. He tried to speak sense with her and placate her with sarsaparilla and horehound candy, but she spent her days in her rocking chair or wandering the gardens with her hands over her ears.

It happened one day that a load of orphans was dropped at the prison's door. They were the children of carnies who'd been caught picking pockets at the county fair. The boys the Warden took straight to the stone fields, but the girls . . . well, he had something different in mind for them. And from the way the prisoners and the guards eyed the oldest girls, it was clear they had ideas of their own.

The Warden's wife took one look at that wagon of little girls and said, "I'll leave if these young ones walk through these doors." And the Warden, he knew she meant it. He thought fast and came up with the perfect solution to his quandary. He loaded his wife in the children's wagon and had the driver take them all to a cottage deep in the adjoining woods. It was used for conjugal visits and the occasional state dignitary who came to hear the stones sing, but the Warden decided to just give them his lonely bed in the main house to sleep in when the time came.

He settled his wife with the children and an armed guard and told her she could run the house as she saw fit, knowing she'd love the chance to let her highbrow notions out to play. He saw the wisdom of his wife's demands only he and John Josaphat, his oldest guard -- who'd lost his hobnocker in the war -- see the girls. The Warden had a whole den of foxes who wouldn't mind ravaging the oldest chickens in the henhouse. He would watch his wife and his charges with his silence, even from the distance of his home in the prison. As the weeks dragged on and the stones continued to sing, the Warden knew other men would right the situation with more forceful measures. But he wanted to earn his wife's love, not take it. When she rewarded him with a tender kiss, the Warden knew he'd made the right decision. He knew it wouldn't be long before he could enjoy all the sweetness her arms had to offer.

So eager was the Warden for another taste of his wife's lips that he dismissed the John Josaphat's unsettling stories of strange meals around the cottage dinner table, odd prayers, how the children shoved books behind their backs whenever he appeared around the corner. The Warden knew an old, jealous fool when he heard one. And at each visit, the Warden found a group of well-behaved young ones in pin-neat aprons. They presented him with the kind of apple pies that made a man remember the scent of his mother's skin.

Even the prisoners found themselves swinging with a little more energy when the Warden came back from the forest and that cinnamon breeze curled around their faces, especially the carnie boys who labored alongside the prisoners, dreaming of home and their missing sisters. Soon the singing stones echoed throughout the entire state, and the visitors that came to hear their song brought back tales of the perfect pies—and their mysterious bakers—to their duly elected officials.

The State Superintendent paid a visit to see what all the fuss was about. He came with promises of promotions and improvements, new wonders to celebrate the Warden's success. And then the Superintendent changed his tune.

"Folks say funny things sometimes. Like a wagon of children that vanished off God's good earth a few months back." The Superintendent drummed his fingers on the table, and the little pile of stones the Warden kept in a candy dish jumped to the rhythm. "I wonder what happened to all those young ones."

The Warden's housekeeper carried in a pie. The Superintendent took one whiff of a fresh-cut slice and began to drool.

"Who baked this astonishment?

The Warden hemmed and hawed about townswomen, but the Superintendent raised his hand. "I wouldn't mind a taste of something sweet," was all he said, but the Warden knew the man's appetites full well. He understood exactly what sort of skin the Superintendent's teeth wanted to bite. He set off for the forest that evening with a heavy heart and explained the matter to his wife.

"Please pick out your best baker," he said. "She can carry the pie herself."

The Warden's wife exclaimed her horror. She knew the child would not return with her spirit intact.

But the Warden shook his head. "This is the way of things," he said. Simply. The Superintendent was his senior and not to be gainsaid. He felt no need to embellish such an implacable truth with fine words or regret.

The next day, the Warden rose early and waited by the gates for the fresh arrival from the house in the woods. But instead of soft curls and a dimpled smile, John Josaphat staggered into the courtyard. Shreds of his uniform clung to his shoulders. Blood dripped from a gash just below his heart. His throat worked around some terrible story, but the words refused to come out until he loosed his dying breath. The Warden had to cup his ear over the poor soul's mouth to hear it. "She took them."

The Warden got in his motorcar and flew to the cottage. When he got there, he found spoons in bowls and a pot of stew on the stove. A pile of charred animal bones lay on the hearth. But no one was in the house or in the surrounding woods.

The Warden sped back toward town to call for a search, and he passed Old Jebediah Pickmaster at the crossroads. He pulled over and rolled down his window. "Did you see where they went?"

Jebediah spat out a hunk of chew and crossed his arms over

his chest. His dirty index fingers pointed in opposing directions. "Take yer pick."

The Warden Makes a Daughter

The Warden searched high and low for his wife, but he had a prison to run so eventually he had to call off his search and return to work. Folks talked it over and decided, all in all, he'd recovered just fine. He might have a little shine of whiskey on his breath now and then. But still. He'd moseyed straight back to his old bachelor habits, as if he'd never carried a bride across his threshold in the first place.

One day, he opened his door in answer to a knock and found a basket on his porch with a bright red bow on the handle. He looked inside and found a beating ox heart. A little notecard dangled from a string around that heart. "Feed Me," it said.

Now the Warden and his wife never had enough separation to warrant a loving correspondence—prior to her disappearance, that is—but he'd been so lonely for her spirit that he'd taken to reading anything to which she'd set a pen, and he instantly recognized her schoolmarm letters. He went tearing through the yard, searching behind all the singing stones. But all he found was a rusty pickaxe. He threw the basket into the woods and went to bed and blamed the whole thing on a bad batch of hooch.

When he opened his door the next morning, he found another basket on his porch. The ox heart was back, but now it was slightly wrinkled and beating weakly. "I'm Hungry," the little tag said.

The Warden took the basket into his kitchen and searched his shelves, but he had no idea what kind of food to offer a heart off wandering on its own. So he tucked an apple next to the heart and set the basket on a log deep in the woods for the foxes to manage.

Now the Warden was sure that after the foxes had their say, he need never fear another of his wife's gift baskets on his porch. But the next morning he woke up and found a shriveled chunk the size of a rotting peach on his wife's old pillow. The heart was so small now that the tag fell off.

"I'm Starving," it said.

The Warden ran out to his truck in his suspenders and drove to the crossroads to ask Old Jebediah Pickmaster what to do.

"Feed it, son."

"I don't know what it's hungry for."

"Well, if you're that stupid, I better just manage this for you," Jebediah said. He dug a hole in the center of the crossroads with the bottom of his walking stick. Then he dropped the heart into the hole and spat a line of chew on it.

"What are you doing?" the Warden exclaimed.

"Hush."

Now folks say that the Devil does his work in a cloud of sulfur and that God does his in a flash of light. Jebediah just kicked dirt over the heart in the hole with the flapping toe of his broken old boots. When that cloud of dust settled to the ground, a little girl stood in the crossroads. She had his wife's eyes and his own coal-colored hair. The Warden crossed himself.

Jebediah used his walking stick to knock the Warden's hand away from his chest. "What good is that going to do you now, fool?"

"I abjure you, Satan," the Warden said.

Jebediah rolled his eyes. Then he plunged his walking stick through the Warden's breast for all the world, like he was thunking a straw into an orange for a long, tasty sip. The stick came away clean as a whistle.

"See. I told you. No point praying, son. You ain't got no heart to cross."

The Warden prepared to brain Jebediah for the affront and the loss of his Sunday shirt. But just then the girl smiled. Her laugh sounded exactly like the stones singing in the prison yard.

His heart kicked to life, encaged in her ribs.

It was disorienting, to say the least, but the Warden soon got used to the sensation. But he never acclimated to the danger of tethering his heart inside another, and he clung to his daughter to keep it as close to the safety of his chest as possible. The arrangement worked well, and for many years her laughter rang a rich duet with the pickaxes cracking outside her window.

It was better than the sound of a lark to the Warden's ears, and he soon found himself forgetting his wife's voice, the wheat-grass fall of her hair. What need had he for the touch of a woman when he had his daughter's smile to warm his heart? Had he been a thinking man, he would have consoled himself with thoughts of her comfort and happiness and the circumstances of her birth. Where else could a girl born of stones in the Devil's crossroads live but here? But he was not a man given to plumbing the depths for the slipperier kinds of truths, and it never occurred to him that she could leave the circle of his arms.

But there's a cycle to life, and every sapling wants to branch into a tree. The Warden's daughter soon noticed how a particular pickaxe followed the lead of her laughter, punctuating the peaks and valleys with a merry jingle. She followed the tune to the back of the stone fields, where a young carnie boy had grown into a strong-backed man with a raven's head of hair and cobalt eyes. He handed her a rough-hewn heart hacked from a veiny piece of rose quartz.

"Now you can return his," he said.

Now the Warden's daughter was young, but her mother's blood ran through her veins, and she was no fool. She saw the sharp edges and ragged cuts all along his offering, and she knew if she pulled her father's heart out of her chest and replaced it with the boy's, she'd still spend her life tied to a man's rib. But she was soul-sick of dust, of her frilled window seat, high above the yard, where she watched the prisoners crack the stones in two. She could bear no longer the touch of her father's breath on her neck. His scent. His ear on her door at night to make sure she stayed within.

She shrugged and tucked the young man's heart into her apron pocket. The weight of the stone promised to be a bother each time she stooped the wrong way or leapt across a stream, but better out than in.

The next morning, the Warden found a beribboned basket on his doorstep. A notecard was tied around the handle. It said, "I'm back."

Inside lay a desiccated red oval the size of a prune. When the Warden tried to pick it up, the shriveled thing dissolved in a puff of red dust.

The Warden carried the dust carefully in his palms to Jebediah.

"Can you bring her home?"

"What does your heart tell you?"

The Warden, mindless, reached up and touched the concave dip in his chest, scarred with tissue from Jebediah's long-ago violence. Red dust rained down from his fingers. The last of it flew over the crossroads and blinded a raven's flight. The raven was not amused by this disruption and cawed a curse for the ages.

"Well, isn't that a fine kettle of fish." And Jebediah threw back his head and laughed.

The Warden's Granddaughter Comes to Call

The years rolled by, as they are wont to do, and the Times, well, they all circled back to tap each other on the shoulder. The Warden watched politicians in suits make speeches about progress and principles, carnie-faced young ones barker about justice and liberation. The Warden observed, without fight or comment, as the stones went silent and the prisoners went to college. He simply sat in his chair in the high window of his office, overlooking the yard. Watched the fence fall in and his wife's forest creep closer day by day. Some may say that he'd acquired a few drips of wisdom from the changing world around him. Others that his constitution was too weak to fight the tide of change. More likely, his collapsing chest and rust-stained fingers were the cause of his languor.

Whatever the reason, nothing could jolt the man into action, even when the State Superintendent—a new one, also carnie-faced and full of his wife's high notions and fiery ideals—came to close the prison for good. The Warden nodded to each item on the agenda, but he paid the Superintendent the same amount of mind he offered his housekeeper. He peered out the window and noticed how his wife's forest had, overnight, sent shoots and tendrils through the fence and into the yard.

Once the Superintendent had pulled in the slack of his jaw and left, the Warden crept out into the whispering darkness. By then, the trees had reached his doorstep. A line of stones led through wood, rich with the menace of life. And then he saw a wheat-gold tumble of curls disappear around a bend.

"Wife," he called as he tore down the path.

He ran until a stitch bedeviled his side and he had to stop to exorcise the demon. Once his wheezing breath settled, he heard it. That ringing laughter of metal-struck stones. A sweet cotton candy scent on the wind.

"Daughter, Daughter. Wait for me." He ran, skidding on rocks, until the path abruptly ended in a clearing and he found himself standing before his wife's old cottage.

A stranger stood before him, knife brandished in her fist.

"I know how to cut. Don't try me."

The Warden took her in. There, his wife's golden hair, his daughter's stone song laugh. Could those be his coal-black eyes on her face?

"Granddaughter?" His voice shook in such a way that he realized, for the first time, that he was an old, old man.

The girl lowered her knife. "Who are you?"

"I believe you are the child of my blood."

She tilted her head and eyed him curiously. "Maybe. I never knew my father. Either way. Welcome to my house." She surveyed the grounds with obvious pride. "Would you like to come in?"

The Warden's jaw set. "I'm afraid there's been some mistake, my dear. This house belongs to me."

"You must be thinking of another cabin," she said. "My mother left this house to me. Her mother left it to her." Her chin lifted. "And *I'm* going to rebuild it."

The Warden was flabbergasted by this girl, by her resolute pride, her firm hold on the doorknob. He tried to seize the reigns of the conversation: "Well, my dear, technically, this land belongs to Stonesong Prison."

Her lip curled with distaste. "That place died years ago." And then she turned to him, her face soft. "Why don't you come in? I'll get you a glass of water and call someone for you."

It took the Warden a moment to understand the source of her kindness. She assumed he suffered a meandering mind. It was too deep a cut to bear. "What makes you think *you* can help *me*?" he spat.

The Warden watched all the warmth slowly melt from her face.

"Good question," she said.

Now, this dusty state wasn't particularly known for the damp kinds of weather, but nevertheless a mist began to rise between them. First, he lost sight of the house. Then the outlines of her body. Then her face.

"Goodbye," she called through the impenetrable fog. "Thank you for the stones. They're sure to come in handy."

The Warden stumbled backward into a path empty of the stones that led him there. He stumbled down a trail one way. Then another. Each way dropped him back into the crossroads.

He fell to his knees. "How can I get out, Jebediah?"

Jebediah spoke around a pipe clamped between his teeth. "You made these roads, boy. Don't you know your own path when you see it?"

But the Warden was rabbity with fear and beyond such wisdom. "Help me! Show me the way out."

"Alrighty, Warden. For old time's sake." Jebediah spat out a hunk of chew and pointed.

The Warden gasped with horror. "But that's the way to hell."

Old Jebediah Pickmaster lifted his trouser leg and showed a cloven hoof. He looked at the Warden and laughed so hard that all the crows in the forest took flight.

"All roads lead to hell 'round here, son."

TRACIE MARTIN is a fiction writer who also loves to feed birds, wave jump in Lake Michigan, and throw marshmallows straight into the fire to watch them burn. She hails (Yes!) from Michigan

(Go Blue!) and lives with her husband and two children just outside Chicago. It really is as windy there as they say.

One last bite from Tracie Martin...

Ironically, I started this story with the Warden. As I wrote him, I started to wonder what it would be like if a fairly decent man grew corrupted by his need for love. And then, as the story grew, I explored how the women in his life fight back against him, how each generation would grow and learn to take control of their lives in the most direct way. The women who came before us gave us so much from their strength and experience. I hope my story honors those gifts, at least a little.

It's hard to pick a feminist lit favorite, but I *do* have a favorite author: Shari S. Tepper. She wrote marvelous sci-fi, where the best feminist fiction lives (come argue with me about this on Twitter: I dare you). TRY GATE TO WOMEN'S COUNTRY and SINGER FROM THE SEA.

SHADOWS

DEMITRIA LUNETTA

June 13, 1998

D r. Janet Sayre,
        The women of this small village have developed a society completely devoid of male influence. Women provide everything for themselves and take the responsibilities that other native tribes have delegated to men, including hunting, protection, and all leadership roles. They have remained undiscovered and untouched from modern ideas and ideals. They live their entire lives within a twenty-mile radius of their birthplace, and they seem to exhibit no curiosity about the outside world. They are exceptional among all other cultures and present us with a unique opportunity to study what has in the past only been a hypothetical: What path would a society take if it were women, and not men, who ruled the world?

THE LETTER WAS THE LAST CORRESPONDENCE I'D RECEIVED from Dr. Harvey, sent in a brown paper–wrapped package that also included his journal. Dr. Harvey—Peter—was a friend and colleague and had been missing for four months now, and presumed dead.

I was following in his footsteps, traveling to South America to continue his work. He had discovered these tribal women and had alerted me as head of the department of anthropology. He'd sent no validation, no tangible evidence that such a tribe of women truly existed. Just coordinates and a request not to tell those bastards at Cornell just yet. He wanted the credit to go to our program alone.

Flimsy, but Peter was not a fantasist. I needed to find him. To find them. If it was true . . .

It had taken months of convincing, of calling in favors and doing back-door deals. I had also done my fair share of groveling and batting my eyelashes at trustees. It was worth it to swallow my pride; Peter had always taken my side during department power struggles. I could trust him to give me a heads-up with what was going on elsewhere in the university.

Luckily, I hadn't had to resort to bribery or blackmail. Peter's word was good in the academic community. He was respected, and thus, even the hope that his research had merit allowed for me to receive a grant, with more money to follow when I had made contact with this allegedly wholly self-reliant lost tribe of women.

I met up with Cassandra Jones in Peru. Cassie was a linguist who did her undergrad at McGill in Native American studies. She was currently at Princeton researching similarities between various South American languages. She was at the top of her field and at ease conversing in Spanish as well as Quechua, the native language spoken in Peru. I had feared she wouldn't be interested. Turned out, I needn't have worried. She had been extremely easy to convince; if the prospect of discovering a new language wasn't bait enough, I had waived my grant money at her and made promises of dual authorship on anything I published relating to language, provided she served as translator and scribe.

It was easy enough to find the coordinates Peter had notated. We had our guide drive us as far as was possible (Peru was not known for its well-maintained roadways) and hiked the rest. It was difficult going, but I was determined. Cassie seemed . . . less so. When we had made these plans, she had assured me that she was in good shape and often camped (she was a Canadian, after all!). But in truth, she seemed ill at ease in the wilderness.

She complained first about the heat, then her new shoes, then the humidity, then the weight of her pack. In addition to our survival supplies, we carried cameras and extra batteries in order to document any discoveries. Cassie had wanted to bring her laptop, but I had told her that the battery life would not be worth the extra weight. She was likely grateful I'd insisted she leave it behind.

To change the subject from Cassie's constant litany of complaints, I suggested we discuss the women and guess at their lifestyle. We slipped into the habit of saying "if they exist" each time we mentioned them.

"*If they exist, I bet they worship a vengeful goddess and sacrifice all males to her.*"

"*I wonder if they still get PMS, you know, without men around to be bothered by . . . if they exist.*"

It amused us to speculate.

It was three days before we crested a hill, which Peter had indicated in his notes, and looked down upon the area where the alleged women-centric tribe lived.

"Do you see anything?" Cassie asked, excited.

"Trees." I smiled.

"Trees and vines." Cassie laughed, a tight almost hysterical chuckle. "And birds."

"Don't forget the insects," I reminded her.

"How could I ever?"

We began our slow descent down the hill and into the jungle.

Cassie and I set up our tents and ate our cold dinner cold in the dark, the tree canopy shielding us from the light of the night sky. We discussed our next move. Cassie believed we should let the women (*if they existed*) establish contact with us, after we made ourselves known to be in the area. I agreed. It would be no good to go charging in, acting as if they should be grateful for our intrusion. If I knew Pete, he would have pulled something like that, which may have contributed to his disappearance. From his notes, he had made it clear that he had not found the women—naked and unarmed as they were—to be a threat. I would not make the same assumptions.

We decided, finally, to go to the river in the morning and wait for contact. The women would need to fetch water for their village and to bathe. If someone did not appear tomorrow, we believed they would come the next day or the next. We might have to be patient, but it would be worth it for the discovery of this century. I slept fitfully, worried about insects piercing the netting of my tent and snakes slithering into my sleeping bag. If I dreamt at all, my imaginings were fleeting, and I did not remember them in the morning.

I woke to the same noises of the rainforest that I had fallen asleep to. I changed my clothes quickly in my small enclosed tent and went to wake Cassie. I stepped out onto the soft earth of the jungle.

"Cassie?" I called softly.

No answer.

"Cassie!" I could hear the panic in my voice.

"What?" She poked her head out of her tent, her face showing sleep and confusion.

I pointed at the ground. "Footprints."

Cassie grinned. "Well, I guess they exist."

"Or we're being stalked by a different unknown tribe." I dropped down to study the footprints.

"Yes, I'm sure there are *two* previously unknown native tribes living in the region your colleague specifically indicated."

I laughed. "Yeah, and if we're extra lucky, at least one of those tribes will exhibit cannibalistic tendencies."

"A girl can dream . . ." Cassie also knelt to examine the tracks. "Let's follow them!"

I shook my head. They were meant to make first contact.

"They know we're here," Cassie said. "We should present ourselves to them."

She had no doubts about what should be done. I, on the other hand, was not so sure.

"They know we're here," I said, starting to document the footprints with the camera. "But they don't know why . . . or that we're aware of their existence."

"If they wanted to," Cassie said, beginning to pack up camp, "they could have harmed us last night."

"The fact that we weren't attacked could just mean they do not see us as a threat. Who knows what they will think if we march into their village—" I stopped mid-sentence. Cassie froze as well.

The woman stood before us completely naked, save for a belt of corded fiber, on which hung several stones of various sizes. Her black hair was tied in a long braid that hung across her shoulder and down her breast. She had a faint smile on her round face and held her hand out palm up. In a fluid movement, she tilted her hand upward, moving her arm toward her chest, and spoke an unintelligible word. She nodded once and disappeared into the trees.

I looked at Cassie. "It doesn't take a linguist to understand that."

I grabbed my pack and ran after the woman. Cassie's footsteps padded close behind.

THE WOMEN WERE SURPRISINGLY ACCEPTING OF US. THEY welcomed us into their village, giving us food and a communal hut in which to sleep. They saw our clothing and electronic equipment as oddities, something to poke and gasp at, then to forget just as quickly. Cassie attempted to communicate with them, but the process was slow and difficult.

She tried to ask about the males, about Peter, but to no avail.

"It is like no language I have studied, but a combination of Culle and Andoque both extinct," she admitted. "I can only understand about a tenth of what they say. I've never had to learn a language from context. I am going to write such a paper." She scribbled constantly in her journal, as did I. "Very exciting," she would mutter under her breath.

Very exciting, indeed. I myself thought of the articles I would publish. A tribe of women – fifty of whom we've seen so far, but I know there are many unseen - completely self-contained and independent. The Ayhua, Cassie told me they called themselves. I was living among them; Cassie and I their only point of contact with the outside world. It was one of the most important discoveries of modern times.

While Cassie painstakingly went about the task of learning their language, I studied their day-to-day activities—their village life. They slept in self-made huts, some with as many as five or six women, like the one in which Cassie and I had been allowed to stay. A few women preferred to live in smaller groups, some in couples, and some alone. Each woman slept on a woven mat, which I was surprised to find quite comfortable.

A few huts were reserved for the children. The village took on a communal mother role. Cassie explained that the children called all the women "Ahhie," which means mother. If the child was speaking with someone roughly her same age, she would address her as "Kuma," or sister. There were no male children.

"Cassie, can you ask them where the boys are?" I said. "Do you have enough of their language?"

Cassie spoke with the women in our hut as I listened. I did not understand them, but I loved the way their language flowed like a river across the landscape. After a while, Cassie turned to me.

"They don't understand what I'm asking. They keep responding that the only children they have are daughters. Quenta: it means daughter and child at once."

"But they must have some form of male contact. Where do the children come from?"

They had to have occasional access to men in order to have so many children. How was it possible that these women only gave birth to females?

"They say that they become with children in the dream-time." Cassie shook her head. "I don't really understand what they are telling me. I need more time."

"Okay, we can wait," I agreed. We were learning much about these women, but there was still a great deal to uncover.

I DISCOVERED THAT THE SAME TITLES HELD TRUE WITH the women: older women were called mother, while younger women were called sister. There was one exception, a woman named Chira, whom everyone called mother though she could have been no older than twenty-five. The other women seemed to confer with her often; she was clearly the chieftess of the Ayhua. It was surprising to me when she invited me to share her meal. Though we did not understand each other, she was very gracious, pointing to each item in her hut, saying the Ayhua word for each, expecting me to repeat it. She patted my head in dismissal when she had finished with me and sent me on my way. This became a daily ritual, and hour by hour, I learned more about these women and their language.

I sat with Cassie, as we did each night to compare knowledge learned that day. I was thumbing through my notebook, reviewing one of my early journal entries:

The women have distinctive Native American features, bronze skin, dark hair, with little to suggest contact with Latin America, which leads me to believe that their society was untouched by colonial influence. This dates their culture at the very least, 300 years, though I believe it to be much older. Whether by luck or design, they have remained undetected and unconquered for centuries, if not longer.

The women are surprisingly tall, more than half standing over six feet. This suggests that their diet contains much protein, as well as a gene pool that predisposes them to height. I still have not come into contact with men, and short of parthenogenesis, I have no answer to the question of how these women become pregnant. This theory, that an egg can be fertilized without sperm, is a highly unlikely, though not impossible explanation.

It is clear they value their children and work very hard to protect them, while teaching them to be self-sufficient, useful members of the village.

All the women, without exception, are naked, save for a belt with which they suspend various items. Some hang stone knives, some rocks of varying sizes, some herbs and flowers. The flowers may only be decorative, as I have seen several women wear them in their hair.

"THEY ARE SO VARIED IN THEIR STYLE," I TOLD CASSIE, closing my journal and looking up.

"I know, you would think that women without clothing would have no fashion, but they definitely take pride in their appearance." She was riffling through her own notebook, adding knowledge and crossing out misinformation. "Kiya, for example, takes great pleasure in braiding her long hair, while Jhut shaves her head clean daily."

Kiya and Jhut were definitely a couple, if not evident by their affectionate touches and loving embraces then by the fact that they shared a hut together, just the two of them.

"Jhut also wears a stone knife on her belt. I think she is a protector of the village," I said absently, thinking also of Kiya and that day we first saw her at our campground. She was small and beautiful, easily the gentlest person I had ever meant. Why had they not sent someone more imposing, like Jhut?

"Wait a minute, you think Jhut is a warrior? We've seen no evidence of violence, no need for—"

"Protection? This is a village of women. If they didn't have some form of defense they would not have survived for very long."

"I suppose so," Cassie agreed reluctantly. "But I have not heard them use a word for violence or war or even disagreement, for that matter."

"Phimuan. I learned it yesterday." I looked at the floor, ashamed I had failed to mention my progress with their language to Cassie, the linguist.

"Phimuan?" She wrote it in her notebook.

"Chira taught it to me. Two children were fighting and one

pushed the other onto the ground and pulled her hair. Chira chastised them and explained that fighting within the village was not tolerated."

"Hmm." Cassie chewed on the butt of her pen. "You are learning a lot from Chira. Can I see your journal to compare?"

"I'll write down any new words for you," I promised her quickly, not wanting her to read all my private thoughts. I know I should share everything with Cassie, but I felt protective of my relationship with Chira.

"You know," I told her to change the subject. "Chira offered us our own living space."

"Why would we want that? We are gaining invaluable information by living in the communal . . . Oh." She looked up. "They think we are lovers." She blushed slightly and laughed. "Did you explain?" she asked casually.

"I told her that we were very happy to live with the other women and needed no more time together than we already had. I think Chira understood. Her offer was a way to ascertain our relationship, while my response would have given her the answer she needed."

"Kiya and Jhut." She laughed, picking up the thread of our earlier subject. "Talk about an unlikely couple."

I shrugged. "Not so unlikely, they each want what they are not."

Tagging along with Chira, I learned that each woman performed a different task in the village, though none were assigned. Each did what needed to be done, to the best of their ability. Kiya was good at weaving belts and mats, while others went into the rainforest to harvest the materials. Some women cooked, while others watched the children. They took pride in what they were good at, and only the children occasionally complained about their chores. They all worked, except one. Chira introduced me to her one day.

"This is first mother," Chira explained. I was learning the language, but they still spoke to me as if they were speaking to a child. For this, I was grateful.

"First mother?" I asked, not understanding.

"Most mother." Chira tried again; she was always very patient with me.

"Oh," I exclaimed, understanding. "Many, many children?" The woman called Ah Ahhie nodded proudly.

"How many?" I was still amazed at the number of children in the village and the ease at which these women handled labor. Three births in the two months I'd been there, and the women up and about a few days later, their babies happy with the other mothers whose role it was to take care of the daughters.

The woman held up nine fingers, one for each daughter she had birthed. As an afterthought she closed her hands and held up six fingers, saying a word I did not understand. I looked to Chira, but she repeated the same word.

I called to Cassie, who was speaking with a few of the older children, interested in a game they had been playing.

"Cassie, have you heard this word before?" I made the woman repeat it.

"No, but it sounds like the Culle word for shadow." She wrote the word in her ever-present journal and looked up at me expectantly. "What is the context?"

"Childbirth. She has had nine daughters and six . . . could it be miscarriages?" The women here never spoke of infant mortality or stillborn births, but that didn't mean they didn't occur.

Cassie spoke with the woman, asking her as best she could

about her birthing experiences. They spoke many words I did not understand.

"They have a word for miscarriage, a phrase actually . . . 'the sadness of loss.' These shadows are births that don't result in daughters." In that moment, we both understood. She looked up at me, her eyes searching my face.

"Boys," I whispered, and Cassie nodded. "But . . . where are they? The shadows?"

Cassie and I agreed not to jump to conclusions or judgments and to continue with our research, though I must admit I could think of no other explanation than infanticide. At the same time, I could not believe that these women were capable of such an act, especially Chira, who I had come to think of as a friend.

Despite our feeling toward these women, Cassie and I had decided to check in every two weeks with our respective departments. Before we'd left, we'd arranged a boat that would meet us up river and take us to Iquitos. The journey took three days round trip. Though I hated to make Cassie take sole responsibility for the check-ins, I soon found that I was making too much progress to leave so often. Besides, Cassie didn't mind the breaks. She would return to civilization for a day, recharge batteries for the cameras, and make phone calls. We had told the American embassy in Lima that we were botanists and if we didn't report in every two weeks to contact the university.

"And if I don't show up?" Cassie asked of me one day. "Do we want people to know where to find us . . . where to find them?"

We were watching an older girl teach the younger girls to

braid hair. The older girl was almost a woman and would soon be moved from the children's hut.

"We could leave directions on how to get here, but what if there is an accident involving us and the wrong people get that information?" I said. People who would not come here just for research.

"When we release our findings, every ethnographer, linguist, and amateur anthropologist will want to study them." Cassie definitely wanted to err on the side of caution; we didn't want a delay to jeopardize our research, even hypothetically.

"I feel we would have more of a say over what happens here when we report our discoveries. But if we're not around to explain . . ." I hated to think of the Ayhua being exploited.

"Fine," Cassie finally agreed. "But if we discover that they leave their baby boys in the jungle to be eaten by jaguars or that they actually sacrifice men to their fertility goddess, I'm on the first plane back to New Jersey."

"I suppose linguists aren't taught not to judge another's culture based on American societal norms."

I hadn't meant to sound disparaging, but Cassie looked hurt.

"Of course we are." She folded her arms across her chest and shook her head. "Anthropologists don't have a monopoly on ethics."

"I'm sorry." I put my hand on her shoulder. "You know what anthropologists do have a monopoly on?"

"Bitchiness?"

"I was going to say arrogance, but that will do." I laughed and elbowed her gently until she smiled.

She dropped her arms and sighed. "Something is wrong; you know it, and I know it. If they kill their baby boys . . . why wouldn't they kill us if we got in their way? I just don't want to die here, as much as I have grown to love them." She looked at the girls, who groomed each other happily, oblivious to the world outside their village.

"I don't think your life is in danger," I assured her. There was no evidence that either of us were anything but an accepted part of their community.

"And if it were . . . If there was some indication that we were in danger, would you leave?"

I didn't answer. She knew I would stay. I would stay until my research was finished. This was the turning point in my career, in my life. There would not be another opportunity like this. Cassie and I stood in silence.

The girls we were watching tired with braiding each other's hair, and the oldest girl stood up.

"Come along daughters," she told them. "Let's bring flowers to mother Kiya; she will make us rings for our hair." She helped the younger girls up, holding the smallest by her chubby hand. She could not walk as quickly as the older girl and stumbled.

"Mother," the girl whimpered. She was scooped up into the older girl's arms and comforted.

"Cassie, did you see that?"

"Yes, I've noticed the younger children call the older children mother. There seems to be no distinction between genetic mothers and just a girl who is older. I suppose if you're not worried about inbreeding, it doesn't matter who your actual sister or mother is. Although with a quarter of the village adults exhibiting same-sex mating habits, you would think they would make some effort to keep track of who is related to who."

"No, Cassie, look at the girl's hair, the youngest one." The one the older girl was still cuddling.

"Why," Cassie gasped. "She's blonde." The girl's hair was dark, brownish-blonde at best, but golden streaks shone through. How had we not noticed this before?

"And none of the older women are." I frowned. "Where are the men?"

I had wrapped this village and its people around me like a warm blanket, cozy in their comfort. But now I was chilled to the core. That little girl, her hair reminded me of Peter's . . .

Chira beckoned me then to attend to her. I shook the unease from my shoulders and let the sun warm away my concerns.

———

CHIRA WAS MORE THAN THE CHIEFTESS. SHE WAS THE medicine woman and the midwife. She also performed religious ceremonies, such as during the birth of a daughter or when a child became a woman. Cassie and I had the opportunity to witness a Womanhood Ceremony firsthand, the same night I found out what was being done with the baby boys.

Two of the older girls had started their menstruation earlier that day. All the women had their period on the same four days each month, and Cassie and I were soon on the same cycle. During this time, most of the women of the village rested and chewed herbs that eased cramps. The older women did all the cooking. I'd noticed that Jhut and a few of the other women did not rest. I asked Chira for the reason.

"They take the leaves of a special flower, crush them in water, and drink the mixture. They do this daily and have no need to rest once a month. They also do not become pregnant." She spoke as she prepared herbs for the ceremony that night.

"Pregnant how?" I asked, hopefully.

She looked at me with her dark eyes. "Were you never taught this in your land? How you become a mother?"

"I was . . . but . . ." I stammered. There was no word for men. I didn't have the vocabulary to ask the proper questions.

"Jhut will not bleed nor become pregnant while she takes

the tincture."

"And she wishes this?" I myself had taken birth control, but I was surprised because the Ayhua women gave so much respect and admiration to pregnancy and motherhood.

"They have important work elsewhere." She used a few words I did not understand.

"Do they not want to be mothers?" I pushed.

"They are mothers." Chira stopped what she was doing and grabbed my shoulder. "We are all mothers here."

I nodded uncomfortably, and Chira went back to her work. For the first time I felt useless, being an observer and not an actual member of the community.

"Chira, teach me to make . . ." I couldn't think of the word for medicine, was not even sure if that was what was being prepared. "Teach me to make plants," I finished lamely.

Chira smiled and pointed to the herbs before her, naming each one.

THE WOMANHOOD CEREMONY WAS NOT WHAT I EXPECTED. The village women formed two circles around a fire; Cassie and I sat in the back, though I yearned to be up front. The inner circle seemed to be reserved for the older women. The two girls stood in the center with Chira. They were clearly excited to finally become women, smiling at each other and giggling with excitement. Chira was holding a long pipe, the first I had seen in the village. Each girl smoked and coughed and smoked and coughed until Chira was satisfied. The women began to chant, words neither Cassie nor I understood.

The girls began to shake slightly. Chira took the cord that the women used as a belt and tied it around each girl's waist. The girls were shaking more violently now, and Chira had them sit, then lay on mats on the ground. She took a bowl of liquid and soaked her hands in it. She then took the first girl and lifted her knees. She reached out to the girl and placed one hand on her pelvis and the other between her legs.

"What is she doing?" Cassie asked, horrified.

"Chira is breaking the girl's hymen," I explained.

"What?"

"Calm down. A few ancient Middle Eastern cultures would do the same," I whispered. "It takes the power of sex away from the men, making them unable to determine if their bride is a virgin or not."

When Chira was finished with the first girl, she washed her hand in the bowl and moved on to the second girl. The women continued their chant, and I could feel Cassie becoming more and more uncomfortable.

"It's really not that bizarre a practice," I assured her. "It makes a woman's first sexual experience less painful and therefore more pleasurable."

"But there are no men." Cassie no longer could whisper if she wanted to be heard. The women's chanting had become progressively louder. "If there are no men, why do they need to do this?" She was practically shouting now.

Before I could answer, a scream pierced the night, and the chanting stopped. I and every other woman looked for the source. Ah Ahhie stood, clutching her swollen stomach. She was the First Mother, and she was about to give birth.

Chira stood and walked directly to me. "Take her to my hut. I need to fetch a special plant."

I nodded, and Cassie grabbed my arm before I could get up. "Are you her apprentice now?" she asked archly.

"No, we are friends." I shook off Cassie's grasp. "I am learning firsthand how these women live. Isn't that why we're here?"

Cassie nodded, her face pinched. I shook my head and went to help Ah Ahhie. Cassie would have to learn to deal with her own inhibitions.

———————

THE GREAT MOTHER'S LABOR DID NOT TAKE VERY LONG. Ahhie had given birth many times and did not bother to fret. After her initial scream, she only grunted on occasion, biting down firmly on the piece of wood Chira had given her. As well as having a medicinal purpose, it was a physical release of her labor pains.

Within an hour, the birthing was over, and Chira adeptly caught the newborn baby and cut its umbilical cord. She quickly wrapped it in woven tree bark strips, while the child wailed.

A few more gasps and pants and the veteran mother had expelled the afterbirth. She looked searchingly for Chira.

"A daughter?" she asked urgently. "Do I have another daughter? Is she well?"

Chira came and held her hand. "There was no child, Great Mother. I am sorry."

I looked at her horrified. The baby still cried softly from where it had been placed on the floor.

"Ah Ahhie, the child is fine." I had no idea why Chira would say such a thing.

"My daughter? Give her to me at once!" Ah Ahhie said, trying to rise.

"No, this woman is confused." Chira pushed Ah Ahhie back down, gently, yet with all the authority of her position. "There is no daughter. Only a shadow."

The Great Mother nodded her head in understanding, and I sat back on my heels, shocked. There was a baby boy. A boy. I hadn't seen a male of any kind for months, and this woman had just given birth to healthy baby boy. Asexual reproduction—as much as a long shot as that theory was—was now officially ruled out. Such a child could only be female.

Chira gave me a pointed look, a sharp expression I had never before seen on her face.

"Stay here; comfort her," Chira ordered me.

"Where are you going? Where are you taking . . ." I couldn't continue. They had no word for him. No male words at all.

Chira looked at the exhausted woman, who was already sleeping. "I will be back by sunrise." She disappeared, and I had only a moment to decide. I left the recovering woman and followed Chira.

IT DID NOT TAKE LONG FOR HER TO NOTICE ME. THERE WAS a slight path out of the village toward the river; as soon as Chira stepped from it, I was at her mercy. I had to keep her in my line of sight. I did not trust myself not to become lost in the rainforest.

"I know you are there, daughter." Chira called over her shoulder. "You might as well walk with me."

"Yes, mother." I was used to calling this younger woman mother. I looked at my feet, so as not to trip. "I left the Great Mother alone. If there is a problem . . ."

"She will be fine. She has given birth many times before and will most likely be pregnant again before the new moon. It is her role." Chira glided along the jungle floor, never unsure of her footing.

"And the daughter?" I had no better word. Child and daughter were the same.

"There was no daughter," Chira explained patiently. "Only the shadow of a daughter."

"What will we do with the shadow?" I was acutely aware of the *we* I had just used.

"We have far to walk, and you are slow." Chira sighed.

Though I believe she did not mean to insult me, the words stung. She wanted me to be quiet.

We walked for several hours without stopping to rest. My legs ached, and I was thirstier than I had ever been in my life.

"Water," Chira said, as if reading my mind.

"What?" I had not looked up from the ground for a while.

"We are nearing water. We can drink and rest," she explained.

We came to a lake, and I drank hurriedly, expecting Chira would want to move on quickly.

"We can wait here a moment," she told me. Then the baby began to howl. The whole time it had been silent, sleeping, tired from being brought into the world. Chira was unconcerned with its cries. She made no move to comfort it.

"Chira, if you need to take the . . . shadow somewhere to leave it, maybe I can . . ."

"Shhh," she hissed and stood suddenly, facing the trees. I did not see anything at first, but I heard footsteps. A woman emerged from the forest, carrying several cloth bags. She was short and sturdy, shouldering her bundles with ease. She wore a plain buttoned shirt and a pleated skirt, not exactly the latest fashion trend but definitely modern.

Wordlessly, she dropped the bags at Chira's feet, hardly sparing me a glance.

"You are fortunate you were not here yesterday. I only just arrived back." The woman's words formed strangely in her mouth, but they were of the same language I had so painstakingly learned this past year.

"I have often waited much longer than a day," Chira said.

She handed the baby to the woman, who placed it in a sling

over her shoulder. The woman nodded once and turned without a backward glance.

Chira grabbed the bags, throwing one over each shoulder. "Drink as much water as you need; we will return home now."

I tried to take one of the heavy bags from her, but that slowed us down even further, and once again I was struck by my uselessness. We did not speak in the hours it took us return to the village, but a great weight had been lifted from my shoulders. Chira was not a murderess. They did not kill babies. They just did not want the boys. How is it different from parents in other countries giving their daughters to orphanages?

When we returned to the familiar village, Chira and I went immediately to check on Great Mother. She was recovering quietly and needed only to rest.

"It is difficult," Ah Ahhie confided, as I wiped the sweat from her head with papery bark that Chira had given me. "To have false births. I wish there were no shadows."

"I feel your sadness." I didn't know how to convey to this woman just how sorry I was. "But you have had many daughters and will have many more."

This seemed to comfort her, and she soon drifted back off to sleep.

I looked up to find Chira watching me.

"Do you wish to know what we have carried?" Chira asked.

I nodded eagerly, and she motioned for me to open the bags. I crawled excitedly to the bundles and undid the ties. I was confused at first, the course white substance before me was unlike the table version I was used to.

"Salt?" I asked in English, not knowing the correct Ayhuan word.

"It is from a place I have never seen. The pregnant women greatly crave it," she explained. "There is a village near a very large lake that we have been trading with for generations. They value shadows; we need salt."

"How far is this village? Have you never been there?" I thought the women had no outside contact.

"No, I do not go there. That woman travels many days each way. That is just our meeting place. She has a shelter there and waits for me. That is how she serves her village." She began to crush a plant in a bowl with a stone pestle. "Here, I will show you how to prepare the herbs for women who have given birth. To make them strong and fit."

I stood beside her. "Thank you Chira. I value your knowledge."

"I know what they do with their boys, Cassie."

"You do?" she asked wide eyed. "Is that where you were last night?" She grabbed my arm and pulled me into our shared hut. "What happened? They don't . . ."

"No, they don't hurt the babies. They don't just leave then in the wilderness either." I assured her, guilty we had ever thought as much.

"Well, that's a relief."

I paused then, hesitant to tell Cassie the rest.

"So . . . what *do* they do?" She was so curious that her fingers twitched around her notebook.

"They . . . well, Chira, actually, takes the babies a few hours walk southwest, as far as I can tell. She meets up with a woman from another village and gives her the boys. The woman's village is on the coast, a few days walk. But, Cassie . . ." I looked at my feet. "The woman wore modern clothes."

"Oh, dear God, do you think she puts them on the black market?" Cassie looked horrified.

"There is nothing that would suggest that," I said. "As far as we know, the woman takes them to her little village on the coast where there is a happy abundance of males, thanks to the Ayhuan women. I mean . . . Chira thinks she's getting the better end of the bargain; two bags of salt in exchange for a thing she doesn't even see as human."

"Salt?" Cassie asked, confused.

"They trade their babies for salt." Saying it aloud made it sound so much worse.

"How can they?" Cassie was clearly disgusted, her face scrunched into a scowl.

"Cassie, we can't judge them. I mean, look at China, they send their girls to orphanages, or worse, in hopes that they will eventually have a boy. How is this different?"

"They sell their children for seasonings." She knit her eyebrows together. "I just can't believe these women would do something like that."

"And you have no criticisms of our culture? Picture-perfect America?"

"I'm Canadian," she pointed out.

It was not meant to be a joke, but I couldn't help but laugh. It was an awkward explosion at first, and I tried to stifle my giggles, but once I started, I couldn't stop. Cassie narrowed her eyes, then smiled, relaxing.

"Point taken, but I don't like it," she told me.

"You don't have to like it. The question is can you live with it? Can you not let it affect your work?"

She nodded, crossed her arms, and stared up at the thatched ceiling. "I think . . . I think I need a break from this. More than a few days. I want to go home for a month or two, collect my thoughts, publish my findings . . ."

"But not this location." It was not a question, and Cassie knew it.

"No, of course not, but you're going to have to come back too. My research means little without yours. My department is salivating over my findings. They thought I would be here for six months, and it's been thirteen."

"I'm expected to be here for three years." It had seemed like such a long time to be gone, and now I understood it would not be enough. "The papers and images I've sent home . . . I have a feeling they think it might be a hoax."

"More the reason for me to go in person," she said eagerly. She hid her homesickness well, but now it all gushed out. "Just for a month or two."

"Of course, go." I had a sudden urge to hug her. She alone here understood the outside world. There was no one else to talk about old movies with, or worry about the world economy, or lament our lack of indoor plumbing.

"You will come back though, won't you?" I offered her my hand, and she held it. In the real world, I would have thought this odd, holding hands with a woman who was a friend.

"I will. I'm sure that after I share your research they'll probably want me to turn right around."

We packed Kiya's woven mats, Jhut's stone knives, and Chira's herbal medicines for Cassie to take home. She also took several belts, examples of what different women wore. The village understood that Cassie was leaving for a long time, perhaps for good, and even the children were quiet, less joyous. My eyes caught on the little blonde girl. Where was her father? Where were any of their fathers?

It would be a full year before Cassie returned. We would welcome her back as a sister.

———

I KEPT BUSY IN THE YEAR OF CASSIE'S ABSENCE. I LEARNED

much of the intricacies of the Ayhua's language, as well as their society. I became Chira's unofficial apprentice; she was happy to mentor me and share knowledge, teaching me as she did many of the village children.

When Cassie left, I felt very lonely at first, unable to share certain thoughts about the culture I was observing. I couldn't very well tell the basket weavers that they possessed skill that even Martha Stewart would envy. I didn't know how to explain to Chira when one of her herbs reminded me of a scent—cinnamon or sage—from my other life.

I became friendly with Kiya, the small, sweet woman who was so good at handiwork and weaving. She chatted with me about her day and the children while I tried unskillfully to follow her lead and weave mats. My inept attempts always resulted in an inferior product, which Kiya would happily unravel and expertly redo.

Kiya was one of the few younger women who had not gotten pregnant during my time in the village. The others whom I'd yet to see with child had all been the ones I thought of as warriors, such as Kiya's lover, Jhut. Those women seemed too preoccupied with their duties, leaving the village for days at a time on unknown missions, to be slowed down by pregnancy. But even one of those strong women was growing heavier, her stomach stretching.

"Kiya," I tried to ask casually one day. "Why have you had no daughters?"

She looked at me, her large black eyes sad. "I have many daughters. All the children are my daughters, and I am their mother."

I didn't want to alienate my new friend. "I only meant . . . I have not given birth either. I was wondering if it was your choice or . . . something else."

Kiya smiled then. "I have tried to get pregnant, many times, but . . ." She shrugged. "Nothing."

My throat dropped to my stomach, and I stopped working on the mat I was muddling. I had been prying at Chira for the better part of a year as to the origins of the village women's pregnancies. No one spoke of men in any way or even sex other than the contact that occurred between women.

"If I wanted to," I asked, "how would I become pregnant?"

"The same way where you come from, I should think," Kiya answered, guarded. She worked furiously for a moment, her hands moving with a dexterity I could never hope to match.

"Do you not trust me?" I asked, suddenly understanding.

"I do," she assured me, most likely not wanting to hurt my feelings. "But . . ." She leaned toward me and whispered, "We are supposed to wait for Chira's permission. If you were to have a child here, and then leave . . . we could not stand for you to take our daughter away."

All those dodged questions, all the times Chira brushed away my inquiries and swept me out of her hut like dust on the floor. They accepted me, in their way, but they knew I was not here to stay and did not want me messing around with their society.

"If I wanted to stay here, and Chira said that it was okay . . ."

"That would be a very happy time." Kiya smiled and then hugged me excitedly. "Many here would like for that to happen."

"I am concerned about becoming pregnant." I tried a different tact, feeling slightly guilty for trying to manipulate Kiya, but only slightly. "What if I cannot do what needs to be done?" I asked as vaguely as I could.

"Where you came from, did you not try to become pregnant?"

"No," I answered honestly. I had never engaged in sex with the intent of procreation.

"Well . . ." She looked doubtful. "The thing itself is rather nice." She looked around to make sure no one was listening. "I will tell you a secret."

I nodded my head eagerly.

"Jhut does not like that I attempt to become pregnant, even though I know that I cannot."

"Why not? There is always the chance."

"No." She shook her head. "I have tried so many times that I should have had many daughters, as many as Ah Ahhie."

"Then why does Jhut not want you to try?" I whispered, wrapped up in Kiya's predicament.

"Because she is . . ." Kiya said a word I had never heard before. But I didn't interrupt. "Jhut thinks that I enjoy it too much, and I enjoy it very much indeed." She laughed then, a girlish laugh.

"Well, there's nothing wrong with that, Kiya."

"Don't tell Jhut." She looked genuinely concerned.

"Of course not," I assured her.

Later, I asked Chira the meaning of the word Kiya had used.

"It means to desire something that is not yours," she answered simply. Or someone. I had learned the Ayhua word for jealousy.

FROM THEN ON, I WATCHED KIYA LIKE A HAWK, TAKING note of when she was gone from the village for any length of time. I knew it took about twenty minutes to get to the river and back, but one day Kiya disappeared for more than two hours and came back flushed and happy.

It made sense. I had been so preoccupied with learning, with acclimating, with my notes and journal and papers that I missed what was right in front of me. All the women and children in the village went to the river at least a few times a week, if not every day, to bathe and gather water for cooking or to drink. The men had to be just past the path. I also realized that Jhut had left the village the day before, and Kiya was taking advantage of her freedom. I knew Jhut would be gone at least another day and hoped Kiya would once again seize her opportunity.

I stayed with her when I could, but Chira would call me away now and then to complete a task or learn something new she was teaching one of the daughters. It was during one of these lessons that I spotted Kiya heading toward the river. I was stuck. I couldn't risk offending Chira, but I didn't know when Jhut would once again be gone from the village long enough for Kiya to feel comfortable in her pregnancy attempts.

"I haven't gathered enough machi," Chira said suddenly.

"I will fetch some," I volunteered, already turning to leave.

"Only the leaves, not the stalk," Chira called after me, as I raced to follow Kiya.

I was reminded of that night long ago when I had stalked Chira to find out where she was bringing the wailing baby boy.

As I had thought, Kiya walked to the river and into the jungle. I sighed. I was better at navigating the rainforest than I had once been, but I was still unsure of myself. I didn't have to worry. Just beyond where the river path ended, a new one began. While I had bathed or washed my clothing, I'd never thought to go further into the jungle.

I followed the new trail, not knowing how far I trekked. Walking an unknown path always seemed longer than traveling down a familiar one.

Eventually I came to a large hut. Two women stood in front of the entrance, talking. I recognized them, but they were rarely in the village. The one with a distinctive long Mohawk that fell down her back was named Hennek. The other woman, whose head was shaved clean, was Babu. Hennek was much smaller than the other women I had come to name as warriors. She was shorter than me, but her naked body was well muscled. There was no doubt she had earned her position.

It was Hennek who saw me first and grabbed the knife from her belt, while Babu, her reflexes only a moment behind Hennek's, took a stone from hers. I'd seen women throw these smooth stones with deadly accuracy, killing a lizard or bird from twenty feet. I was now not so sure of my plan to simply follow Kiya.

"I . . . I was looking for . . . I . . ." I stared at the ground while Babu tossed her stone in the air and caught it expertly. "I wish to become pregnant," I blurted. I continued to look at the ground, hoping they would take pity on me.

"Did Chira send you?" Hennek asked, sounding calm and friendly. She would be the more sympathetic of the two.

I contemplated lying but knew it would only get me into more trouble. "No," I admitted. "I learned of sister Kiya's desire to become pregnant, and I followed her. She did not know," I added quickly. I didn't want Kiya to be in any danger for me overstepping my bounds.

The two women looked at each other, and then Hennek put away her knife.

But her companion continued to play with her stone, eyeing me and smiling wickedly. "Chira told us that you would come when you were ready, and we were to let you pass."

"But," Hennek continued, "she wanted me to tell you that you can also leave this place and return to the village. This is your choice." Her voice was somber. "Just know that any daughter that you birth here is a daughter of the village."

My choice? How could I truly understand these people I have lived with for so long without knowing this last crucial piece of the puzzle. This mystery had been put before me, and I could finally solve it. In truth, I was dying to see the men, to hear of their experiences. They were the missing link. Even if I could talk to them only once, I could publish my results, not only in academic journals, but in newspapers and magazines. I could win a Pulitzer. I had enough material for at least three books.

"I wish to enter," I told them confidently. Would this be seen as an act of rebellion or as a desperate attempt to provide daughters to the village? I could be banished by Chira, but Hennek had said the choice was mine. Perhaps Chira trusted me to make my own decision.

Hennek nodded and moved aside, but Babu stood her ground. As I walked past them, a sudden fear overtook me, and I believed for a brief moment that this was all a trick and Babu had been told to club me and Hennek to slit my throat. In a moment, I reached the entrance and pulled the heavy hanging mat aside.

The first thing I noticed was the light, or rather, lack of. The darkness was in stark contrast to the bright sun I had come from. As my eyes adjusted, I realized it wasn't just the dimness. There was a strange scent. It gave the air a smothering quality and made my head foggy.

There were many people in the room, perhaps fifteen. I searched for Kiya but did not see her. Most of the figures were hazy. Some lay on mats, some sat. Most were smoking. I looked closely at the figure lying nearest the door and gasped, which made me cough from the heavy aroma.

I dropped to my knees and crawled slowly toward the person, stopping inches away. It was a man. A completely naked man. Hairy and sinewy, with a broad chest and narrow hips. He turned to look at me and smiled. I fell back on my heels.

"Peter?"

His face clouded with confusion at first, but then recognition dawned, and he once again smiled. "You received the journal I sent you? I knew they had spotted me, and I wanted to share all this." He reached up and motioned vaguely around the room. "With you."

"Pete, we thought you were dead." English sounded strange to my ears. Since Cassie had left, I had seldom spoken it.

"Dead?" he asked vacantly.

I looked at him properly for the first time, my eyes finally adjusting to the dim light. "Dead, yes. It's been nearly two years since you disappeared. I came down here as quickly as I could. I've been living with these women for over a year." I felt horrible and almost began to cry. He had been here the whole time, while I had been playing villager.

"No, no, no." He held my head in his hands and studied me with his piercing blue eyes. "Don't be sad. Here . . ." Still stroking my cheek, he reached his free hand toward the pipe beside him on the floor. He brought it to his mouth, inhaling deeply. With a smile, he exhaled into my face.

I recoiled, coughing violently. "Pete . . . your wife . . . she had a funeral for you. We all thought you died out here."

"I'm fine," he assured me and shrugged. As if that would end it.

"Peter, what happened?" I still couldn't believe he was here. I felt the need to repeat his name, making him real.

He said, "I was watching them and thought that I was being very clever, but they were more clever by far." He took another drag from the pipe. I was starting to feel lightheaded. "They came to my camp while I was asleep, and I woke up here. That . . ." He motioned to a man across the room. "That is my translator. Though he's not much use; he doesn't speak their language."

The man waved happily at us. Most of the men were either sleeping or smoking. At the far end of the room were several curtains; grunts and giggles could be clearly heard.

I tried to ignore the smoke and the noise and concentrate on Peter's face.

"I will get you home somehow," I promised him.

"No, no, no." He looked suddenly upset. "I like it here. I am content for the first time in my life."

"You are not content! You are complacent," I whispered loudly. "They are drugging you! What about your wife?" I tried to appeal to the Peter I remembered.

"I am happy here. We are well fed." He tilted his head slightly. "I spend my days high and have sex with many women. What more could a man want?" He laughed loudly, like he used to when telling a favorite joke.

"I honestly had no idea, or I would have done something sooner. I would have gotten you home." I ignored his declaration of contentment; he was clearly not in his right mind. After just a few minutes in the hut, I could barely think straight. He had spent years in this smoky haze.

"I can leave when I want," he told me softly, the pipe still between his lips.

"No, there are guards."

"They let us leave whenever we feel like it, but only in one direction. No one has run away, but we all need to bathe as well as other necessities." He worried the pipe between his teeth. "I think the security at the door is mostly to keep the women in line. They make sure there are not too many in here at one time or that they are not exclusive in their choice of lover. They don't seem to value emotional attachments."

"Not with men." I'd finally had it. The answer to my question, and it was as simple as a hut full of doped up, oversexed males. I could feel the tears begin to flow. I was so full of disappointment, of dashed expectations.

"Oh, don't." Peter took me in his arms and pulled me to his chest, stroking the back of my neck gently. It had been so long since I'd seen a man, been touched in this way, that I melted into his chest and breathed in his odor. It was there, under the smoke smell, a distinctive musk. My sadness and frustration drained from me as I inhaled deeply.

Suddenly another feeling rose up inside of me, long dormant. Peter was rubbing my shoulders and had begun to nuzzle my neck. I felt another pair of hands massaging my back.

"Wait . . . I . . ." My head was clouded, and I couldn't properly focus. Someone was unbuttoning my shirt, and I did not possess the will or desire to stop them. I felt Peter's mouth on mine and that ended my protests. Later, I would run all the way back to the village before I realized I had left my blouse behind; I wore only my bra as a top. As no one else in the village wore any clothes at all, I hardly found it important enough to go back and fetch it.

I FOUND OUT THAT THERE WAS MUCH KNOWLEDGE THAT Chira had kept from me. The women of the village knew that a man was necessary for procreation; they just did not see his value for anything else.

"They are merely the shadows of women," Chira told me when she had been alerted of my visit to the men's hut. "They have but one purpose. Many of the village women go and visit the hut to become pregnant, smoke their pipes, and do what is necessary with little recollection of the event itself. It is better this way."

"You hold the men against their will," I said.

"We give them a choice: to stay or to go. I have known none to leave." She grabbed my chin and held it between her thumb and pointer. "Do you wish to become pregnant?"

I frowned, still ashamed of what had happened, and shook

my head slightly.

"Then chew a pinch of this." She handed me an herb bag. "One at daybreak and one at sundown for five days. You will not be with child."

"I thought all the women here wanted to be pregnant, except for the protectors," I told her, shocked into curiosity. They took herbs to prevent pregnancies; I had never heard of anyone using an after-the-fact remedy.

"Most, but not all." She smiled at me like the child I felt I was. "A few wish only to go for pleasure. They enjoy being a mother as I do, without the hardships of birth."

That was the first time I'd heard Chira refer to pregnancy or childbirth as anything but a blessing. I had thought of leaving, had in fact convinced myself that after what happened I could not stay; those men were being used for sex, being raped if I was being honest, and I myself had participated. I was ashamed and covered in a blanket of guilt.

But those feelings soon softened. After all, I had inhaled of the same drug, had been in the same stupor. It was not completely my fault. And now Chira was being so candid. There were so many things that I still had to learn. I'd seen these women in simple terms and had therefore thought them to be uncomplicated. All along, they had been testing me, to see if I was worthy of sharing their knowledge.

"Chira?"

"Yes, daughter."

"May I stay here in the village with you?" Had I passed the test or failed horribly?

"Yes, you may stay. For now."

Her last sentence chilled me. Chira rubbed the goose bumps from my arms.

I HAD BELIEVED I WAS ACCEPTED BEFORE, BUT I NOW TRULY was. I thought back to conversations, to lessons, and realized how cautious the women had been with their words. Even sweet Kiya had kept things from me.

These women, using the plants from around their village, had mastered birth control. They had herbs to hasten menstruation or to stop it all together. They knew what to eat in order to become pregnant and to avoid it. That's why Kiya had known beyond a doubt that she was sterile; she had done everything in her power to increase her fertility to no avail. She was saddened by this knowledge, but not as bleak and empty as the word would imply. She was still mother to many, as were we all.

Chira also explained more about their religion. There was no central goddess, as I had expected. Instead they honored their ancestors, their Great Mothers. The ceremonies they performed centered around childbirth and menstruation. There was even a ceremony for when a woman felt she was too old to continue to become pregnant. There were several deaths, of both the young and old, but Chira remarked that they had been fortunate in recent years. There were few miscarriages, and many of the elderly were strong and healthy. There were a couple that could not care for themselves, but there were plenty willing and able to look after the aged.

I did visit the men's hut a few more times, I'm ashamed to say. The first time I told myself it was to speak with Peter, to convince him to leave this place and go home. But there was very little conversation, and I eventually admitted to myself that I simply wanted to be held by a man. To touch and be wanted by something that was not female.

It was no coincidence that the woman called when they became pregnant the dreamtime. The plants the men smoked were a mild hallucinogen that also produced a calming, mellow mood. Chira believed the smoke made the men more potent, but it also made them docile. Women who had not been raised with men would be affected by the smoke and not see them as people. Most women smoked from Chira's long pipe before visiting the dreamtime, allowing them to use the men without thought to their origin.

Chira and the protectors of the village alone seemed to know more about men. "We find the shadows in our territory and bring them to the hut. We feed them, provide them with a pipe, and let a few women visit them. They are happy."

Chira also explained that when a shadow had been with them for ten seasons, they let it go. She said long ago, a shadow was kept for many seasons, longer than some of the young women had been alive. There were many sick babies, some died in the womb, some were born unable to function in the world and died soon after.

They understood, in practice at least, the need for genetic diversity. I wanted to know where they sent the men when inbreeding began to become a threat and asked where they took the shadows.

"We take them into the forest," Chira said.

"And leave them?" How many died out there, after years of being cared for passively?

"Most we find here know the jungle. They find their way back to their people, or they don't." Their indifference frightened me, and I couldn't make this fit with their loving, open nature.

I spoke with Peter about the women's plan for his future. I tried to scare him into action. He remained unconcerned. "Then I will go visit Mary and Brandon, I suppose. I do wish sometimes they would let me see my children. Do you think I could post a letter to them?"

"I don't know if that will be possible."

"No worries then." He shrugged and took me in his arms.

"I'm glad you come to visit me." He kissed the top of my head. "The other women aren't much for conversation."

"They do not think you are worth conversing with." No matter how blunt I was with Peter, what I told him about his situation, he remained unconcerned. "The women accept me now; they want me to stay."

"Good," he said simply and began to kiss my neck and shoulders. I let the dreamtime once again take me away.

⁂

DESPITE MY GUILT FOR USING PETER SO SHAMELESSLY, I did love my newfound status in the village. Chira used me more than ever as an apprentice, often referring minor complaints to me. Just like the rest of the women in the village, I began to wear a belt. Kiya proudly presented it to me one day, showing off her fine craftsmanship. She had designed it with many small bags attached that could be easily taken off or replaced. She even included a stone knife for cutting plants and a small pestle for grinding.

I had taken to wearing less and less clothing, and even stripped down to my underwear, I felt overdressed around the rest of the women who were completely confident in their nakedness. I continued to wear shoes though; my feet were tender, and I could not get the hang of going barefoot. Kiya often laughed good-naturedly at me and called me "soft feet." Hers were as tough as rubber; she could walk through jungle, riverbed, and paths littered with tree branches or stones and not be affected.

I had gone down to the river to gather water when I heard hurried footsteps behind me, followed by loud laughter. I turned.

"Cassie!"

"I am so glad to see you." She beamed at me. Then she took in my appearance.

"They have accepted me completely," I quickly explained. "It would be strange for me to continue to wear clothing." For the first time, I was uncomfortable in only my underwear and hiking boots. "How long are you staying?" I tried to change her focus.

"Six months," she told me, making peace with my attire. She closed the gap between us in a few strides and hugged me happily. "You are the absolute talk of academia. Those reports you sent. They're calling you the most important ethnographer since . . . well, ever." She stepped back and grinned.

"You presented our evidence then? It was well received?" I heard yells from the village, children screaming at one another.

"They nearly wet their pants." She grabbed my arm. "When you get back, there will be such a media circus. They want the whole world to know about your Gynocracy."

"Gynocracy?" I asked doubtfully.

"Do you like it? That's what they're calling the Ayhuan women's society. I think it's a bit crass sounding but accurate."

We were closer to the village, and now I could tell the screams were not those of a child. I looked at Cassie.

"Is someone giving birth?" she asked.

"That is not what childbirth sound like." I began to run, with Cassie following close behind.

In the village, women were gathered in a circle, staring at something. Or someone, I realized, as horrible wailing emanated from the middle of the group. I pushed my way through, hoping that everything was all right, but I knew from the ghastly weeping that it was not.

On the ground, Jhut straddled someone, her knife in hand. She held it high over her head, the hilt faced down. She brought it down again and again, all the time crying her horrible loud wail.

"Who is . . ." I started to walk forward, but someone held my arm.

"She will kill you in her rage," Chira warned. "Let her be."

I felt sick to my stomach. Nobody was doing anything to stop Jhut. They all watched as she pummeled her victim. I once more tried to move forward, but several women reached for me, holding me tight.

I do not know how much time it took for Jhut to tire; it seemed like hours, but it may have only been a few minutes. Eventually, she collapsed in the dirt, held her knees tight, and wept. Her hands were covered in blood, her stone knife tossed aside. She moaned inhumanly and rocked back and forth to her own rhythm.

In front of her lay Kiya, her neck and face a gruesome mess. Her motionless chest was covered in a red-brown mixture of bloodied mud. Her eyes stared heavenwards, unseeing. I knew it was Kiya because of her hair. Her beautiful black hair still held the flowers I had helped her pick earlier. She had placed them with such care.

"No," I tried to shout, but it came out as a whisper. I nearly collapsed, but strong arms held me. Many hands helped me to stand, and I cried on a shoulder, not bothering to find out whose it was. My friend Kiya was dead.

———

"SHE WAS PREGNANT," CHIRA TOLD ME AS I DRANK THE calming tea she had prepared.

"That is a joyous occurrence." Kiya would have been so happy. She would have wanted to share the news with Jhut right away. I remembered her smile and began to cry once again.

"Jhut was always an aggressive woman. She was jealous of the pleasure Kiya received from her attempts at pregnancy. Jhut asked her to stop. I believe she may have secretly fed Kiya plant roots to prevent her from being with child." Chira's face fell. "I told Kiya to eat only communal food and to gather her own water. I had no idea the anger that Jhut held in her heart."

"What will happen to her?" I asked, not bothering to disguise in my voice the venom I felt toward Jhut. "How could she have done such a thing?"

"She will be banished, tomorrow, after we send Kiya to our Great Mothers." The Great Mothers were dead ancestors. Kiya would now be a Great Mother.

"Why tomorrow? Why not now?" I hated Jhut with all my being. She had killed my friend, a woman full of good who had only wanted happiness.

"She will say goodbye to Kiya. She loved her."

"She killed her."

"And Kiya loved her in return. Do not forget that."

I nodded, miserable. "I should have stopped her."

"And if you had tried, tomorrow we would have sent you to our Great Mothers along with Kiya."

"How will you make her leave?" Jhut was a strong woman.

"She will go."

I HAD ATTENDED AYHUAN FUNERALS BEFORE, AND BEEN saddened by them, but nothing compared to the pain I felt when we laid Kiya to rest. We wrapped her in large leaves of a mastic tree and carried her far from the village into the heart of the rainforest. The entire village attended, even the old and children who could not walk very fast. We were in no hurry.

We lay her body where wild maca grows. This root plant

was known for its fertility, its ability to thrive under any condition. We said to farewell to Kiya and left her body to the rainforest. Her remains would be gone before morning, cleared away by the jungle.

After the funeral, all the women went to the center of the village, and I followed, glad to see Jhut leave for good. She stood, staring at the ground, despondent and resigned to her fate. The women formed a loose line with Chira at the front.

"What should we do?" Cassie asked me. Since Kiya's death, she was scared to stray far from my side.

"Stay in the back. I don't know if there will be a ceremony." Or a fight.

I moved to the back, but Chira caught my eye and motioned for me to stand by her.

"You were one of Kiya's closest sisters," she said simply, taking my hand.

Chira approached Jhut with me in tow. Jhut raised her head then but made no other movements. Her face was gaunt, lined with sadness and guilt. Her tears had run a path down her dirty face, creating muddied contours.

Chira reached for the knife in Jhut's belt, making my heart leap from my chest. Chira was not a weak woman, but Jhut could so easily hurt her. Jhut remained motionless and once again stared at the ground. Chira grabbed Jhut's belt and cut it away from her, throwing it in the dirt. She then grabbed her arm and made a clean, straight horizontal cut at her shoulder. Jhut winced slightly but did not retaliate.

Chira turned and handed the knife to me. I looked at it uncertainly, then to Chira.

"Kiya was our sister, and Jhut no longer is." Chira nodded at me to proceed.

I felt the blade in my hand and thought of Kiya. She was kind and talented, a valued member of the village. She had been a friend and sister. Jhut was a monster. I approached her and stood until she looked me in the eyes.

"You stole my sister." I could see the sorrow looking back at me from those eyes, but I could muster no sympathy for her. She destroyed someone she should have loved. I made the cut across her arm long and deep.

Chira pried the knife from my grip and handed it to the next in line. Some women told Jhut of their pain and disappointment; most were quiet and silently left their marks on her arms and torso. I watched her become more and more bloodied, satisfaction spreading through my body with each slash.

"I will not do this." Cassie's voice interrupted my thoughts. She was standing next to me and was the last woman to receive the knife. She shook her head but had spoken in English. Everyone watched her, expectantly.

"I think you have to."

"It's not right; look at her. She will not survive this." It was true, Jhut's eyes fluttered, and her legs quivered. Her blood trickled down her arms and dripped to the dirt below, dying it rust-colored. "This is torture."

"She killed Kiya. You saw her." I did not understand Cassie's hesitation. She still looked doubtful. "I do not know how these women will take your refusal," I told her, honestly.

Cassie looked around, now frightened. She had come back thinking it was the same village she had left. But it was different. I was different.

She walked slowly over to Jhut and took her hand. I saw her squeeze it before she made a thin, shallow cut across the palm. She turned to me, her face twisted in disgust. She dropped the knife at my feet.

"I am finished," she told me, pushing past me and walking determinedly toward the communal hut.

Meanwhile, Jhut had begun to stumble from the village, away from the river path. Chira put her hands on my shoulders.

"She will die," I said. There was no doubt, with all the blood she had lost.

Chira shook her head. "She is no more and never was."

"Only a shadow."

CASSIE LEFT THE VILLAGE FOR GOOD THAT NIGHT, THOUGH I urged her to wait until morning.

"I can't," she said. "Not after what I saw. The violence." She shivered through the air was hot.

"What will you say?" I asked.

"I will report this," she warned. "Exactly as it occurred. I think it's long time these women understand how the rest of the world works." She was determined. "You still want to stay?" she asked, uncertainly.

"I have to . . . my research."

She knew it was just an excuse.

"Well, good luck," she said. "I hope that you are okay until my replacement arrives."

She hugged me and hollowly wished me the best. I assured her I would be fine.

I FOLLOWED HER FOR OVER A MILE. IT WAS EASY. SHE WAS out of shape from her year away, and it reminded me of our first hike into the jungle, before we knew about the women, before we knew about the village. I was sad and anxious and full of nerves, but I was still quiet. Chira had taught me much.

Cassie didn't know I was behind her until the stone knife

was at her throat. I couldn't let her destroy these women—my mothers, my sisters. The blade cut through her throat so easily, it startled me. I lowered her to the ground and held her while she died. My face covered in tears, I cooed to her and told her that she was my sister and that it would soon be over.

When her breath was gone and her blood soaked the earth around her, I stood and cleaned my knife on the bark of a nearby tree.

With one last look at Cassie and my old life, I stepped into the shadows.

DEMITRIA LUNETTA is the author of the YA books THE FADE, BAD BLOOD, and the sci-fi duology, IN THE AFTER and IN THE END. She is also an editor and contributing author for the YA anthology, AMONG THE SHADOWS: 13 STORIES OF DARKNESS & LIGHT. Find her at demitrialunetta.com for news on upcoming projects and releases.

One last bite from Demitria Lunetta...

I often wondered how society would work if it were run exclusively by women. Would there be less violence? Would things be as peaceful as I would like to believe? Or are women just – at heart – humans. Messy, violent, complicated humans. SHADOWS is an exploration of a gynocracy and all the things women do to keep themselves safe.

My favorite feminist authors are Margaret Atwood and Octavia E. Butler. Go! Read everything they both have written. You will not be disappointed.

@THEGUARDIANS1792

JENNA LEHNE

It started with a hashtag.

Well, it started about five years earlier—the first time Billy Ruperts noticed that I'd hit puberty. We were sitting in the hallway, working with a few of our friends on our final history project of grade seven. He looked at me, then at my chest.

"Savvy, you're growing." He leaned forward and flicked my pint-sized breast.

That was the first time I felt it. That subtle stomach-churning twirl of rage. I shoved him into the lockers.

He split his forehead open on a rusted hinge.

I got an in-school suspension, even after I told them what he did.

Billy got stitched up and a break from homework for the rest of the week.

I kept my head down after that, and my anger simmered in the back of my mind. I ignored the leering gazes and comments about my blossoming body, but I didn't forget.

Social media kicked up that summer. Suddenly I started getting messages like:

Wanna meet up?

Ur cute. Sup?

Send me ur #

I didn't reply to any of them.

They turned vile.

Ur a bitch.

Ur ugly anyway.

You better hope I don't find you alone.

By the time I was in high school, it was happening to all of the girls. Text messages. Voice mails. E-mails. Friend requests. Tumblr pages rating the girls in our schools. Voyeuristic Instagram accounts dedicated to the library stairs. Boys made up hashtags like #ThongThursdays and #Back-to-School-BootyShorts.

The guys in my school stopped snapping bra straps and started swapping our nude photos. I sent a photo of myself in the tub to my boyfriend at the time. Everyone had seen it by lunch the next day.

I got summoned to the principal's office.

My boyfriend-turned-ex got a stern lecture.

I should've learned to ignore assholes like Billy Ruperts, but yesterday he struck again.

IT'S A NORMAL DAY IN THE CAFETERIA. I'M STANDING WITH my girlfriends, all of us staring down at our phones. Billy sneaks up behind me and tugs my pants down. My panties go with them. He must've tipped off half the kids in the cafeteria because most have their phones out and set to video. So over a hundred people get a video of my bare ass.

Stupid tears immediately prick the back of my eyes. It takes a dozen blinks to keep them from falling. It isn't that big of a deal. At least it shouldn't be after my previous photo debacle, but I can't stop myself from freaking out. I yank up my pants, grab my stuff, and run.

I should've stayed and pretended it didn't matter. I should've grabbed the nearest container of molten cafeteria soup and splashed it in Billy's face. Instead all I do is swallow the ball of fire-hot rage and bolt.

I make it into my car before I start crying. I punch the steering wheel, hating myself for letting some asshole like Billy affect me so much. I grab my phone, not quite sure what to do. Billy doesn't have a girlfriend. He hasn't hooked up with anyone I know, so I can't even post any unsolicited dick pics of him. Besides, that'll make me worse than him.

So I launch Twitter.

Forget Dumbledore (RIPiloveyou), I need the #Feminist-Army. Some douchenozzle just pantsed me in front of a hundred people. How can I get back at him?

I send the tweet, turn off my phone, and leave. There is no way I'm going back to school. I opt for retail therapy and bury myself in the deepest corners of the local thrift shop. I buy vintage button-fly jeans and a couple of cute belts even though my dad is the only one I know who wears one. I don't care if I'm off trend; no one will be yanking my pants down unless they're invited to.

When I turn my phone back on, it lights up like a Christmas tree. Dozens of texts from my friends telling me that I was overreacting. That everyone thought it was hilarious and more than one person said how nice my ass is. That a certain captain of the football team is thinking of asking me to prom. The only person asking if I'm okay is my good friend, George. He even offers to beat Billy up. My knight in plaid armor.

My Twitter timeline is a different story. A few tweets

echoing that Billy was, indeed, a humongous douche. And one odd tweet that says:

Follow us. We'd like to help.

I click the profile. The user's icon is the smiling, featureless face of the V for Vendetta mask, but the mouth is smeared in hot pink lipstick. The handle is @TheGuardians1792.

I click the follow button. Seconds later, a message pops up in my DMs.

What that pestilent little creep did was unacceptable. Please send us his full name and link to his accounts. We will do the rest.

I stare at my phone. Is what Billy did worth a viral flood of online shame? Was it really that bad? My phone dings, and already someone has made a meme of my ass. I copy all the links I can find for Billy's online accounts, all while repeating one mantra in my head over and over again:

These assholes can't get away with this shit. It's not fair. It's not right. Fuck them. Fuck them all.

Then I DM the links along with two words:

Billy Ruperts.

I walk into school the next morning and find the hallways eerily quiet. Small clusters of people flit around with their phones out. Teachers speak in hushed tones.

My favorite person on the planet, Sam, grabs my hand the second he sees me and hauls me into the staff washroom. Luckily it's empty.

He thrusts his phone into my hand. "Did you see the news?"

The screen is lit up with a story from our local news website. There's bright yellow caution tape, an ambulance, and a police car all parked outside the town's loan convenience store.

A torn plastic bag along with a couple cans of energy drink, a burst bag of chips, and a large, crimson stain decorate the sidewalk. A few more red splatters complete the gory picture. "Shit, who did that happen to?"

"Billy Ruperts," he says. "Someone jumped him last night. They beat the shit out of him with a bat. He's in the hospital."

The beige-and-grey bathroom tiles twirl into a kaleidoscope. "Sorry, what did you just say?"

"Billy is in a coma," Sam says. "The doctors don't know when he's going to wake up. He's hurt really bad."

My phone buzzes in my pocket. I pull it out and check it. It's another mysterious DM from the Guardians.

You're welcome.

I bolt for the toilet and empty my breakfast into it.

"Shit, are you okay?" Sam asks.

"I'm sick," I manage to spit out.

I leave school and go straight home, thankful that my parents are already gone for the day. I lock myself in my room. I grab my phone and click on the Guardians' Twitter account. There's no way they're responsible for what happened to Billy. They can't be. They can't.

I HARDLY SLEEP. EVERY CREAK AND GROAN OF MY SETTLING house forces me out of bed to double-check the locks on the doors and windows. If the online vigilantes were able to find Billy that quickly, I have no doubt they know where I live. As if the fear wasn't enough to keep me awake, I also have an annoying seed of guilt planting itself firmly in my stomach.

I'm awake when the sun rises, and even though I'm exhausted, staying home isn't an option. I have debate practice this afternoon, which means I have to stick around school for the entire day. People are still rattled about Billy. There's lots of quiet weeping and sad selfie taking.

I mean, I get it. It's sad, Billy in the hospital and all. But do we have to make such an excessive show of grief? Aren't the vague, *"I can't believe this happened to you . . ."* Facebook statuses enough? Must we throw ourselves into cool steel and collapse on dirt-streaked, squeaky linoleum floors to show everyone how sad we are that some kid in our three-hundred-person graduating class got jumped? It's annoying as fuck. Billy's friends—his true friends—are another story. The girl next door, who he grew with, hasn't said a single thing on social media, but she's been to the hospital. She quietly weeps into her locker in between periods. It looks like she hasn't slept either. She is the only one making my stomach ache with guilt. Not the fakers. Not Billy, but her.

Sam is waiting for me at my locker after the last bell rings.

"You lasted a full day," he says.

"Unfortunately." I grab my backpack and slide my phone into my pocket. The Twitter vigilantes haven't said anything else since their cryptic messages the night before. "Big plans?"

"Just the usual volleyball, homework, and dinner with the family," he says. "My sister is in town, so I have a full evening of being compared to the greatest human who ever lived. So if you want to swipe some liquor and meet me at George's party later, I wouldn't say no."

"Oh, right. I forgot about that. Yeah, I think I have some vodka stashed in the back of my closet. I'll meet you there. Ten sound good?"

Sam nods. "Everyone should be love-drunk off my sister's GPA by then. I'll text you when I'm on the way."

"Good luck." I gather up my crap and head to the library.

A dozen or so kids mill about a group of tables. A lone

teacher sits in a chair, his scuffed dress shoes resting on one of the empty chairs in front of him.

"Hey, Mr. Fisher," I say.

"Hey, Sav," he replies. "I thought we'd spice things up a bit so it's random topic day – no notes allowed. We drew names out of a hat already. You're up first."

"Great." I groan. "Topic?"

He grins. "The wage gap between men and women."

Fanfuckingtastic.

"Who am I up against?" I ask.

"Taylor. Whenever you're ready."

I glance at Taylor. He's decked out in his usual polo shirt and jeans, his hair swooped to the side like it happens naturally, even though we all know he's got more hair products than half the girls at school.

He winks at me as I take my place at the makeshift podium across from him. He begins, "I'd like to start off by saying that this topic is a complete waste of breath. For in just a few moments, you'll realize that the wage gap is merely a myth shoved down your throat by lying, vicious feminists."

I roll my eyes so hard they nearly disappear into the back of my head. "So Feminists—who simply believe women should be treated as equal—are to blame for women making twenty-five percent less than men?"

"Oh, come on, Savannah," Taylor says. "In general, women take on jobs that naturally pay less money but ones with a greater social return. They work in careers like teaching and social work; jobs they will enjoy doing. Men aren't afraid to do the boring, harder jobs like engineering and architecture. There are reports showing that college students studying those subjects are much more likely to be male than female. So of course the men are getting paid more; they're doing jobs that require more education."

"There's a higher percentage of women graduating college then men, you idiot," I snap.

"Sav, let's keep this professional." Mr. Fisher wags his finger at me like I'm a toddler.

I grip the podium, digging my nails into the chipped, painted wood. "How do you explain a man and a woman, working the exact same job, but one of them getting paid less? They have the same amount of education and experience, yet the man gets paid more. How do you justify that?"

"Easy," Taylor says. "Chicks get months off for maternity leave. Where's my paid year off? I want to sit around the house in my sweats all day too."

"Paid year? Try three months at best. Besides, men can take paternity leave too," I say.

Taylor rolls his eyes. "Like any self-respecting man is going to stay home to take care of the kids."

"Your father clearly didn't. That's why you're such an insufferable asshole."

"Savannah." Mr. Fisher says my name like it's a warning. "Don't let him get under your skin so easily. Use facts and data."

"Sav runs on rage, not facts," Taylor says. "Did you know that Equal Employment Opportunity considers women a protected class?"

"Sure, the EEO but not the actual U.S. Constitution," I say. "And despite EEO protection, we still get paid twenty-five percent less for doing the same job."

"There are plenty of childless, young women making more money than men," Taylor says. "Look it up."

"We're not debating a select demographic, Taylor. We're talking about women as a whole."

"Wait, so you agree that I'm right about those women making more than men?" Taylor grins at me like a complete idiot.

"I didn't say that . . ." I rack my brains for a rebuttal, but it's too late.

I've lost him.

All of the guys—and a depressing amount of girls—cheer. Taylor circles the room, high-fiving all the guys.

He approaches me with his hand held out.

I take it, not wanting to look like that sore of a loser.

He yanks me forward into a tight hug.

"Losing looks good on you, Sav," he says, breathing into my ear. "If you want to lose anything else, come over later."

I push away from him and shudder, but he doesn't seem to notice. That or he doesn't care.

We all file out of the classroom, and I beeline for my locker. I spin the dial on my lock, grab my shit, and slam the door shut.

Taylor strides down the hallway, a gloating smile on his face. He sidesteps in front of me, blocking me.

"Move it, dickhead."

"Relax, Sav," Taylor says. "Someone will get you pregnant one of these days, and you'll realize that you ladies make just as much money as we do if you compare the hours. The system works in your favor. Trust me, babe."

"I'm not your babe." I shoulder past him.

Taylor lets me by but not before smacking my ass. "Keep wearing jeans like that, and I might knock you up myself."

My hands move on their own, reaching for my phone. I turn away from Taylor and furiously punch out a tweet.

Misogynistic prick in my class is severely pro wage gap. How do I teach him a lesson in equality, #FeministArmy?

Again, my phone chirps moments later. It's @TheGuardians1792.

Name?

I take a deep breath. I can't do this again. Taylor's a jerk, but he doesn't deserve to get beat up.

Taylor squeezes my hip and brushes his lips against my ear. "I meant what I said about you coming over. I know what that ass looks like thanks to Billy."

I jump out of his grasp and jog down the hallway without another word. The second I get into my car and lock the door, I pull out my phone. I type Taylor's name into the reply bar and hit send.

"I hope they break your jaw," I mutter.

I WAIT UNTIL MOM AND DAD ARE SNORING IN UNISON before I uncover my secret bottle of vodka.

I sneak out my window, carefully climbing down the oak tree growing beside our house and start the short walk to George's house. I check the news on my phone, but there's no report of anyone getting beat up. Maybe my guilty conscious is wrong; maybe Billy getting jumped is just a happy coincidence. I shove my phone in my pocket. I'll find another way to get back at Taylor.

Sam is waiting at the end of George's sidewalk. He has a red party cup in each hand. "Warm keg beer?"

I wrinkle my nose and take one. "My favorite."

"So what do you think about Taylor's little friend?" Sam laughs into the wide mouth of his cup.

"His little friend?" I ask.

"Apparently someone got a hold of all his online profiles and sent out copies of his personal messages, photos, booty calls, and everything. But the dick shots have to be the worst." Sam passes me his phone. A slightly blurred photo of a fully erect, micro penis fills the screen.

"Oh my god." Panic surges again. "Do they know who did it?"

Sam shakes his head. "No one is taking credit for it. Fake accounts are sharing the photos. Each time they get taken down, another two pop up. I almost feel bad for the guy."

"I don't," I lie. I can still feel his condescending hand grazing my ass, but that doesn't make the guilt twisting my stomach disappear. "Now, where's our host? I want some of the good stuff I know he's got hiding in there."

The party is an all-out rager. George, former loner, now popular hipster, has went above and beyond the usual parties we're used to. There's a keg in the bathroom, manned by the cheer team. They can pull off the most gravity-defying keg stands I've ever seen.

George spots me and waves me over.

I leave Sam and weave through the crowd toward him. George and I been friends forever—way before he got cool for wearing skinny jeans and toques in the summer.

"Hey, stranger," he says. "What took you so long to get here?"

"Homework and parents," I say. "The usual. Hey, I need to talk to you about something. Can we run up to your room?"

George nods and grabs us a couple of drinks. "You know the way."

———

GEORGE'S ROOM IS DIMLY LIT AND MESSY AS HELL. I SHOVE a pile of clothes off his bed and sit down. His custom-built computer hums from its home beside George's bed.

"Sorry about the mess," he says. "I was up until three in the morning coding and didn't get a chance to clean. I didn't think I'd have anyone up here."

"Don't worry about it." I take one of the drinks from George. It's strong—like nail polish remover and fruit punch.

"So what's up?" he asks.

I hug my knees to my chest. "I think I hurt someone really, really bad."

He waits for me to continue.

I recap what happened to Billy. I leave out Taylor, for now. By the time I'm done, my stomach hurts and I'm a bit sweaty.

George's expression is a mixture of disbelief and laughter. He shoves his perfect, black curls out of his eyes and sighs.

"You're kidding me, right?" He grabs my phone and clicks through it. "You think that some random Twitter account tracked Billy down and beat him because he, what? Pulled a little prank on you?"

"A little prank? He humiliated me in front of half the school."

George winces. "Sorry, I didn't mean it like that. I know it was embarrassing. But you can't really believe that some keyboard warrior tracked Billy down that fast and roughed him up, right?"

"I told them his name," I admit.

"Unless you told them the serial number of the tracking device you implanted in his arm, it doesn't matter what you told them. Listen, it's totally normal to feel bad about someone getting hurt, even if you don't like them. But you and your Twitter pals aren't responsible, okay?"

I let out a deep breath. George is right—he has to be. I mean, there's no way they'd be able to track Billy down that fast. They could be in Guam for all I know. And even if they did have people close by, they'd probably just egg his car or something. They wouldn't mangle him just because I complained about his asshattery on the Internet. I tell myself that a few times, but I can't force myself to believe it.

We go back down to the party. Sam and I drink and dance and drink some more. Even as people trickle out, George keeps our glasses full. It isn't until Sam falls asleep on the sofa with one hand in the chip bowl and the other wrapped around a half-drank beer that George finally puts the bottle way.

"What do you want to do now?" George asks as we half-assedly shove empty cups into garbage bags.

"I want you to help me find out who the Guardians are," I blurt out. "I know you don't think they're the ones behind the Billy situation, but it can't just be a coincidence."

"Not this again," George says. "I don't know what's going on with you, Sav. Did you fall down some weird conspiracy rabbit hole or something? Start smoking your dad's medical bud?"

I laugh. "I'm not making this up or stoned. Seriously. It's not just Billy either. I tweeted about Taylor this afternoon and bam —instant karma."

"That's exactly what it is. Karma. Do you know how many girls he's pissed off? There are dozens I can name off the top of my head that'd do this to him."

"That can hack all his accounts too? And his phone?"

George nods. "A few, yeah. I'll talk to them tomorrow and find out who did it, okay? In the meantime, I've got leftover pepperoni pizza with your name on it. Want to hang out for a bit?"

I don't want to give up on my search, but if George won't help me tonight, no one will. I yawn and check the time on my phone. "Sure, I can stay for a bit. Should I get Netflix loaded?"

George nods. "I'll get food."

George wanders into the kitchen while I tuck Sam in on the loveseat. I pick a lame movie we've both seen already and hop on the couch.

George comes back a few minutes later with a plate full of food.

"What time is it?" Sam jerks upright, swiping at a string of drool. His black T-shirt has cheesy fingerprints all over it.

"It's almost two," I say. "Want some pizza?"

"Can't," he mutters. "I gotta get home before my parents realize I'm gone. Want me to walk you home?"

I look between him and the mouth-watering deep dish. "No, that's okay. I'll hang out for a bit and then head home later."

"I'll make sure she gets home safe," George says.

"Sounds good. Night." Sam walks out of the room with his eyes half-closed.

"And then there were two," George says. "We're always the last to go to bed."

"That's only because your parents travel and mine are far too trusting. Everyone else has curfews and security systems."

"Good point."

We start the show and settle into the couch.

George shifts a few times. Arching his back or stretching his legs. With each minor movement, he gets closer and closer to me.

What the hell?

George never pulls this shit, not even when he's drunk. And now that I think of it, I don't think I saw him drink anything more than that first drink.

I pretend to fix my pants, sitting up a bit and moving away from him. It's not that I don't like George, but we're friends. Just friends.

He doesn't get the message. By the time the first car chase scene is over, he's only a few inches away from me. I try to focus on the screen, but I can feel his presence humming against my thigh. I lean away from him, but he just moves closer.

"Hey, you're coming dangerously close to popping my personal bubble," I joke.

"That's uh, kinda the point." George rubs the back of his neck nervously before stretching his arm across my shoulders.

"George, no. I'm sorry. I'm just not feeling it tonight. I'm tired and a bit drunk and just want to hang out, 'kay?"

George doesn't move his arm. "Come on, Sav. You don't have to pull this coy card on me. We can have a little fun. I won't tell anyone, I promise."

"It's not about that." I lean forward until his arm drops off my neck. "I love you, George. You know that. But we don't do this. We don't fuck around."

"But we should," he says. "It'll be good for you too. I promise. We don't have to do anything you don't want to do."

"Great." I give him a forced smile. "Then I don't want to do anything but eat pizza and watch a movie."

"You're such a tease. I know you want me."

"What the hell is wrong with you? Don't talk to me like that."

"Why else are you here then? You know I don't buy that bullshit about some Twitter army. It's obviously an excuse to get some alone time in. But you don't need an excuse. I want this."

"I don't." I stand up and reach for my sweater.

George grabs my wrist and pulls me down. "Just try it for a few minutes, then decide."

He slams his mouth into mine, his teeth mashing against my lips. He grips the back of my neck and holds me still. I struggle, whipping my head to the side and shoving him. He grabs one of my arms and shoves me onto my back with his chest. He's lying in between my legs. His mouth is still covering mine. It's all happening so fast.

"Stop." I groan. "Please, stop it."

"Shut up," he grunts. His teeth bang against my own.

I drive my knee into his crotch.

"Bitch," he snarls.

I do it again and push him off me. I grab my bag and sprint for the door. I don't stop to look back. I just run. I lose my flip-flops along the way home and scale my tree with my bare feet. I lock my window and quietly move through the house, making sure the other doors and windows are locked as well.

Moving keeps the panic at bay. When I crawl into bed, I shake. I shake so hard I can't hold my phone still enough to type. Even when my hands stop trembling, I don't know if I should send the tweet. He's my friend. At least he used to be.

"Fuck it, and fuck him." Anger swells in my chest, and I send one, single tweet.

#FeministArmy. Attempted rape. George Connors. Please help.

No one faves or replies. No mysterious DMs or anything else.

I turn my phone off and shove it under my pillow. I pull the blankets over my head and for the first time in years, I cry myself to sleep.

FISTS POUNDING ON MY DOOR WAKE ME IN THE MORNING. I stumble out of bed and unlock my bedroom door. Sam bursts in, a tornado in denim and plaid.

"You've got to stop turning off your phone." Sam looks like he hasn't slept at all. "George is dead. He killed himself."

I fall onto my bed. I grab my phone and turn it on. *They didn't. No. They wouldn't do that. Not for a stranger. Not because of a tweet.* I frantically mash buttons and delete the tweet. But it's too late. I check my DMs.

You're welcome.

It's followed by another.

You'll hear from us soon.

Shit. Shit. Shit. What did I do?

"How?" I whisper. "How do they know someone didn't kill him?"

"He hung himself. He left a note saying he was sorry." Sam sits down next to me. "I don't remember much of last night. Did he seem weird to you?"

I sit on the edge of the bed. Hot tears leak out of my eyes. I let them fall.

"I left right after you did. He was fine. Drunk, but normal." I hate lying to Sam. I rub the back of my neck and wince. There are tender circular spots on either side—most likely from George's fingers. If the cops see these, they'll have questions. I pull my hair out of its messy bun. "He did seem stressed about his college acceptances though. He was worried about his grades or something."

It's a lie. George was brilliant. But even the smart get stressed.

Sam nods slowly. "I think I remember him talking about that last week. This is the worst. George was such a good guy."

"Yeah, he was." I nod. "I'm going to shower. Can I call you later?"

Sam gives me a hug. "Text me if you need me."

He leaves. My e-mail chimes three times.

The first is a Bitcoin account being opened in my name along with a website for everything from drugs to hand guns.

"What the hell?" I click to the next e-mail.

Next is the name of a man from the nearby town. His photo, address, make and model of his car, and phone number are included, along with a list of offenses. He's wanted on both sexual and physical assault charges.

My palms itch for the feeling of his throat in my hands. It's a foreign feeling that catches me off guard, but it doesn't scare me. Instead, it floods my veins with fire and fills my stomach with nervous, excited energy.

The last e-mail brings a small smile to my face. It's signed with the painted mouth of the V for Vendetta mask.

Savannah,

You've got debts to repay.

Here is your first target.

Let's see how you do.

Welcome to the Guardians.

JENNA LEHNE is a tea-sipping, carb-loving mom from Calgary, Alberta (in the Great White North). She's a fourth-year Pitch Wars mentor and kidlit writer extraordinaire. You can find her over at MidnightSocietyTales.com where she blogs with her friends about all things horror. When she's not hanging out with her two boys and husband, you can find her crafting everything from bath bombs to inappropriate coffee mugs.

GRAVITY

KYRIE MCCAULEY

I am born *sunny side* on my mother's sixteenth birthday, which means she labored in her back and bore me face side up.

When I arrive, the doctor says, "She's smiling," and as soon as he says it, I laugh.

My mother had more warning of me than most teenage moms ever get. She knew because her mother had raised her to trust her body and its movements, its hungers and desires, and that sensation like a stone in your stomach when something is off, but you don't know quite what it is.

My mother had to trust her body because she couldn't trust her feelings.

She claims that she was so in tune with her body that she felt the precise moment of my conception—like a bee sting deep in her womb. And as soon as she felt it, she knew three things: that I'd arrive near her birthday, that I would be a girl child, and that, like her, I would be cursed.

It is the smile on my newborn lips and the laugh that bubbles from my infant throat. It is the curse of every woman in my family, more tradition than travesty at this point, though that doesn't mean it is not a burden.

We bear the curse of levity. Laughter. Humor and mirth.

But we cannot stop it, so even when things go wrong, a feeling of joy surges over us, like a wave obliterating a sand castle. One crest of foaming water, and our pain is erased from the world forever. That is how our sadness feels. Temporary. Gone before it ever reaches the surface.

Also, we float.

It isn't flying, exactly. It is the absence of gravity. Nothing about us can be kept down—our moods or our bodies. As soon as I am born, startling the doctor with my laugh, he reaches to hand me into my mother's arms. But his palms are open at the last moment, and I begin to rise—*up, up, up.* Gravity has no hold on my small body, and I don't stop until my little toes grace the ceiling, and the umbilical cord, still attached somewhere deep inside my mother, tugs against whatever force is lifting me, and I bob for a moment, not entirely unlike a balloon.

One of the nurses screams.

Another passes out.

And one very smart nurse says, "I'll close the windows."

My mother tugs me back down, and clasps me tight. She slips rings around my ankles. They are the same ones she wore as an infant, and her mother before her. They are just heavy enough to keep us near the earth. In a few months, I'll start to hover, and she will put a new and slightly heavier set of anklets on me. "To keep you safe," she whispers as she changes them.

The curse breaks naturally on our sixteenth birthday. Mom teases that it would have been considerate of me to come the day before her own curse broke. To let the potency of our curse mask the pain of childbirth; she would have felt everything just the same, she just wouldn't have cared.

I've heard rumors, whispered among my cousins when

our family gathers. Rumors that some in our strange lineage fought the curse. But when Aunt Cordelia catches us talking about it, she scolds us severely. She wears at least one ring on each finger—each bent out of an old spoon— and as she gestures, they clink against each other. "Don't be foolish, girls. No one ever broke it early. My Aunt Marie tried and was lost to the sky. Sightings for a day or so and then . . . nothing."

On the last word, Cordelia waves her hand in the air, like she's brushing away smoke and not the memory of a girl who reached for a star and fell off the earth.

These days, our mothers raise us to wait it out. To smile and bear it. And to always be vigilant with our weights.

WHEN I AM EIGHT MONTHS OLD, I GET SICK. MY FEVER climbs, but my mother misses it. Even looking for the signs, knowing that her baby daughter won't cry out in pain, she doesn't notice until it is the middle of the night, and she lifts me to her breast, and I am on fire. One hundred and four degrees and still smiling.

When I am seven years old, I hit a crack in the broken side-walk outside our apartment building, and I flip over the handlebar of my bicycle. I skin my forearms, my thigh, my cheek, and knock out my two front teeth.

I grin at the mess.

A group of neighborhood kids has already gathered around, but when I smile, they step back in unison. A moment later, I giggle, and they all scatter at the sight of me: blood pouring through my laughter.

Even by my own memory, I am a frightful creature in that moment. Some internal part of me knows it isn't good, that my body is a little broken, but that wave crashes down, and all I feel is joy.

Everyone runs away, except Odette.

Odette takes my hand, opens my palm, and hands me my teeth.

Odette was my first friend, and after I flip my bike, she becomes my only friend. Odette's eyes are the deep blue of ripe summer blueberries, and she is bold in ways I've come to admire: with her gaze, her posture, her confidence. She's barely one year older than me, but she moves through the world like a small queen, immune to cruel whispers.

She loses friends when she is kind to me, but it never stops her kindness.

My twelfth year is memorable because it is when I learn how to break my own curse—albeit only temporarily. It goes away when I am submerged in large bodies of water. Our town is far from the ocean, and we never could afford a pool membership, or else I might have discovered it sooner. I suspect my mother and grandmother must know about this cheat in the curse's code, but they never say a thing. They let me find it for myself. And I'm glad they do, so that when it happens, I am alone. I'm walking home, and it is the height of summer, sweltering over one hundred degrees. This time, when I reach the local quarry, rocks long submerged in a makeshift and murky lake, I decide to go in.

It doesn't happen until I'm nearly neck high, and then it crashes against me: a tidal wave that carries all of the pain of twelve years striking me at once. And this time, I don't have to laugh in response. I couldn't summon laughter if I tried. Instead, for the first time, I cry.

I sob.

I stand there, my feet sinking in mud and scraping on stones, and I cry and gulp and scream my frustration. I tell that murky, disgusting water every sad thing I've ever thought and felt but couldn't express. It feels like rage, and then it feels like grief, and then it feels like relief. A tide in retreat. It is only when my body is thirsty from the crying that I finally climb out.

———

THE NEXT WEEK, I JOIN THE SWIM TEAM. IT'S THE ONLY way to access the rec center pool year-round. I can't spend every day in the quarry, and now that I know this great secret, I don't want to spend a day away from water. I learn that, in addition to feeling my true emotions, water keeps me from floating away. It grants me a fraction of the gravity that my body has always been denied. I lower myself into the cool water, unclasp the weights on my ankles, and sink. I cry into the water and rise for air, and by the time the other girls get there for swim practice, I've put the weights back on and climbed out. The feeling is fleeting, but when I stand on the block, waiting for Coach's whistle, I feel at home and whole in my body.

I swim hard, finding grace in the water that I've never known on land.

I swim through the months and then years, until I am fourteen years old and my muscles have grown long and lean. As I swim, I wonder if I'd feel like this if I took my weights off and went up—up—into the sky. The water shows me how I could feel all the time, and more than ever I crave a way to break the curse. I think often of my Great Aunt Marie who never broke hers. I wonder if she found freedom in the sky's embrace before she was lost to it forever.

One evening, I sit at the dinner table with my grandmother and mother, measuring their moods. There is this quality with the women over age sixteen in my family, a direct inverse of their childhoods: they rarely smile. Tonight I can see they are not upset, but only thanks to my familiarity with the lines of their faces. I know all of the places they carry their worry and grief and, most of all, their anger. But Marie has been on my mind all day, and I finally ask what would happen if my weights came off.

My grandmother's flat mouth somehow straightens more, and a little puff of air escapes her lips.

To a stranger it would look like anger.

I see grief.

"That's not what this is. It isn't a gift. Don't ever try to make it something it isn't. You can only get hurt."

She rises from the table, gathering dishes into the sink and ending the conversation with running water and the scraping of silverware.

That night my mom comes to me. She sits on the end of my bed, her hand resting on one of the weights at my feet.

"It was meant to protect you."

"The weights?" I ask.

"The curse. It was meant to protect all of us. From predators."

"Like a wolf?"

"Yes, like a wolf. Like a man. Your smile eases your way. Your joy spares you from the pain women bear in this world. Your lack of gravity could lift you up out of their reach if you needed it. Our curse isn't born out of punishment. It is born out of love. A desire to keep us safe."

I turn on the bed, finally meeting her eyes. I want to ask about my father, who only loved her when she smiled all the time. I want to ask about Marie, who couldn't wait for sixteen. But mostly, I just want to know how to be free.

"So I just have to wait?"

"It's too dangerous to try and break it. And you are so close now. You have swimming, and you have Odette."

She doesn't say it directly, but I hear between her words: *Don't ask for too much. Don't go too far. That star you want is out of reach.*

Before she leaves, she kisses my forehead like she did when I was very little.

When I sleep, I dream that I am running in the forest, chased by wolves. My feet nearly lift off the ground so many times, but it's been too long.

I've forgotten how to fly.

IN THE MORNING AS I WALK TO THE BUS STOP, I'M STILL consumed by the dream—by thoughts of flying. Maybe I would float until there is nothing left, a vacuum where there once was oxygen. Maybe I could move through the air like I move through the water. A bird set free.

I pass an older man sitting on his porch near my bus stop. I'm unaware of the smile on my face until he says something.

"What a pretty smile," he says. "I see you walk past here every day smiling like that. I wish all girls smiled like you."

No, you don't, I want to say, but the phrase dissolves inside of me like the sugar cubes my grandmother drops in her tea. Men who want all girls to smile at them don't really care if the girls want to smile.

Men who are like wolves.

I wish men knew what it meant for a compliment to feel like a threat.

I see you every day means *I've been watching you.*

What a pretty smile means *I want to eat it up.*

I wish all girls smiled like you means *Girls owe me their joy, real or not, a flash of teeth in a pretty face. It's only polite.*

When I climb the stairs onto the bus, the weights on my

ankles feel heavier than ever. The smile on my face feels like a painting.

I SWIM LIKE EVERYTHING DEPENDS ON IT. I BRING HOME gold medals, and my grandmother hangs them on our walls. If I obsessed over anything else to this degree, my family and teachers would intervene, but because I am good at it, they call it talent. They say I have discipline. I smile in interviews and break inside.

Some nights I lock the door to my bedroom and check my window is shut tight, and I take off my weights. I float along my ceiling, reaching and stretching, willing my body to go back down. I try bracing my feet against the ceiling and kicking with the all the power of my strong legs, but I only make it a few inches, and then I rise again. Hours of this, and no progress, until I'm shaking with exhaustion and crawl my way over to the posts of my bed to pull myself down and slip my weights back on.

I don't know how to make close friends besides Odette. My smile is the first and second and last thing everyone knows of me. Some must think I'm silly and some might think I'm stupid, but after a while they all decide I'm too strange. You can't get close to people when they only see one side of you, and one side is all I have.

Odette never wavers.

One morning she is waiting for me, perched at the end of the pool. We are swimming the backstroke, so I didn't have to climb out onto the block to start. I left my weights abandoned at the very edge of the pool, but when I stop in front of Odette, I see they now rest in her lap. She runs her fingers along their curves, almost mindlessly.

But it isn't mindless, because later that day when we sit on the rocks over the quarry, she finally asks me what they are.

I tell her the truth. I tell her that my joy isn't mine, and my sadness even less so. I tell her that I want to feel everything, but I can't—but that I know the feelings I'm missing out on, because of the water. I tell her about Great Aunt Marie and why my mother's smiles are so rare when mine are so common. I end with words I've practiced in my head ten thousand times but have never spoken out loud until now.

"It's a curse."

Odette listens in silence, nodding, and when I am done, she pulls my hand into both of hers and holds it tight.

"The happiest sad girl I've ever known," she says, so quietly that I'm not sure she means for me to hear it. "Or maybe the saddest happy girl."

Same.

But different.

Then she leans in closer. "Don't fly away," she says. This is the summer she cuts her hair short, and when she leans in to whisper, the ends of her hair tickle my ear and my neck, and despite the summer heat, a shiver runs down my whole body.

I smile, and this time it is a soft smile.

A barely there and not at all cursed smile.

A smile not for the consumption of wolves.

A smile just for Odette.

Once the summer sun dries my hair, Odette wordlessly begins to undo my French braids, tangling her fingers against my head, tugging and pulling until my scalp tingles and my hair is free. The sensation of those tight braids coming loose feels like when I take a breath after being underwater a very long time.

It is how I imagine breaking my curse will feel.

THE NIGHT BEFORE MY SIXTEENTH BIRTHDAY, I SNEAK OUT to meet Odette at the quarry. I usually swim with my hair in a ponytail, quick and effortless, but I remember Odette playing with my hair in the summer sun, and I take the time to braid it again.

It takes longer, but that's all right. This summer—these last few weeks, really—I've needed my time in the water less and less. I wonder if I'm imagining it, but as my birthday gets closer, there are times when I wonder if that feeling I have, for just a moment, might be gravity. A force that will eventually outweigh a curse.

I pause on my way out of our apartment, checking the mirror. The braids are slick and so tight that my head already aches.

I can't wait for Odette to take them out.

When I reach the quarry, it is silent as a churchyard. The dark water below is still. Last summer a kid got hurt jumping in, so the township added a fence to try to keep people out. The lattice wires were cut within the week, and the trespassing signs ignored. Tonight, as I climb through the hole in the fence, my eyes flash across bold red words on the sign nearest to me: DANGER—KEEP OUT.

I plant myself on the ledge, my feet swinging back and forth in a way that makes the weights shift and rub against my skin. It hurts, but this time I don't fight the swell of the curse as it washes away that unpleasant feeling. Soon I will be rid of both the curse and the damn weights.

And then I'm not alone. Odette is there by the edge, sitting down next to me. "Happy birthday," she says, and her voice reminds me of the way I used to wish on stars long after I should have been asleep. It sounds like a secret. The kind we trust the dark to keep.

Odette leans into me a bit, resting her head on my shoulder

and pulling one of my hands into both of hers, a habit of hers that always makes me feel grounded—like this must be the exact place I'm meant to be in this moment. "How do you think it'll feel when it breaks?"

"Mmm, I dunno," I answer. "What does gravity feel like out of the water?"

"It's hard to describe. It's all I've ever known. It feels like my body is doing it, even though I know it's not. It feels like part of me. Of everything."

"Everything but me." I laugh, but I don't mean it, even when the smile lingers on my face. Odette always knows which ones are real. She squeezes my hand in reassurance.

"Yeah for . . ." She glances at her watch. "Eight more minutes."

A bright light flashes between us, illuminating my arm in this perfect way that shows how every single hair is standing straight up after whispering in the dark with Odette. The light bounces.

"Hey!" a voice yells from the fence. "No trespassing!"

"Shit," Odette mutters, scrambling to her feet. The security guard is unlocking the fence gate, reaching for his baton where it is strapped at this side.

Odette never lets go of my hand as she stands, pulling me up beside her. I start to laugh.

"C'mon," she says, starting to run.

When I glance behind us, the guard is through the gate and after us, his flashlight trained on our ankles as we move.

We reach the fence and begin to run alongside it. The hole cut into the chain-link fence is too far ahead.

"Stop!" the guard yells. He sounds so close.

"We'll never make it," I say, breathless. "Here." I stop abruptly, tugging Odette back into me, where she stumbles and grabs onto my hips to steady herself.

"Here what?"

I reach down, tugging off one weight, and then the other, throwing them over the fence. My legs flip out from under me, and I rise, a foot, two. Enough to reach the top of the fence.

"What are you *doing*?" Odette says.

"I've got it," I tell her as I wrap my hand around the top of the fence. "Jump!"

She listens, her feet lifting, and my lack of gravity is just enough to leverage her body weight up. She hauls her torso over the top of the fence.

"That was really dumb," she says.

"It worked." The security guard is right below us, reaching for us. "Hurry."

Odette swings her body around and begins to lower herself down the other side.

"I said *stop*!" screams the guard, slamming his baton against the top of the fence; it hits my and Odette's interlaced fingers, and we both cry out, our hands breaking free.

I begin to move up.

"No!" Odette cries. She claws at the fence, reaching. "No!" She screams again, as we both realize I'm rising too fast. I stretch my arm, but there's a clear foot between us already, and I'm still moving. Up. Away.

The guard backs away from the fence, his face bewildered and his pursuit forgotten.

For a moment, fear takes hold. I think first of Marie, and I imagine drifting forever. Will the loss of oxygen be subtle, less and less until the air is as thin and vacant and empty as the smiles on my face these last sixteen years? Or maybe it will feel sudden and tight, a seizure of my lungs, robbing me of breath like the laughs I never meant.

And then I remember that I have only minutes until my birthday. Minutes left of this curse. How high will I be by then?

At midnight, will I crash back down to earth? A girl turned meteor.

And Odette will watch the entire thing, helpless from the ground.

I feel a familiar surge within me, and I hate it. My fear is about to be replaced by happiness, and I'll probably fall back to the earth with a stupid smile on my face.

But it isn't laughter that fills my chest to bursting and rises in my throat.

It is a sob.

Choking and angry, and filled with regret that Odette would never know me as anything but cursed. Tears form in my eyes for the first time out of water, and they run up, into my hairline, because I'm floating upside down toward the clouds. Tears like a wave crashing, breaking my curse into pieces.

When I open my eyes, I am suspended for a moment, weightless, in a void between curse and freedom.

Then I begin to descend, and I feel it in my bones. In my organs. In the blood in my veins and in the oxygen in my lungs and in the saltwater tears that have changed direction with my body and now run freely down my cheeks.

I feel gravity.

Not to the earth.

To Odette.

I am the tide, made up of salt and things lost to the water, but Odette is the moon and she's pulling me toward her. Closer, closer.

Until our fingers touch.

Odette's nails dig into the palm of my hand, so sharp that it hurts. So sharp I could cry.

I could cry.

When I'm finally in her arms on the ground, I do cry.

Because I can and because I want to, and I don't stop until the alarm on Odette's watch begins to chirp.

It is midnight on my sixteenth birthday, and for the first time in my life, I start to laugh.

I've beaten my curse in its final moments, and it feels like taking a deep breath after being underwater for a very long time.

It feels like braids coming undone.

KYRIE MCCAULEY lives just outside of Philadelphia, where she can be found with a notebook in hand and one of her young children tugging on her sweater. She loves all things cozy, books that make her cry, and girls who resist. Her background is in advocacy and social policy with a focus on domestic violence. Kyrie's debut novel, IF THESE WINGS COULD FLY, will be available Winter 2020.

One last bite from Kyrie McCauley...

GRAVITY was inspired by the classic Scottish fairy tale, THE LIGHT PRINCESS. I believe a story retelling begs the question: what about the world is different from when this was written, but also, what is the same? And the idea of a girl who must smile even when she doesn't want to felt very relevant today, as did the precious balance she maintains between freedom and safety. She must learn to navigate a world (or a curse) that forces her to always choose between the two, a choice familiar to many women.

My current feminist read is HER BODY & OTHER PARTIES by Carmen Maria Machado.

THE GUARDRAIL DISAPPEARS

MELODY SIMPSON

An unfamiliar skin sits in the driveway.

When I go out with Mom for errands, she usually sets the skin from her phone before we even get into the AV, changing it to the sunrise I once told her reminded me of cotton candy. A sunrise that I could taste every morning. She places it over the original exterior black paint job. I love that I don't have to ask even though it's her autonomous vehicle and she prefers a skin that mimics the stage of her favorite symphony greeting her. But this skin is neither of those. It's new. This isn't her AV. And this isn't an errands trip.

"Mom?" I turn back toward the house, watching as she sets the alarm to lock the door.

"Yes, honey?" she says softly, her back toward me, a slight smile in her voice.

I walk forward with my red suitcase in hand, tattered gloves in the other. A knot forms in my throat.

Mom drinks lavender tea every morning and sorts her socks every other night. She crochets after school, a pastime, and keeps my classmates off our lawn while listening to the volume of the symphony on high. Mom doesn't do surprises. But there's one taking up the entire driveway. *This is different.*

The skin of the AV displays endless fields with tall, unkempt weeping willows clustered together toward the back wheel.

I walk on the beet brine covered path melting the snow, past a yellow stain left by the neighbor's cat. I notice on the AV skin a tiny cabin home not too far from what looks like a river—one that might overflow if the storm clouds ahead are any indication. I hope we're not heading wherever this is.

"Where are we going?" I ask, the cold catching my breath in the air. "This is the last chance to let me know if I'm missing anything. You didn't tell me how to pack." Or for how long, but I imagine I can't miss too much of school.

She waves a hand as she passes me, the door creaking behind her. Her weekend bag is light on her arm.

"It's a surprise," she says, for what must be the hundredth time, as if surprises are a thing she ever does. She doesn't enter the code. Instead, she gestures toward me. I enter the code for her vehicle, but this isn't her vehicle.

"Try your birthday," she says, unmoving. February 3. Today. I enter my full birthdate. The AV unlocks, and the sliding doors open. I walk in.

"Good morning, Samara. Please set up your Touch ID."

"Wait. This is mine?" Tears well up as I sit in front of the center console. I place my index finger on the home display screen. "You said we couldn't afford another AV."

She says we can't afford a lot of things. And she never let me forget it when I asked for a new AV, always going on and on about how her mother didn't let go of their Airstream until every mile possible was used on it; only then did Granny trade it in for the first-generation AV.

"It's a glorified family-friendly miniature party bus," Mom once said to me. "It can wait."

It didn't matter that everyone else was jumping to get AVs.

"Holding onto a good thing while it lasts is important," Mom always says. Their first-gen AV looks slightly bigger than Granny's old Airstream in pictures, and this AV is at least two inches taller than Mom's current AV.

"What are you going to name her?" Mom asks.

"Stay in the hive, you're too young to fly. The worker bee survives when they comply." Her mantra for me from when I was little rings in my ears.

Home by five after my club meets. Dinner at six. Homework finished by eight. Family hour if homework doesn't take longer. Retire to our bedrooms. This is every single night, if I don't go to a game and dinner afterward. Even that's a hassle, with her having to approve everyone I'm going out with or telling me to come home early. And forget about sleepovers. *"We don't know what people do in their homes."*

The worst was when she pulled me out of orchestra once they started traveling across the country. There were six chaperones. Even the underclassmen call Mom "Ms. Lila Bird" because she's one of the only parents in the school who hovers so much.

Our weekends aren't for day trips into the city or mother-daughter excursions I hear other girls talking about in homeroom. I wonder about those. What's it like having a mom who takes her daughter out just for fun? Or a mom who volunteers to chaperone a school trip, singing along with you to the same songs playing in the background instead of our tunes being decades apart and worlds away? What's it like having a mother who's free?

I'll take this fancy chamber for my birthday and see how far

I can really go. I can look after myself. This AV will be my protection instead of her. My shield. My shell.

"I'm going to name her 'Shellie,'" I say, activating the AV.

"Would you like to connect a device?" Shellie asks.

As the AV senses the weather outside and warms up almost instantly, I hang up my coat and shove my gloves into one of the pockets. Below the coat hanger sits a tiny stack of magazines that I subscribe to. I riffle through and count. Mom read all nine of my monthly subscriptions and only approved of me reading three this month. She claims she's storing the ones she disapproves of for when I'm "ready for that content." Not even a free pass for my birthday to read whatever she deemed too R-rated for me to see. I pull out my phone while Mom brings my luggage inside the AV. It takes ten seconds for the phone to sync with Shellie.

"I need to connect my phone as well, honey," Mom says. "I don't want you to see where we're going."

We could be going anywhere. I've only been outside of the state once, and we're an hour away from Manhattan. For my thirteenth birthday, she took me into the city to see a play that I wouldn't stop talking about. Almost everyone in drama brags about which plays and musicals they see before the Tony Award nominations. Sometimes, they pool all of their saved allowance money onto the floor and map out how many shows they can afford to see that semester. I just sit in my seat. Alone and empty-handed because: *"You don't need an allowance, honeybee. You come to me to ask what's allowed."*

"How long is the drive?" I ask, as Mom walks in and presses the pad to close the doors. She frowns as she sits across from me, tugging her own coat off. Her black gloves remain on.

I wish we could stop at all of the areas we'll pass along the way. Some people call them tourist traps. Overcrowded, overpriced hype that Mom would never shell out extra funds for.

Take me to the traps the sightseers fall into. I want to see. I want to fall.

I'm stuck in this town because: *"There are dangerous people out there, Samara. You're safer close to home. Close to me."* Because: *"I don't know what I would do if something were to happen to you. Or to me! What if I had another heart attack and you were too far away? All we have here is each other. Why would you ever put your mother in that position?"*

Grace's house burned down two summers ago, but her parents don't have her on fire patrol duty every waking minute. The question should be, why would she put me in that position?

Before today, I clung to the Reality Tracks app every time I got into Mom's AV. *"You can visit wherever you want from the comfort of your own seat. You know the rules,"* Mom always says.

The rules.

My weekends are filled with chores and whatever I can do from the comfort and safety of home. Mom runs errands on the weekends. If I tag along, it's only for the local runs like the grocery store and the post office.

"When people leave their houses, they're only looking out for themselves. You're too oblivious, Samara, you can't protect yourself. You don't have any street smarts."

Whatever that means. We're in the middle of the suburbs.

At home, I choose my own adventure in my favorite fantastical worlds from the television. But in the AV, with the wheels underneath my feet, the forward motion of a destination, I set my Reality Tracks to the live feeds of whatever city or province I want to explore next. Currently, I'm halfway through the twenty arrondissements of Paris. But today, I want to experience a reality with her. One last hurrah for the big *one-eight*. Because after today, I will step into the reality she's always shielded from me. She doesn't know it, but after today, I make the rules for me.

I try again, more stern this time. A different approach. "Do we have enough time for a musical?"

"Maybe . . ."

Maybe means "no" in the Stokes household. In her presence. Safe mode is off now that the parental locks are gone, and I'm done waiting until I'm alone in my room to watch the musicals that I've heard out of context a millions times in school.

"You might have enough time to watch two if you want," Mom says. "Something clean, of course."

There it is. The monitoring never stops. I'll pick one that appears clean until we're in too deep to turn it off, lest she ruin my day. Enough time for two shows means this is about a four-hour drive.

"First," Mom says, "We have to head to the Charge Stop because I took Shellie out for quite the spin before I came home with her last night."

I let out a laugh.

"I'm glad you enjoyed yourself," I say, with an edge. "In your gift to me."

In my AV. I hope you had a great joyride, because you won't be invading this space again. You're not the only one with ultimatums. I'm eighteen now. *Try me*. She doesn't respond. I look up and down the driveway and then along the front of the house. "Mom, where's your AV?"

"Ride-sharing begins now. And all through college while we share Shellie until you leave your dear old mother."

Until I'm officially out of her nest. She's thought of everything. But I'm not waiting to be kicked out of the nest, because with her, I'll be waiting forever. She can keep her AV.

"Shellie can ride-share on campus and pay for my classes while I'm in them," I say with confidence. "She'll get more rides there. But thanks for offering. Keep your AV. It's easier, and we both win." I force another smile, satisfaction sweet on my tongue. She can't argue with that.

She's there for me, everywhere I look, every talent show, every science fair, but I haven't gone anywhere. Just nearby places like the Meadowlands Fair every summer. There, I get hypnotized and let someone else control me for fun instead of what's best for me. There, I gaze at the fireworks, waiting for green to light up the sky. Waiting for permission to go, go, go, as far and as fast as I can. I was saving up for my own AV after freshman year, for my own freedom, but here it is. Eighteen is my green light, and I'm going.

Mom tightens her lips, hesitant not to say the wrong thing and bring the mood down on my day. She reaches low behind her seat and pulls out a small jewelry shaped box. "Part two of your surprise."

Her muddy brown eyes fix on me. I grab the baby blue box and open the lid. A navy blue watch.

I showed her this watch, a full moon inside of it, six months ago, after helping Grace look for watches for her dad. I showed her the watch and told her all about my date with Grace that day, being her cheerleader while she got her first tattoo. It's an ambigram which reads "BEAUTY" on the inside of her arm when looking to the right and "REALITY" if she turns her head to the left. I talk to Mom about my dates all of the time. The watch wasn't even the coolest detail. I didn't think she was paying attention.

I love the sound of watches. I can always hear the ticking, each second passing by closer to a moment I want to be in. A moment of making choices to go somewhere without having to ask for permission and getting shut down.

A moment of freedom.

Graduation is months away, and I refuse to not know

freedom for another year when I've reached my savings goal. After three years, I'm tired of designing worlds for a fan fiction app and hoping the money I earn and leave sitting in another app doesn't get miraculously hacked. I'm done inching toward free; it's time to take leaps.

Finally, I can move that money to a bank. An actual account and one that Mom can't touch, one she doesn't even know about. I'll have enough savings for a year on my own in addition to whatever else I can save with an on-campus job. It's a good start. A good start is all I need.

I set Shellie's voice to a French accent and turn on French captions so that everything I see in the AV automatically shows an overlay of its French word and pronunciation. I am so going to ace my last French final at the end of the semester. Until then, I practice, talking to Grace during lunch out in increasingly less broken French while she responds in straight-A Italian. Thanks, Shellie. I skip the other settings.

"All done," I say, facing Mom. "Your turn."

I take off my damp boots and put them in the corner, turning the designated heat on the floor beneath them to get rid of the remnants of snow.

Mom begins to connect her phone and sets the home display screen to private so I can't see anything that her phone utilizes through Shellie. When she's done putting in the directions, Shellie asks me to confirm the destination, "*Birthday Surprise*", which appears on the screen. I click "*Yes*", and Shellie begins to pull out of the driveway.

Mom leans back in her seat. "I'm going to finish watching my cooking show first and then take a nap after the Charge Stop, if that's okay with you?"

Work weighs heavy on her eyes. Overtime the past three months has dried her out. Understaffing, she told me. Now I see it was for this AV. She's already sliding her seat down, clutching her heart as she stretches out.

"I still haven't chosen a musical," I say. "But when I do, I'm turning to it."

She hesitates, and her mouth opens a small amount before she remembers what day it is. My day. She nods.

I haven't decided what I'm going to watch so I don't change the interior skin to a theater yet. It remains a bleak extension from the exterior skin, dark clouds, clusters of giant willow trees. I swivel my chair around, lean it back, fasten my seatbelt at the waist.

"Buckle up," I say, patting my belt, now tight across my lap. She waves her hand in a dismissal, putting all her trust in technology.

"Vehicle deaths are a quarter of what they used to be when I was your age," she reminds me, as if she's immune to being in that quarter.

I tell myself I'm taking the other three-quarters for the both of us, doing a once over on my belt, making sure it's snug. I expand the settings so the entire AV is immersed in Mom's cooking show.

The smell of burned milk fills the AV. Redolence. A fully immersive upgrade from Mom's AV. No wonder she wants to watch cooking in my AV. I revel in the contestants' failings before I begin to wonder what other upgrades there are.

I condense the show from theater mode to just Mom's side of the AV and pull up Entertainment on my side. I scroll past my top apps. Story Share has a notification beside it. I downloaded the app in Mom's AV, and it immediately asked me to upgrade our subscription package in order to access it. There it remained, never used again. Along with two hundred other dormant apps that won't wake without an upgrade. This AV has the upgrade.

Instead of watching a musical, maybe I can make my own epic story with someone who's connected right now. I press my finger against the app. No notification prompts stop me. I'm in.

"I'm the Author" and *"Pick a Coauthor"* pop up on the display. I pick the latter. *"Random Connection"* or *"Curated Connection"* pop up next. Spontaneous choices are hit or miss, and I'm not trying to miss on my birthday. I tap on *"Curated Connection."* *"Set Profile to Public"* and below it, *"Return to Random Connection"* appears. An option I've never seen in any of my apps before today. No more online parental restrictions. *Hello, world.* Happy birthday to me. I set my profile to public.

Three dots appear on the screen, and then a wheel of dots surround it, moving counterclockwise for about ten seconds before I'm matched.

Shellie turns into Charge Stop just before the I-95 North entrance and eases into park. Four loud beeps sound as Shellie connects to the platform. *"Charging. 30 Minutes Remaining"* pops up on all of the window displays.

Mom opens the door. "I'm going to make a call and go inside for snacks so we can fill up the fridge. You coming?"

"No," I say.

"Send me a list if you see anything you want."

I open up the Charge Stop app and case their inventory before checking off a few snacks, none suitable for Mom's diet post-heart attack a few years ago which she tried to make "our" diet, and then send the list to her profile. Lila Stokes. The only "friend" I have in the Charge Stop app.

Once I've added a green tea with no honey, dark chocolate, and a few more snacks to the wish list, I go into my general settings, then deeper into privacy settings and make all of my profiles public. *Goodbye, seventeen.* I take a few photos of myself positioned just right to show off my new AV. Then I accept the notification that pops up without reading it, instantly setting my new profile picture across all of my accounts.

I go back to Story Share. The profile of my coauthor appears, but I click the video tutorial first. When the tutorial is over, I open the profile.

Her name is Opal. She's got smooth dark brown skin. Flawless. My brown is a few shades lighter, and I've seen my days of bad skin. She's twenty-four. Six years older than me. Her locations are New Jersey and Sierra Leone. Her languages include English, Krio, French, Portuguese, and Hebrew. Three and a half more than what's listed on my profile. I also have Morse code on my profile even though it's not really a language, but it helps when I team up with other like-minded players in AR games. A notification appears with a preview of a sunrise. *"Accept Photo Album?"* Opal's username sits below the notification. I accept.

The images fill the vehicle with the 360-degree setting. Shades of orange and yellow and pink engulf the screens around me. It's beautiful. Quickly, I condense the album and open up the camera app so Shellie can take photos of my sunrise. We are both in New Jersey, but I wonder how close one has to be for a sunrise to look substantially different? A text message appears.

Mom: *New releases at That Blue Book! Look at the catalogue and let me know if I should borrow anything for you!*

No matter how many times I tell her that I like audiobooks and AR books, she always wants me to take out some raggedy old physical copy. I usually oblige to get her off my case but not today. I don't bother opening the Charge Stop Library app.

Me: *No thanks. No time to read anything on the trip anyway. Entertainment slot has been filled. Please try again later.*

Mom: *Ha Ha.*

No emotion follows as she appeases me.

"Audio Connect with Opal" appears on my display. I accept.

"Hi!" The girl's voice rises. "I'm Opal."

"Hi, Opal! Nice to meet you, I'm Samara. I'm at a Charge Stop now, so we'll have to switch to text when my mom gets back."

"Okay, cool. So how we doing this? Just AR or do you want to shake it up and feel the bumps in the road?"

"I'm sorry? I just got the upgrade," I say, sheepishly.

"Oh, no worries. So, what you're used to is making up the story with the AV based on your surroundings and it's like a movie, but with the upgrade you can co-write—thank you for making me your first," she says, and I can just picture her bowing while saying it.

I laugh. "You're very welcome. Continue."

"And you're also moving on up from seeing your story to *being* in the story. Fully immersive, baby. If you hit a pothole but we're on the beach about to introduce our surfer meet-cute, they'll catch a wave. That kind of thing. It never gets old. I love it."

"Yes. A million times yes." I open up a side compartment to see if there are any motion sickness pills. I take one so that my vitals don't pop up in the middle of the story and give me a warning like Mom's AV does when I get dizzy and lose myself looking up at slow-moving skins.

"My settings are already chosen," Opal says. "It takes about ten minutes to pick everything, what kind of characters you like, settings, tropes you love, don't love, that sort of thing. I'm gonna go finish a game so just message me when you're done and we'll start."

First, Story Share asks general housekeeping questions: "*Do I want the DNA app to connect with my other apps?*" Sure, whatever. I scan my hand on the center console for verification. "*Do I agree to use the data on file for passenger, Samara Stokes, Hair Follicle?*"

"I don't know what I would do if something were to happen to you."

Of course she wouldn't get me an AV without tracking my every move within three miles of it. Well, safety first. Sure.

Then it gets to the good stuff. The worlds I want to build. The stories I like. Choosing my settings only takes five minutes but instead of messaging Opal back right away, I click on her profile. First, I go through her images. AV photography never gets old. The images of the sunrise she sent me, from every angle of her AV, are already on her profile. More 360-degree AV shots from all over fill her feed. She's been to these places. I count zero doctored stamps.

The images start out as nature shots, a new hobby it seems she began to ring in the new year. The photos further back include a mix of nature and friends and people who look like her. Her relatives all have similar dark skin, the same doughy eyes, the same small, wide nose, kind of like mine.

A notification appears. Twenty, actually, from various apps on my dashboard. My apps catch up to the AV upgrade. The DNA app catches my eyes. I tap its icon.

"You've Been Matched! Click to See Relatives!"

I tap. Opal Jones appears. That can't be right. It must be a glitch. I open her profile. This one includes her genetic makeup and family tree.

It includes me. That definitely can't be right.

I tap my name and my family tree, which I could never see before. It's just as complete as Opal's. It is identical to Opal's. I check my genetic makeup. I check hers. I bring them side by side. My eyes shift back and forth. I've never seen a glitch this big. This can't be. But it is. How is this possible?

Immediately, I make an audio call to Opal. I rub my hands together as if I'm starting a fire. My skin feels like it's burning. Like the zest of a kumquat has exploded in my mouth. I am not prepared, but I want more. I need to know more.

"Hey," she says, "you ready, Sam? I'm sorry. Can I call you Sam?"

Nobody calls me Sam. Not now, not in another life. Would I have been Sam in another life? The thing is, I don't want another life. I just need to straighten this one out. Without Sam. I don't like Sam. *Who is Sam?* I ignore her question, rejecting the proposition and moving on to the bigger issue at hand. This has to be a glitch.

"Opal, do you umm, ever think that technology can be too smart for its own good? Like so smart it cracks?" My mouth dries.

"Is this an idea for the story?"

We might not need to make up a story today. "Opal, did you get a notification from your DNA app? Mine just updated. Can you take a look at yours? Like right now." My voice rises. I try not to sound desperate by letting out a laugh, but it comes out strangled.

"Okay," she says, stretching the word out. Her movements are slow. But we've got to make this quick. I need to know. Before Mom comes back inside. How do we have half of the same genetic makeup? How can that be when Mom has never brought up any of the names on that family tree filled with strangers? Updates have bugs. Maybe this is one of them.

"Samara?" Opal whispers.

"I'm here," I say.

"It's you. I can't believe it's you. But that's not the right name. Her name is Zahara. Your name. They changed your name. Are you still in New Jersey?"

"Maplewood. Where are you?" I'm lightheaded. The app requests to sync our family trees. I accept the request. Suddenly, in parentheses next to my name is the one that escaped Opal's lips.

"Piscataway," she says with a great sigh.

"Oh my God. You're so close. You've been so close this entire time." She pauses a beat, but I don't know this song, so I wait for the next verse to come. She catches her breath. "I'm sorry. I can't believe I'm the one to have to tell you this." She pauses again. "This isn't at all how I imagined this happening all of these years later . . . but you were taken from us."

My chest hurts. "Taken?" My body heats. I black out for just a moment. When I come back to, Opal's voice fills the space around me again.

"You were kidnapped. When we were kids. It was July 16, a family reunion. Every four years we switch between Jersey and Sierra Leone. That year it was here on the beach at Seaside. We haven't been to the beach since."

My heart beats faster than it should.

"There were just so many of us. They blended right in and took you in broad daylight. You weren't even a year old. I'll send you the news articles," she says, determined. "Mom saved every one."

July 16. That's the same day inked into the playbill of my first and only play in New York. My first time out of the state with Mom. She said the show was sold out until then. If what Opal is saying is true, Mom took me out into the city on the anniversary of the day she took me away from my neighborhood. Uprooted me from an upbringing I will never know. Miles apart and worlds away from my actual family. I just might have a family outside of Mom.

"How did we get matched through the game?" I mutter. *How did I not know my own birth name?* is what I really want to ask. But that's not a question for her.

"Your upgrade."

The DNA app knows more about me than I know. Four loud beeps sound.

"I've got to get off audio. The AV is done charging, and my... my mom will be back any minute."

Abandoning the interior skin that's been chosen, I change the overlay from a cloudy day to the darkest night. I push my chair the furthest to the edge that it will go. The door opens.

"Ready to go, honeybee?" Mom walks in and places our teas on the center console before putting her bags down beside her seat. She looks around at the new interior skin. "Cozy."

I lean over and take the tea marked with my name. "I know you're tired." I keep my voice as level as I can. I know I can't look her in the eyes even if she wasn't tired.

Out of the corner of my eye, I watch as the blurred image of her takes medication from the pouch of her bag and into her mouth before washing it down with her tea. She needs me more than I need her. It dawns on me that I don't even know when her first heart attack actually was.

Shellie begins to pull out of the Charge Stop, and we make our way onto the turnpike. She starts out in the right lane, gathering her bearings, planning the best route for the trip.

"Where are we going, Mom?" I ask, more urgent than before. I take a sip of the tea. There's too much honey in here. My mouth feels thick, the contents of my stomach sticky. I put the tea down, noting not to pick it up again. I don't remind Mom to buckle up.

She packs the fridge with drinks and snacks, more than we need for a weekend trip. "Do you really want to spoil the surprise?"

"I've had enough surprises for the day," I say.

She perks up.

I bring my hands up midway and wave them in a circle. "This AV is so much better than the old one. I don't want to leave Shellie." I don't want to go anywhere with you. But we're cruising steady.

"I knew you'd love it." She smiles and settles into her seat. She turns her show back on. A message notification pops up on my side.

Is that woman in there with you? Don't say anything to her. Send your coordinates to the police and they can be there within five minutes. If you feel comfortable, send them to us too?

I respond: *Today's my birthday.*

Your birthday is August 16.

August? August 16. Exactly one month after the reunion, one month after the date on the playbill. My birthday isn't in the winter? I'm quite possibly a summer baby. All of those summer blowout pool party birthdays I always envied could have been mine. Did I even enter kindergarten at the right time? Could I have graduated an entire year earlier? Been on my own all this time? Has mom been manually overriding the settings and protecting my account in her AV since my actual birthday?

Shellie beeps. I look up. *"A Lane Drifting"* notification appears. Common for new AVs still adjusting their calculations for not-yet familiar bumpy, weathered roads and routes. Especially icy roads.

I'm recalculating everything too.

Guardrails line the highway, keeping AVs in check.

A stranger lines this vehicle, this town, keeping me from an entire host of people who love me. People who wouldn't lie to me and steal my time for a lifetime of their own happiness. People who wouldn't cheat me out of the best life possible for me in favor of the best life they can glue together like a macaroni art project. People whose hearts bleed like pomegranate, not people who have a gold star that smudges on the surface.

"Everything okay, honey?" Mom asks.

Mom. Lila. Lila Stokes. Opal has had the upgrade. Both of

our AVs can't have the same glitch, can they? Who is Lila Stokes? Who am I if not Samara Stokes? As it turns out, I'm not Samara or a Stokes.

Shellie beeps. There's no *"Lane Drifting"* notification. Shellie beeps again. I look closer at my display screen. My text notification number has gone up. It jumps from two to six to ten to fifteen unread messages. I open the text message thread. Audio messages from Opal. I reach for my audio patches, placing them on both sides of my temples and hit "Play All." Multiple beeps begin to sound, so faint I have to strain to hear Opal's message. Morse code. *"Still public. Private everywhere."*

Mom's phone is still connected to Shellie. I never set up my privacy setting. But she did as soon as she got in the AV. She can see everything I'm doing on her console. She can see Opal. I close out Story Share, turn off my message notifications, and pull up Digital Games. *Be casual.*

Casual.

Act normal. Casual.

Everything is fine. Fine. *Solitaire?*

Before I can make a decision, Mom leans over from her seat to the center console. She swipes a few games over and clicks on The Game of Life.

"What about a Game of Life, honey?"

Life is agonizing. I prefer to stick with Monopoly. At least then everyone gets tired of the false starts, the pipe dreams, and falls from grace at the same time, mutually agreeing to bring the trailing fun to an end. In Life, if one person wants to keep going, I'm responsible for cutting short their personal, most fulfilling fortunes.

Now, I'm not so sure I care. This DNA app can't be an error. This family tree is the truest thing I've ever seen. I can't do it. Not anymore. Not when I am so close to freedom only to discover I could have had it an entire summer ago. I can't answer to Mom's honey this and honeybee that. Not anymore.

Lies are sweet. She wants to fill me up with all that is sweet so I never realize I have a stinger. I know now. And I'm meeting my hive. All that matters now is the imaginary girl that Mom—Lila Stokes—plucked out like a character and placed into her reality. My life isn't a game. But I'll play one last round.

"College or Career."

I choose college.

"You always pick career," Mom says. Her voice never rises.

So I can see the world sooner than you'll ever let me. I grit my teeth. But this is going to be a long ride, and I need time to process all of this. I stare at the *"Mid-Life Crisis"* space mocking my life from the digital board. Is that when she took me? An ache forms in my stomach.

"How was your call?" I breathe out.

"Oh, just work. I had to call off sick for our little trip."

The mischief in her smile is different now. Lonely. Desperate. *You* are *sick*, I think.

"You're sweating," she says, the last of the honey left in her voice. She turns her chair and opens the fridge, pulling out a water.

I breathe in.

"Do you want to save the game?" she asks.

I shake my head. I didn't need saving. *My life is not augmented because of you. Because of this AV. Because of the college tuition you're itching to pay to keep me close to you, only delaying the inevitable.* I sit in silence. Waiting for her next move.

"Part three of your surprise . . . " She pulls out a book from her reusable Charge Stop bag. She extends her hand.

"We're going to Boston," she says with a thin smile. That

Blue Book! Library spine label covers a bound copy of a new play. Two ticket stubs hang out from the pages.

I can't take her smiles. Not after years and years of begging to go to just one local production out of state before a show hit big in the city. Just one trip like that would have meant everything. Just one trip like that could have given me bragging rights for life. Now it's a play she's chosen in a city she's chosen, on her terms and on my birthday. She controls everything.

Not after today.

Now, I have control, and it's time to infiltrate the system that she built just for me so I can find the real me. I dive in head first.

"DNA results don't lie," I blurt out. My eyes turn into daggers. "You changed my name? I have a sister?" I question while not losing my rhythm. "I have a family who looks like me. Who created memories without me. Instead, *you* sheltered me, everyone around me telling me how charming it was. Until the only person you let get close to me didn't even want to come around anymore with all of your hovering and third wheeling." Not to mention, phone call and text spying. Grace's last straw. She said she'd wait for me to get out from under my mom's spell. I couldn't hear it then, but now I see. Two years together is enough time to know that Grace's love blazes higher than Mom's ever will. I grit my teeth.

She raises her chin. Her entire body stiffens. Cold. "I saved you," she says, zero hint of regret trailing behind. "Boys and girls will come and go. No one else can love you like I can. Not Grace. Not those people. Not anyone. No one else can save you."

I turn away from her, close my eyes, and slowly breathe out. I didn't need saving. I didn't need changing. *She changed my name.* Barely. She changed me, entirely. Who would I be if I had never been taken?

"Good morning, Lila. Please set up your Touch ID."

I turn back around and find the AV manual resting neatly on her lap. Shellie is a welcome gift that speaks my name, but I haven't inked my signature onto any documents yet. Shellie has been reset by its true owner: Lila. Everything has been erased. Opal Jones has been erased. She clicks so fast. She blocks Opal from the AV, she blocks her from home. She blocks her from me. I look from her to the luggage, my suitcase packed to the brim, her weekend bag as light as a purse.

"Where are your things?" I say, my eyes moving from her back to the luggage.

"I knew this day would come, but I hoped it wouldn't be on your first day of adulthood. I thought I had more time." She shakes her head too fast, too uncontrolled. "I thought I was enough for you." She looks up at me. "It was a mistake getting you the AV." She shakes her head again. "That's okay. The cabin we're staying at is my cousin's. You haven't met her. My belongings are there from previous visits. We'll extend our stay," she says, matter of fact. "Indefinitely." The innocence in her eyes disappears. "We'll move to Salem."

My eyes well up, and I hold myself back from letting the tears overflow. "No."

"You still need saving, honeybee. It's okay," she hums.

No. I am not moving anywhere with her. I have to find a way to pull her stinger out before more venom seeps in. I have to find a way back to Grace. Back to Opal. Back to free. To whoever Zahara should be by now. I pick up my phone and swipe to open up Story Share. I can't access any of the apps from the AV's upgrade until Lila approves the upgrade on an additional device. Suddenly my phone changes from the Story Share app to my lock screen, asking for a four-digit code. My passcode is six digits.

"We're going off the grid," Lila says, her phone in her hands.

She's locked me out of my own device. Everything is in her name.

"Get some rest," she says, leaning back in her seat and closing her eyes. As if it's handled just like that.

The hell it is. I try her birthday. The phone shakes in dismissal. My birthday. It shakes again. My real birthday. Another dismissal. I have two more tries before the phone completely resets itself and then locks me out for six hours with only a random code that will be sent to her phone to unlock mine. I try July 16, seventeen years ago: the day she took me away from my family. The day she fabricated her own. The phone unlocks. I look up and make sure her eyes are still closed.

Shellie beeps. *"Lane Drifting."* I look outside the window, down the icy slick roads. I slide my seat toward the center console, ready to enter Lila's code. She opens her eyes, and I quickly move my fingers from the number grid to the general settings and start changing Shellie's interior skins as a distraction. I summon interest in the pink, lavender, and blue backdrop. She closes her eyes again.

I split screen and enter her code, opening the settings I couldn't get to before. I scroll, scroll, scroll, up and down. I don't have time to waste, but my vision is blurry, my skin is hot. I scroll up and down again, this time slower. Until I find what I'm looking for. When prompted, I enter the passcode and disable Shellie's automatic brakes system. I won't give Lila the chance to respond when I roll out of the AV. Once safely out, I can call the police from my phone. But why wait? I send an emergency text alert with my coordinates. Now I need to get out. And knock her out so she can't come after me. So the police can, and she can't escape the wrath coming down on her.

I have to span this just right. If I make my move before Shellie makes hers, that gives Lila moments to stop me. I wait until the hydroplaning begins. Then I reset Shellie's passcode. Lila's phone pings. She opens her eyes and looks at her notification. She draws her attention from her phone to me. As soon as she lurches forward, Shellie loses all control on the ice-covered highway.

Like a rag doll, Lila's thrown to the front of the AV. My body jerks, but the buckle keeps me in place. Shellie skids. A piercing screeching from below fills my ears.

I've never been in an AV that has gone this fast before. They're not supposed to. Shellie is out of control. Suddenly, we're off the ground, meeting steel head first. Glass shatters into a million pieces. A strangled scream is cut short. I don't know if it's mine or Lila's. Shellie tumbles twice, four times, faster than cotton candy swirling together on its stick. My vision blacks out with every other blink as the AV becomes a broken shell. My only escape. If I can wrangle my way out. I was supposed to get out before Shellie lost control.

I was supposed to get out.

I'm upside down. My vitals fight to be seen through the static on the shattered screens. I can't make anything out. I look ahead to my right at the only pocket of light ahead of me. A glove lays on the ground. Shellie was supposed to be broken but not beyond repair. *What did I do?*

The guardrail is behind us. Or, now we're behind it. I have to get out. I blink. Black out. I blink. Blink. Blink. Eighteen. Goodbye.

Stay alive. Stay alive, you're too young to die. The worker bee thrives when they look to the sky.

Look to the sky. I can't see the sky. I look to the ground. The glove. The back of her body. Still. Only this stillness is not a choice. And there's no queen to defend the hive she's built. Shellie tore my stinger out, and now I am going to die. I blink. I'm going to fly. Blink. Open my eyes wide. I'm going to stay awake and save myself. I am going to be free. I close my eyes for a second. I'm going to try.

———

MELODY SIMPSON writes about television, movies, books, and Broadway at Hollywood the Write Way. When not writing or reading, she can be found in the audience of a musical or walking around the exhibit floor of conventions. She was born and raised in New Jersey and currently resides in Los Angeles, California.

One last bite from Melody Simpson...

The inspiration for my story came from a focus group discussing autonomous vehicles, which I transcribed and could not stop thinking about. I also had a strong desire to write a mother daughter story. So I blended the two.

That said, I wouldn't have the confidence to write without those who came before me, like Toni Morrison and Octavia Butler, both of whom need no explanation.

GOOD SISTER, BAD SISTER

AZZURRA NOX

I t was the eve of her fifteenth birthday when Dilay saw the red stain on her cotton panties for the first time. Seeing the vermilion spot both exhilarated and terrified her. Unlike her sister, Sanem, who had been blessed with womanhood at thirteen, Dilay had been made to feel inferior. First, by her own mother who worried that there was something wrong with her. *A late bloomer,* the doctor had told her as she fretted over why Dilay hadn't come of age just yet. Secondly, by her peers, as her girlfriends whispered in hushed voices how it was strange for her age, when she had admitted that she still hadn't gotten her period.

Dilay's stomach twisted in pain, and she clutched it tightly. She took a deep breath, trying to curb the feeling to throw up her dinner. She got up from the toilet and opened the drawers beneath the sink in search of some pads or tampons, having a vague idea of what to do. Reading the instructions on the tampon package, she figured it couldn't be that difficult. However, the execution proved to be a bit more challenging. She silently cursed her health ed teacher, Ms. Patterson, who had spent more time demonstrating how to put a condom on a banana than explaining the differences between the various feminine products.

After several failed attempts, she decided to take the easy route and opted for the pad instead. Back in her room, she was hiding under a blanket when her mom barged in.

"You got it?" Her eyes sparkled with excitement.

Dilay nodded from her place on the bed. "How did you know?"

"Sanem told me that you must've gotten your period because she isn't on hers. I saw the discarded packet in the trash."

"This is awful." Dilay groaned in pain.

"Oh no, you're very lucky! Today's an amazing day! You're finally a woman!"

To an outsider, her mother may have sounded way too excited over what would appear to be an ordinary event. But she knew that her mother had spent the past two years worrying that there was something wrong with Dilay for being so late. Now she was genuinely happy that Dilay had reached such an important milestone like all the other girls before her.

Dilay curled into a fetal position as pain seized her abdomen and traveled upward. Clutching her stomach, she took deep breaths, trying to ease the pain. This surely was going to require getting used to.

"Yes, lucky indeed," she muttered, swallowing down bile as she attempted one more time to try to keep her food down as her mother stepped out.

Sanem entered her room with soft steps, not wanting to cause any unnecessary disturbance.

"Here." she placed a little blue Midol capsule in Dilay's palm. "This should help with the cramps." Her voice was soothing.

Dilay recalled other instances when her sister had been

eager to ease her pain. When she was little with a stomach flu, Sanem would always hand her saltines and fizzy water to settle her upset tummy. Or the times when she'd butcher her knees falling off her skateboard and Sanem would help her clean the wounds and dress them with Band-Aids. Her thoughtfulness and empathy was what made many people prefer Sanem. Dilay, on the other hand, had always been more of the black sheep and reckless. It's not that Dilay wasn't capable of being thoughtful, but it was difficult for her to be that way often. But Sanem made it look so effortless.

"Let me know if you need anything else," Sanem said.

Dilay could barely reply a thank you, she was in such a foul mood. Hopefully, this pill would work.

That night, once the pill's effect wore off, she woke up from the pain. Her insides kept twisting like a contortionist during a circus act. Sighing, she reached for the Midol packet that Sanem had left on the beside table. She was going to need another dose if she wanted to sleep that night. Her mother's words haunted her. If this were luck, she was screwed.

THE FOLLOWING NIGHT, HER MOTHER WAS IN HER ROOM again. Dilay wasn't sure what to make of her presence till she noticed that she was holding a scarf in her hand.

"It's about time you wore your hijab," her mother stated as she coaxed Dilay to take a seat on the stool in front of the vanity table. "I was thinking I could help you tonight, so that you can start wearing it tomorrow."

Dilay knew how to put one on; as a child, when her mother wasn't around, she used to try on her scarves, admiring how she looked. But it had been years since she had found herself trying to wear one. She wasn't so sure that she wanted to. She loved her long, mahogany curls. They were the envy of Westview High School. She could still remember how Trevor Bradstock had playfully tugged at a curl simply to see it bounce back in place. Usually, when other classmates had done something similar to her in the past, she had been rightfully annoyed. Being treated like a foreign specimen for being different from the other girls at school often left her feeling uneasy, for their curiosity seemed to be sparked by racial divergences rather than mild interest.

"Nice hair," Trevor had said that day in the library, flashing her his lopsided, charming smile. The smile that made all the girls of Westview High melt into a puddle. Her heart had fluttered, and she had dismissed the initial uneasiness she had felt. Like a boy-crazy fool, she had lost herself in his forest-green eyes that were just as dazzling as his smile. But the one thing that made him stand out from all the other jocks was his fire-engine red locks.

To Dilay, he was perfect.

"T-t-thanks," she had managed to mutter before one of the popular girls spotted the two of them speaking and snagged him away.

Dilay had spent weeks replaying that scene in her head ad nauseam. And now her mother was going to hide the very thing that had made Trevor notice her! This was a travesty!

As a child, she had been eager to copy her mother's look, but now she was more focused on being an individual.

But her mother seemed unaware of the tragedy at hand as she carefully tied Dilay's hair back and pulled what looked to be a makeshift wig cap over her hair; Dilay recalled it being referred to as a bonnet. Dilay didn't pay much attention to what her mother was doing as she had seen her mother doing this ritual every morning and could've easily mimicked the same motions on her own.

"Must I really do this?" Dilay asked.

"You know it's part of our religion and tradition."

"I know, Mom." She sighed. "It's just . . . I really like my hair. And besides I don't want to stand out so much." The thought of going to school with her hair concealed made her feel uneasy. Mostly because there weren't many girls at school who wore hijabs. Sanem was one of the few and none of them were high on the school's social ladder. Besides, she was also a little apprehensive over making herself an easy target for any hate crimes. The thought of possibly getting mauled because of a simple scarf frightened her. Sure, there hadn't been incidents at her own school, but she had read the local news online about a girl who had been beaten by a group of peers because of their ignorant views regarding the hijab. She wasn't so sure she was strong enough to handle the pressure that came with such a responsibility.

"This is exactly why you need to wear this," her mother said. "It's part of who we are, of our spiritual identity. In the beginning of our religion, the only way anyone could differentiate between a pagan and a Muslim woman was by the use of her hijab. You should be proud to stand out. I know you think your hair is an extension of your identity, but you're so much more than that." She placed a large scarf over Dilay's head and began to create folds, pinning them as she pulled the material tight in some areas and looser in others.

Though Dilay had seen her mother and Sanem do this a thousand times, as her mother placed the hijab on Dilay's head, she felt a strange sense of novelty. She couldn't quite explain why. Maybe it had to do with actually *experiencing* it herself rather than watching them; it added a certain validity she hadn't known before. Or maybe it was because wearing it now actually signified something unlike when she had put it on as a child with playful ignorance of its symbolic attributes.

"What do you mean by that?" Dilay asked.

"What I mean is that it's not easy being true to yourself. I know how high school kids can be with their cliques. But you should spend less time trying to look like everyone else and more time being proud of who you are. At this age, you're at your most vulnerable. But you're strong. You may not understand your strength right now. But you will in time. Wearing the hijab not only honors our traditions but the women that came before us. Strong women who were proud to distinguish themselves in a crowd. Some may be afraid of our strength. But I want you to embrace it and not shy away from it. I want you to receive the attention you crave for the right reasons. Not to be viewed as one who blindly follows the crowd."

Dilay knew that her mother was right, but at fifteen she wasn't sure she had the strength to stand out. Some days, she was grateful for her long hair, using it as an armor to blend into the sea of pretty girls. Ever since her father had left them two years ago for his young intern, her mother's trust in men had dissipated to the point of drilling her daughters with the notion that they shouldn't depend on men, rather on themselves, cultivating their inner strength. But Dilay's crush on Trevor knew no bounds, and although she knew some men couldn't be trusted, she was certain that he was different. He *had* to be with that smile.

She looked at her reflection in the mirror and couldn't help but recoil. The hijab only accentuated the baby fat in her cheeks. Without her curls, she felt naked. She couldn't hide her disappointment as she stared back at herself.

"I don't feel myself without my hair," she said.

"I could get you prettier scarves that you could use," her mother suggested. "Sanem's been wearing the hijab for much longer than you and she never complained."

Dilay absolutely hated it whenever her mother would

remind her how docile Sanem was in contrast to her. Why was her questioning always seen as fault? Besides, Sanem had reached womanhood years before her, and that's why she had worn the hijab for a longer length of time. Comparing the two sisters was ridiculous.

"I'm not Sanem. If Dad were here, he wouldn't force me to do something I didn't want to do," she simply stated as she glared back at her mother with defiance in her eyes.

"If your father cared enough, he wouldn't have abandoned us, so I'm all you've got," her mother said with vehemence in her voice. She pulled the hijab free from Dilay's hair with sudden force. The bonnet was still snug on her head, pins still firmly placed. But then her mother yanked on it, ignoring Dilay's cries of distress. Despite the struggle, she managed to tear it off; some pins fell to the floor while others landed on the vanity table. Before Dilay had a chance to reply, her mother had already grabbed a pair of scissors and snipped off a large chunk of Dilay's hair.

"Mom! What are you doing?" she screamed, horrified.

"I've tried reasoning with you, but you're always so difficult!" She raised the scissors, again ready to snip, and Dilay's vision blurred with tears as she touched her beautiful fallen curls.

If she wanted to salvage her hair, she needed to act now. She jerked her elbow back, hitting her mother and catching her off guard. She quickly stood, getting ready to flee. Her mother went after her with the scissors, still intent on cutting her hair.

"You're crazy! Don't get near me!" Dilay shouted.

Sanem came out of her room and gasped at Dilay's haphazardly cut hair. "What's going on?"

Genuine concern crossed Sanem's features, but this only furthered Dilay's annoyance. She certainly didn't need her sister to mediate. Nor to side with her mother, which was usually what she did whenever Dilay defied their mother's parental authority. And she certainly didn't need Sanem's sympathy either.

"Mom's gone crazy, that's what!" In a frenzy, Dilay grabbed her phone from its resting place on the vanity table and stuffed it in her pocket.

"I won't have you speaking to me in that manner, Dilay!" her mother shouted, quickly approaching her.

But Dilay had a head start and raced down the stairs. She made a mad dash for the front door, unlocking it and running out before her mother had a chance to stop her.

"Where are you going? It's getting dark, come back!"

Dilay heard her mother shouting after her, but she didn't dare look over her shoulder as she continued to run down the street and toward the woods. She knew that her mother would be coming after her in the car, and Dilay needed to find a way to lose her. But she hadn't been in the woods in years. Not since they had found the mangled body of a young girl.

Despite that knowledge, Dilay continued to run, not wanting to stop for fear of having to confront her mother.

She truly regretted reacting the way she had and was certain that her mother would surely ground her for weeks, if not months. She was prone to having a bad temper, and even the most banal statement could make her explode like a hand grenade. Why had she been so stupid? She knew that she shouldn't have provoked her the way she did, especially bringing up her dad.

Dilay's feet crunched gravel and snapped several twigs in two. It was dusk, and night was fast approaching. Although years had passed since she had last walked through the forest, she knew that on the other side of it was a lake, which she was more familiar with. But one thing that Dilay soon realized as she found herself in the heart of the woods was how terrible she was with landmarks. Within twenty minutes, she was already lost. She couldn't even find where she'd entered the woods. Had she always been so directionally impaired or had years of avoiding the woods made her so?

The trees and foliage enveloped her as though they had become denser. She stopped running and took out her phone to use the flashlight to illuminate the path. Cautiously, she took small steps. An owl called out from its place on a limb in a nearby tree. Birds flapped their wings in agitation, and she heard them fly away despite it being too dark for her to see them.

A slight smile formed on her lips; nothing about these animals seemed menacing at all. But her smile quickly faded when a deadly silence fell over the woods. Only a moment ago it had been alive with commotion, and now one could hear a pin drop.

Something, possibly a larger animal, was approaching, causing all the smaller animals to freeze, not wanting to be noticed. Dilay strained her ears as she heard the sound of advancing steps. She didn't have a chance to break into a sprint before whatever it was that had been chasing after the forest animals eagerly pounced on her, causing her to fall face first onto the ground. Her lip bumped a rock, and blood gushed down her chin. She'd dropped her phone, and she no longer had a source of light. Her head throbbed, and she reached up to touch the side of her skull, which was wet. A metallic, coppery scent emanated from her fingers, and she knew that it was blood.

She tried to scream, but the creature was heavy, pinning her diminutive body down to the hard ground. Her fingers grasped at the dirt, attempting to push herself back up, but it was futile. The animal was stronger and had bit down on her left leg.

She cried out. The animal dragged her body across the

ground as she desperately tried to hold onto something—anything. The skin on her cheek felt raw, and her whole body was in tremendous pain. Tears blurred her vision, and she called out for help once more.

Her horrified wails filled the night. Everything around her was cloaked in darkness. Blood filled her mouth as the animal continued to attack, its claws digging into her tender flesh and tearing at it, much like a bear would.

Then it left as quickly as it had come, large paws running across the ground, kicking up dirt and fallen leaves in its wake. Broken and in pain, she managed to roll over onto her back. Gasping for breath, she looked up at the starless sky, the full moon partially covered by clouds barely allowing any light to transpire.

What a waste to die on such a beautiful night.

WHEN DILAY WOKE UP SHE WAS IN A HOSPITAL BED WITH tubes supplying extra oxygen coming out of her nose. Another tube, attached to a beeping machine, protruded from her wrist.

Sanem clutched Dilay's hands. "Dilay!" she exclaimed. Then she nudged their mother, who was sitting in the chair beside her. "Mom! Mom! She's awake!"

"Allahu Akbar! It's a miracle!" Her mother's voice was filled with emotion, and she grabbed Dilay's hands as well as tears streamed down her cheeks. "We didn't think you were going to make it! You've been out for the past two days."

Dilay's head felt heavy. She tried to remember what had happened, but it was proving to be difficult. She lifted the hand that didn't have the tube and touched her head. It was wrapped in bandages. A panic settled in her core and traveled throughout her limbs, slightly shaking them.

"What happened? Why am I here? Why the bandages?"

"You were attacked." Sanem quickly filled her in. "They think it was probably a bear. If Trevor hadn't found you, you'd be dead by now!"

Dilay's heart spiked at the sound of Trevor's name. Trevor had saved her? She could hardly believe it. A rush of warmth overcame her body like being kissed by sun rays on a hot summer day. It was bliss.

"You hit your head pretty hard," Sanem continued. "The doctors had to shave some of your hair off to operate so they could remove the blood clots and relieve the pressure on your brain."

Her mother leaned forward. "When you ran out, I thought you were headed to your usual spot at Craven's Cafe. What were you doing in the woods?" Her mother's voice was stern and laced with worry, a stark contrast to the affectionate tone she had used merely minutes before.

"I was lost," Dilay murmured, fragments of that night slowly resurfacing. She recalled running into the woods and then being attacked by a large animal. But her memories were hazy, and she couldn't say if a bear had been the culprit of her attack. Touching her bandaged head again, she whispered, "I'm lost," and rolled over onto her side just so she could avoid their stares, as she cried over the loss of her hair.

By the time Dilay was able to return to school, her mother had taken her to the salon in an attempt to have her haphazardly shaved hair fixed. But it was useless; it was going to take some time for her hair to grow back.

A part of Dilay was worried that the portion of her scalp that had been cut into and sutured back together wouldn't be able to grow hair again. In the meantime, Dilay decided it was best to keep her Frankenstein head concealed by the hijab. As much as she had been reluctant to wear one in the first place, ironically, now it was helping her look pretty by hiding the stitches.

Her mother, perhaps overwhelmed by Dilay's sudden change of heart, didn't question her true motives. If her mother did have an inkling, she didn't confront Dilay about it. Maybe she'd chalked it up to Dilay being grateful that she had made it out of the woods alive. The doctors and nurses were surprised by her speedy recovery; the bite on her leg had healed in ways that baffled them. There wasn't even a visible scar.

Dilay was walking down the halls of Westview High trying to find the one person she cared to speak to: Trevor.

Sanem was walking beside her and whispered, "They're all looking at you like you've risen from the dead."

"Was I such a goner?"

"You were in such an awful state. I thought they were gonna have to make burger patties out of you."

"Thank you for the gory graphic, sis." Sure, Dilay had been in danger, but she felt amazing now, and it kind of annoyed her that her always-protective sister acted as though she were a wounded child.

That's when she saw *him*.

Trevor's striking red hair was the first thing she noticed in the crowd, and she made her way to approach him. Something about being on the brink of life and death had given her a sudden courage she wouldn't have had otherwise.

"What do you think you're doing?" Sanem pulled her back by the elbow.

"I was going to thank him for saving me."

"Are you crazy? He's a senior *and* popular. Don't embarrass yourself. Besides, it's best you stay away from the jocks; they have such a bad rep."

But Dilay was feeling defiant. How dare her sister try to mold her into a meek and mild girl? He had saved her life, and she felt very much indebted to him.

"That's ridiculous; they're just rumors. And Trevor is different," she scoffed, freeing herself from her sister's grip.

The sea of students parted as she walked over to Trevor. He was standing next to the lockers, chatting to a group of his friends, all of whom were on the football team. His green eyes flashed and settled on Dilay's soulful eyes. Butterflies exploded in her stomach, and she breathed in to calm them.

"Hi Trevor."

"Oh, hey," he replied, his eyes scanning her face, curiously studying her hijab. "I passed by the hospital a couple of times to see how you were doing. I asked your sister about you."

"You did?" She couldn't hide her surprise and wondered why Sanem had kept this hidden from her. Though Sanem might not think there was a reason to tell her. Dilay had been so good at keeping her crush hidden from her sister—from anyone really. What was the point of sharing her secret with her sister when she knew that she'd most likely tell her that he was unattainable and she shouldn't waste her time barking up the wrong tree? And maybe Sanem was right to feel that way about Trevor, but Dilay yearned for things to be different. That maybe once, just *once* she could gain the attention of a boy she liked. Her sister would have simply reminded Dilay of the rumors that circulated around the jocks, like how they couldn't be trusted with girls. Dilay didn't want to believe in anything she didn't have proof of.

"You're wearing a scarf like Sanem," Trevor said.

"Yeah." She touched the hijab self-consciously, wishing she didn't have it on, embarrassed that that was the first thing he had noticed, longing that he hadn't focused on that aspect of her appearance right away. But she flashed a smile and tried to carry on. "I just wanted to thank you. I heard that you were the one to find me in the woods."

He closed his locker and turned back to face her. "Yeah, I did. I was jogging back from the lake." His nonchalant demeanor had a way of enticing her. Like saving girls for him was just the norm. Nothing special.

"In the dark?" she asked.

"What were you doing there?"

"Inspiration. Nature inspires me." It was a dumb reply, but she couldn't control the words that left her lips when she was nervous.

He cracked a smile. "Cute. And I'm glad that you're doing okay."

"Thank you." Her eyes studied his model looks and settled upon his lips. If only she could ever kiss him. Was that too much to wish?

He turned to leave, and it was like the sun was abandoning the sky. But then he turned around once more. "It's good to see you at school again, Dilay. See you around."

"Thank you!" And she raised her hand halfway in a parting greeting.

Trevor Bradstock had *remembered* her name.

Life was good.

It was a week after her attack in the woods when Dilay noticed something peculiar about her teeth.

"Are you sure they're longer?" Sanem said. "I can't see the difference. Maybe it's a hormonal thing."

"Don't be stupid, Sanem. Hormones don't make your teeth

change." Her canines seemed to have elongated. She studied herself in the mirror, huffing in annoyance. It wasn't readily noticeable to others, but her canines seemed to have elongated. It wasn't her imagination, they were longer and sharper than before.

"That's not true. Don't you remember Ms. Patterson in health class talking about how sometimes if your hormones go haywire you can be more vulnerable to gum disease, plaque, or canker sores?"

"No, I don't remember."

"Well, I'm just saying, maybe you should have a doc check it out if it gets worse. Hormones can really mess you up."

"She's ignorant," Dilay replied, exasperated. Once again, Sanem's concern for her was getting tedious. Although, she did vaguely recall Ms. Patterson passing out a worksheet that described all the horrible things that could happen to women due to unbalanced hormones.

Dilay wasn't sure if hormones were to blame for her dental changes, but she was noticing other slight differences. Attributes that weren't there before. Her hair was glossier than usual, and her chestnut brown eyes had a hint of amber to them now. Her sense of smell had become heightened, and she often recoiled at scents that she used to be fond of or noticed those that previously hadn't been so perceptible.

But the most astounding change of all was the incredible strength she had gained. Before, lifting heavy objects would've been difficult for her, but now she found that she could easily lift her bed from the ground on her own.

Her discovery came by accident, when in a fit of fury over her mother not allowing her to go out during a school night with her friends, she had grasped the headboard in anger and found herself being capable of suspending it from the ground. The other day, when she got pissed in math class over Mrs. Arnold giving her a hard time for not doing her homework—reminding her that when she'd had Sanem in her class, her sister had always come prepared—Dilay had barged out and hidden in the bathroom, in a fit of anger, she had punched the wall, and with a gaping mouth had looked at the hole she had made in the cement structure. Surprisingly, her hand had remained unscathed.

Afterwards, she lit up chain-smoking up a storm. For some reason, lately the ritual of lighting up and smoking was the only way to simmer down, something else that was different from before.

She began to notice that anger made her particularly more violent and increased her strength to extraordinary levels. But she hadn't shared this with anyone as she wasn't sure how to address this uncommon strength. And honestly, this newfound skill both fascinated and scared her immensely.

Sanem was still speaking, and Dilay regained focus, trying to push what had happened at the bathroom at school as an anomaly and not the norm.

Brushing out the kinks, Dilay tried to style her short hair in a way that would hide the part that was still buzzed. There were no traces of scars from where the stitches had been, but to her dismay her hair hadn't yet grown back. She vowed to keep it hidden until it looked presentable again.

"At least your skin hasn't acted up yet," Sanem said. "Mine is always terrible before and after my period."

"Lucky me," she replied, turning away from the mirror. "Why didn't you tell me that Trevor had asked you about me?"

Taken aback, Sanem's cheeks flushed. "It just slipped my mind."

"Really?"

"Yes, I mean . . . we'd just spend study hall together talking about you and your progress. Nothing beyond that. But he has a good heart. At first I didn't trust him. I didn't know him that well before your attack, but I can see why you say he's different from the other jocks. I just didn't want to admit that maybe you were right about him. Why? Do you like him or something?"

Now it was Dilay's turn for her cheeks to flush. "N-n-no . . . of course not. But if you feel that way about him, why did you warn me?"

Sanem looked away, embarrassed. "It's just . . . look, I don't want you to get hurt."

"I see. Well, like you said, he's a senior; it'd be impossible anyway."

"Are you sure?"

"Yes! Jeez, can we put this to rest?" She wasn't sure why she had lied to her sister, but maybe she didn't want Sanem to be overprotective toward her as always and give her unwanted advice. Besides, being put on the spot that way about her feelings had just made her feel uncomfortable.

That night, Dilay was plagued with dreams of running through the woods. She could feel the crisp night air moving through her hair and was filled with a sense of freedom that she had never felt before. Her heart was pumping with adrenaline and excitement, and when she woke up, she was astonished to find her feet dirty with soil.

———

THE DAYS THAT FOLLOWED FELT STRANGE. DILAY BEGAN TO notice little details, such as being able to hear people speaking in the next room or being able to see clearly in the dark. Maybe these small alterations weren't so alarming but paired with her recent bigger changes, it gave her reason to pause and wonder what exactly was happening to her.

Her head pumped furiously too, as it did now in biology

class, and she plopped it down on the desk. Sanem entered the room and sat in front of her, turning to face her. Dilay would've ignored her, but her curiosity was greater than she liked to admit. She reached down to grab her sweatshirt out of her backpack. Then she folded it on her desk like a makeshift pillow, and rested her chin on it as she looked at her sister while stroking her aching temples.

"What are you doing here? Don't you have U.S. government right now?"

"Yes, but something incredible happened, Di!"

Her squeals only made Dilay cringe in pain. She hadn't seen Sanem this excited since she won the Juniors State Championship for Academics last year.

"Let me guess, you got an A on your English paper," Dilay replied with a tinge of annoyance laced with sarcasm.

"Well, I *did* get an A on the paper I turned in yesterday, but that's not why I'm here. You won't believe who asked me out on a date!"

"Who? Gumball Watterson?" The notion of Sanem actually going on a date seemed so foreign to Dilay, not because her sister didn't have the looks, but she simply never seemed interested.

Dilay heard a few girls snicker, but she refused to acknowledge them. She just buried her head further into the sweatshirt.

"Trevor Bradstock!"

Dilay's head snapped to attention. Her fingers curled under the edge of the desk in sudden rage. "What did you say?"

"Trevor asked me to the movies."

"You said that jocks were bad news."

"Yeah, but you said it yourself that Trevor was different and that the rumors aren't true."

"You're such a backstabbing bitch!" Dilay knew that her outburst wasn't fair, as she had blatantly told her sister that she wasn't interested in Trevor, but at the same time, she couldn't contain her jealousy.

Heads swerved in their direction; suddenly the two of them had become the center of attention. Students who had been preoccupied with their phones only seconds ago were now staring at the two sisters, enthralled by the spectacle.

"What's wrong with you?" Sanem cried. "It's just a date, and you said you didn't even like him that way!"

A hush fell over the room. Dilay's whole body felt ablaze with rage, and before she knew it, she had risen up and pounced on Sanem.

"Fight, fight, fight!" A few students began to chant, loving the idea of possible bloodshed. It was even more compelling since they were sisters. By the time Mr. Sanchez had managed to disentangle Dilay from Sanem, Dilay's face was the hue of beets and her fist was full of ripped out strands of her sister's black hair. Sanem's hijab was lopsided to the left, and a few locks of hair had spilled out. This sudden outburst of violence was uncommon for Dilay, and the teacher didn't know what to make of it. Flustered, Mr. Sanchez had them stand apart from each other, and while he reprimanded them in a stern voice, Dilay's eyes narrowed and focused on her desk, which had visible nail marks imprinted on the wood like claw scratches.

THAT NIGHT, DILAY DECIDED SHE'D GO TO BED EARLY. Her mother had revoked her privileges for hanging out with friends and had changed the Wi-Fi password, so Dilay was locked out of using the Internet. Besides, she was plagued with intense abdominal pains courtesy of her monthly flow, so hitting the sack early wasn't so terrible.

As she began to change into her pajamas, she heard voices

outside. She moved to the window to see Sanem leaving for her date with Trevor. A lump formed in Dilay's throat as he opened the car door for her.

Angry, Dilay pulled out her hidden pack of cigarettes from her desk and lit one. She knew smoking at home was a big risk, but how much more trouble could she possibly get into at this point?

Her ears perked up at the sound of Trevor.

"You look beautiful," Trevor said to Sanem. Dilay looked out the window to see him flashing her sister his winning smile. She wished she didn't have this new supersonic hearing.

It was true though; Sanem looked beautiful. She was wearing a new dress and had applied makeup.

Why did everyone love Sanem over her? Her mother, her teachers, and now even her crush. Was there something truly wrong with her? Was she just so unlovable? Unlikable? Sometimes she felt like she was going insane.

Dilay took a drag, wiped away the tears that kept falling, and then shut her eyes real tight. A storm of emotions etched into her features as she exhaled the smoke into a cloud above her head. Her heart felt crushed. She finished off the cigarette and turned away from the window.

Before sobs could escape from her lips, she buried her head under the blankets and fell into a restless sleep.

SOMETIME AROUND MIDNIGHT, DILAY WOKE UP. SANEM must've returned home because Dilay heard her enter their shared bathroom. But something was amiss. Sanem was dragging her feet, and then the sounds of her sister throwing up could be heard through the door.

Curious, Dilay got out of bed. She knocked cautiously on

the bathroom door at first, not wanting to wake their mother. Sure, it still stung that her sister had gone on a date with Trevor, but it also had been her own fault for not speaking up about him when she'd had the chance. If Sanem had missed her curfew, Dilay didn't want to aggravate the recent strain between her sister and her by ratting her out. Clear minded now, she was certain the two of them could work things out. Or at least she hoped so. She couldn't allow things to sour over a boy. Maybe if she explained to Sanem how she truly felt about Trevor, then she wouldn't continue seeing him.

"Sanem? You okay?"

"Yes!" she hissed from the other side. Then more coughing mixed with sobs.

Despite her better judgment, Dilay went ahead and opened the door. "Oh my God!" She gasped the moment she saw her sister.

There she was, sitting on the floor, the long floral dress she had worn for her date with Trevor was torn in several places, and there was blood running down her exposed leg. Her hair was in tangles and her makeup smeared. Black tears marred her complexion. Dilay also noticed a small cut on her sister's lip.

"What happened? Did someone mug you?"

But Sanem couldn't speak. She simply shook her head, and tears rolled down her cheeks.

Dilay went to the sink and ran a cloth under the faucet before approaching her sister. She crouched down in front of her and delicately washed off the blood from her lips. "Wasn't Trevor there to help you?"

She only cried harder at the mention of his name.

"Sanem, what's going on? Please, tell me. You're scaring me."

"Trevor . . ." she whispered, hiccupping sobs.

"What about him?"

"He did this to me."

Dilay's mouth dropped open in shock while the wet cloth she was using to wash Sanem fell out of her hands. *No,* she thought. It felt like a lead anchor had plummeted in the pit of her stomach, causing her to feel sick.

"That . . . that can't be true," she murmured, unable to contain the rogue tears that hurriedly rolled down her cheeks.

"But it is." Sanem looked directly into her eyes, and that's when Dilay noticed a certain pain she hadn't seen in her sister's gaze before.

How many times had Dilay stared at Trevor's yearbook photo and sighed at his perfect features?

And now this.

Her stomach burned with an intense outrage, and she wiped away her tears. So stupid. She had been so stupid!

"Trevor did this?" Dilay shouted.

"Shhh! Don't wake up mom! I don't want her to know!" Her eyes were pleading. There was something about Sanem that broke Dilay's heart. Although Sanem was older by two years, in that moment, bloody and broken, she resembled a little girl.

A frightened little girl.

A hurt little girl.

Something stirred inside of Dilay. All those times where Sanem had always looked after her came to mind, and now Dilay couldn't fathom seeing her sister so broken. Her heart imploded, and any affection she might have had for Trevor quickly dissolved as though thrown in acid. How could she have been so stupid? Why hadn't she seen the danger? Had she really been so blinded to not see his potential to be brutal? She shouldn't have dismissed the hushed rumors that passed through the halls at school. Rumors of how jocks from the football team were known to get a bit rough with girls who weren't agreeable to their advances. But she didn't want to believe them, at least when it came to Trevor. After all, he had *saved* her life and had come to see her in the hospital. But none of those nice gestures meant anything now.

They were eclipsed by this act of violence.

Dilay had had *enough* of girls becoming hapless victims simply because they had mistook charm for kindness. A sudden rage rose up in her like a venomous serpent ready to attack anyone in sight. She could feel the anger rushing through her veins, pulsing at her temples. Her nostrils flared.

"Where is he?" she said.

"What are you going to do?"

"Just tell me where he is!"

Her sister gulped and whispered, "I last saw him by the lake."

Then it suddenly dawned on Dilay. The reason why Trevor had been able to save her in the forest was because he had been coming back from the lake. The infamous lake where it was rumored that the jocks brought girls so that they could do as they pleased. The mere thought made her skin crawl in disgust and ire. Her feelings hadn't allowed her to connect the dots, and because of that, Sanem had paid the price.

Guilt gnawed at her insides, thinking back at how she had defended him when Sanem had brought up the rumors surrounding the jocks. Her infatuation for Trevor had brought upon grave consequences, and now she wasn't sure how to undo the damage. To think that she had been so angry when he had asked Sanem out, only for this horror to happen now.

"How did you get home?" Dilay asked.

"I walked to Craven's Cafe and got an Uber."

"That was smart." Her anger was moving through her limbs; she could feel her strength increasing tenfold. Suddenly, she was hit with the desire to punch someone.

Trevor had to pay.

"Okay, I'm going." A little smirk formed upon Dilay's lips, "Now it's my turn to play."

THE MOON WAS ENGAGED IN A GAME OF HIDE-AND-SEEK peeking behind the clouds when Dilay cut her way through the woods. A strange instinct overcame her senses as though her feet knew where to go even if her actual memory was limited. Despite the vague notion, her feet knew the way. She was running, just as she had been a month ago the night she'd been attacked. Running the same way she recalled in her dreams. And as she ran, she felt something inside her change. Her movements were becoming more fluid, faster, and suddenly she was gliding through the trees, a low growl escaping from her mouth. In her distraught jealous state earlier, she had fallen asleep in her hijab, and now the dark scarf flowed freely behind her.

The closer she got to the lake, the more the scent of fear clung to the trees. She could smell the crime that had been committed. Her sister's fear and Trevor's lust. A part of her was afraid that she wouldn't find him where Sanem had left him. That perhaps he'd already gone home. But when the lake came into view, she saw that his car was still parked near the banks and that he was sitting on the hood, smoking. Beer cans littered the ground. Initially, he didn't hear Dilay approaching. Her movements were stealthy, calculated.

A lopsided grin spread across his face when he saw her. "What are you doing here?"

"What do you think?"

His grin only widened, like a grotesque clown ready to devour someone. He continued to smoke, the cloud above him slowly spreading. Dilay moved closer to him. She kept her fists balled, trying to contain her anger. Her nails dug into her palms till she felt blood pouring through the wounds.

"Whatever your sister told you, it's not true. She wanted it."

"Are you sure that's how it *really* went, Trevor Bradstock?" Her eyes glowered in rage, daring him to contradict her.

He looked briefly away. His bravado faltered.

He took a final drag and threw the cigarette to the ground. She could smell his putrid heart seeping from his pores in the form of a cold sweat. All she felt toward him now was hatred; no remnants of her previous feelings existed. She had been naive to be swept by his charm and good looks. Now she knew better. A beautiful face could hide such an ugly soul.

"Look, I'm sorry," he said. "I didn't do anything wrong! She didn't even stop me! Ask her! She wanted it!"

"Did she, really? Or did you just take advantage of her because you could?"

"I . . . I didn't mean to . . ." He looked confused as though he couldn't possibly understand why her ire was palpable.

"Oh, you *did* mean it. Just like I mean it."

"Wait . . . what?" His eyes widened in horror as rage transformed the young woman before him.

Dilay's features contorted, and her eyes burned yellow. Suddenly, she was unrecognizable; she was powerful and magical, and most importantly, strong.

She struck him across the face, his beautiful features destroyed in one swipe. Trevor toppled and fell to the ground, letting out a cry of pain. Blood gushed from his wound, falling in large drops on the dirt. He tried to push himself up into a standing position, but he was struck again. On all fours, he tried to crawl away, but it was futile. He was too weak to escape this fury he had unleashed, and Dilay suspected he knew it.

He coughed up blood. "Please, stop! Don't!" But it was useless, there was the tearing of flesh and the crack of bones. It

212

wasn't long before she watched him lying on his back, staring blankly up at the full moon.

THE FOLLOWING MONDAY, EVERYONE AT SCHOOL WAS buzzing with the latest news. Trevor had been attacked in the woods and found dead. Again, the culprit for this attack seemed to be an animal, although the police weren't capable of identifying exactly what kind. Some people claimed that it might've been a bear, based on the scratch marks left on his flesh; others thought it might be a coyote from the bite marks.

That morning, Dilay was standing next to Sanem's locker. The dark circles under Sanem's eyes were more prominent than usual, and she wore her typical long skirt, to which she'd matched her hijab.

Dilay knew that it was going to take some time for Sanem to get better. A part of her had forever been broken. But she wasn't alone. Dilay was determined to help her glue back the pieces. Maybe with her help, she could be like one of those kintsugi plates, broken but mended back together by gold.

Dilay, on the other hand, had surprised her classmates a few minutes earlier when they saw that she had personalized her hijab. She had decorated the black scarf with punk spikes and safety pins. That night after she had seen Trevor, a quiet rebellion had surfaced inside of her. Staring at her reflection, she had instinctively painted her lips a deep burgundy, almost black. She had admired her handiwork and smiled. It was that night that she decided upon that look and that she would recreate it for school.

"I heard he was unrecognizable when they found him," whispered a girl to two others standing close to the sisters' lockers. "It looked like he had been clawed to death by the myriad marks they found on his body."

"They had to identify him by his teeth!" added another girl, aghast.

"Such a horrible way to die," the first one said.

"Seems pretty fitting to me," Dilay interrupted.

"What do you mean?" one of them asked, as all three girls turned to face her.

"Karma's a bitch. He must've fucked with the wrong person to deserve that." She hinted at the possibility that the rumors circulating around the jocks could have been true.

All three girls looked at her agape as she tugged on her sister's arm. Dilay left with a smirk. She squeezed her sister's arm for reassurance and then looked down at her own black painted nails. That's when she noticed some remnants of blood still encrusted underneath them and thought, *That bastard ruined my manicure.* A sly smile formed upon her lips. It was only a matter of time before she'd make the rest of them pay.

Her mother was right; she came from a long line of strong women. This was who she was.

A new woman.

A strong woman.

AZZURRA NOX was born in Catania, Sicily and has led a nomadic life since birth. She has lived in various European cities and Cuba and currently resides in So-Cal. Her love for the macabre began at a young age when she discovered horror movies. Her writing draws inspiration from music, literature, and her nightmares. Her latest project is MY AMERICAN NIGHTMARE – WOMEN IN HORROR ANTHOLOGY, for which she is an editor and contributing writer. When she isn't writing, she loves dancing, going to rock shows, and cuddling her two chubby rescue pups, Nico and Lupo. You can find her online at https://azzurranox.com/ or at her lifestyle blog The Inkblotters (https://theinkblotters.com/) where she shares her love of books, films, beauty products, and much much more.

One last bite from Azzurra Nox…

One of my favorite feminist horror films is the Canadian indie, GINGERSNAPS. I wanted to write a story that featured a were-wolf as it did in that film, and convey what initially may seem like a curse, in the end, could also be a newfound strength. When creating the character of Dilay, I knew that I wanted her to be Muslim, because one of my best friends from high school is Muslim. I was inspired to create a character that had her same sense of moral strength and fierce devotion to her loved ones. Those two elements were the springboard for my story.

I don't have a sole favorite feminist author, but I do have several favorite feminist novels. I recommend reading the following: THE HANDMAIDS TALE, I CAPTURE THE CASTLE, THE BLUEST EYE, THE HIDDEN FACE OF EVE, and A THOUSAND SPLENDID SUNS.

VIGILANTE LANE

S. E. GREEN

After my shift at the vet clinic, I pull up outside the Youth Center where my younger brother, Justin, attends summer camp. I park in an available spot and tug up the emergency brake. As I tie my red curls into a quick ponytail, I glance at the time. I've got about an hour before I have to be on campus for my first college class.

Plenty of time.

As I'm climbing out, I catch sight of a man sitting at a picnic table tucked under the trees.

Looking like a dad in jeans, T-shirt, flip-flops, and baseball cap, he sits alone. With his feet planted on the ground and his arms propped atop the table, he holds a phone in his hands. To any onlooker, he's seemingly looking at his phone, possibly scrolling Facebook, Instagram, or the like.

My senses prick to instant alert.

I follow his line of sight and the direction his phone points all the way across the grass and over to the playground attached to the Youth Center. The playground where the kindergarten and first grade students currently play.

Son of a bitch.

I leap from the Jeep, slam my door shut, and march straight toward him. His focus stays solely on the phone, and when I slide into the bench opposite him, blocking his phone from the playground, he jumps a little and glances up.

I don't smile. "Which kid is yours?"

A tentative smile dances across his lips. "Um, none actually."

The idiot doesn't even have the wherewithal to lie. My gaze travels over his green baseball hat and down across his thin upper body before coming back to meet his dark eyes. "Then you need to move," I tell him.

His tentative smile turns into one big, fake, and bright. "Why? It's a free world and all that."

I pluck the phone right from his fingers and turn it around.

He reaches for it. "Hey!"

I want to jab the heel of my hand straight into the tip of his oily nose, but I refrain and instead level him with a dark gaze. Apparently, he realizes I'm not a girl to be messed with and glances hesitantly at the phone.

I bring it up in front of my face, keeping partial focus on him, and begin scrolling through the pictures he just took of the playground and the kids. At this distance they're not the best photos, but still.

I don't bother to finish browsing the portfolio because this man is so done.

"D-d-do I know you?" he cautiously asks.

I look back to his wormy eyes. "No, and you don't *want* to know me." I lean closer, and he has the smarts to tilt back. "I am here every day, and if I ever see you again, I will not be this nice."

A terrible fake laugh comes out of him. "Y-y-you've got the wrong idea."

Lightning quick, I jab the heel of my running shoe into the

top of his right flip-flopped foot and cram my thumb into the ulnar nerve on his forearm. He gives a satisfactory cringe. "Listen, asshole, I know who you are." I apply more pressure to both points, and he hisses in a breath, trying to pull away.

"I'm different now," he whimpers. "I did my time. You all aren't allowed to do this."

He must think I'm a cop or something. Fine by me. I give him a sharp intimidating leer. "From the outside you look normal, but you haven't changed. You are who you are."

His bottom lip quivers. "My brain isn't flawed. I can control my compulsions. My past is not a prologue for the future."

Sounds like he's quoting something a counselor told him. I release my hold and stand, taking his phone with me. "I ever see you around again, I won't stop with a couple of harmless pressure points."

"But my phone," he blubbers.

I smack him across the face with it, ignoring his yelp, and walk off.

My brain isn't flawed. I can control my compulsions. My past is not a prologue for the future.

His words ring a little too true for me. Except I would never hurt a child. If I had the time, I'd follow this pedophile and get more information. Really teach him that lesson I threatened. But I have other things to deal with right now, like picking up Justin, getting to class, and making dinner for my family.

I do have Mr. Pedophile Oily Nose's phone, though, which means I have his contacts and personal information. I can easily find him if I want to.

How many times have I sat here in Judge Penn's court? The smell of cleaning products lingering. My favorite vent directly above me always blowing cold air. The sound of his gavel determining the direction of a person's life.

My sanctuary.

Plus I love how the bailiff always greets me with a simple nod of the head and my name: *Lane.* No idle chitchat like, "How's it going?" Or "Looking forward to college?"

Innocent until proven guilty. It's a holistic approach, and one I don't subscribe to. I've been hanging out in Judge Penn's courtroom for years, and though I've never personally met him, I think he and I might be friends. He seems like he would enjoy handing out tough sentences if only the law would let him.

Jurisdiction issues, fancy lawyers, evidence mishandling . . . there are too many people who skirt by, which is where I come in.

I've met many a friend in Penn's courtroom that I later dealt with like The Weasel, the rapist, and Aisha, the drug dealer. And now Mr. Oily Nose, the pedophile.

That's right. We meet again. Last I saw him, he wore a baseball hat, and now I discover he's got an oily balding head to match his nose.

Judge Penn points his finger. "You listen to me, you piece of trash, if I ever see you in here again, I don't care what evidence is or is not admissible, I will take you down. Do you understand me?"

And that right there is why I think Penn and I would be friends.

Mr. Pedophile Oily Nose drops his head, all submissive, and nods his acquiesce. The gavel bangs, and he exchanges a handshake with his lawyer before turning and walking down the middle aisle that leads out of the fairly empty courtroom.

Usually, I keep a low profile, but something drives me to stand, to draw attention to myself. It works because he glances up and his eyes widen when he recognizes me. The shock in his expression has me smirking.

That's right, you ass wipe, I'm coming after you.

I MAY NOT HAVE THE ABILITY TO HACK MY WAY THROUGH whatever network needs to be hacked, but I have my own ways of finding out things. Like, for example, I still have Mr. Oily Nose's phone.

It's amazing how many people don't password protect themselves, and it's amazing what people keep on their phones. Numbers, of course. Addresses. Credit card information. Porn apps. Calendar of events. Personal notes. IM messages with other deviants. Pictures of children . . .

Yes, he may be doing a stellar job of skirting the law, but there is nothing innocent about his intentions. And I fully plan on exposing him.

To the right people.

Biker Dudes Against Pedophiles does indeed exist with headquarters in Texas and several affiliated clubs across the U.S. One here local in DC.

Mr. Oily Nose lives in Annandale, and according to his schedule, he works Monday through Friday from eight until five as a bank teller. What a nice job.

This is my late morning at Patch and Paw, so I park my Jeep a block down from his apartment and watch as he leaves in his black pants, white shirt, and blue paisley tie. So respectable. He climbs into an equally respectable Nissan Sentra and pulls away from the curb.

I let a good solid five minutes go by just to make sure he didn't forget anything and decide to come back. Then I jump from my Jeep and stroll down the sidewalk straight to his brick apartment building.

I wave hello to one person. Give a kind smile to another. *Nothing going on here, folks.*

There are four units total in the small building. Two on the bottom and two on the top. His sits on the bottom and to the right. I don't even use my lock picks. The idiot has a hide-a-key behind the lamp attached to the wall in the upper left corner—a detail he notated on his phone. Not a bright guy, this one.

I slip on my gloves, take the key, and walk right inside. One bedroom. Neat and tidy. Flat screen. Entertainment center. Carpet. Leather couches.

His blinds lay in an open-slit pattern, letting in sunlight. It's enough to see by, and I begin my perusal. Bedroom first, where I find the standard stuff: clothes, family picture beside the bed, light blue sheets, dark blue comforter, dry cleaning hanging in the closet, shoes lined perfectly, and, under his bed, a collection of magazine clippings all with children in bathing suits.

His nightly spank bank entertainment, I'm sure.

I take a Ziploc bag from my back pocket and slide all the clippings inside. Bathroom comes next, and after a thorough inspection, it comes up empty of questionable matter.

On to the living room. I flip on the TV and begin browsing his recent watch lists and movie purchases. *The Human Centipede. The Serbian Film. Irreversible. The Brown Bunny. Lolita . . .*

I can't say I'm surprised.

His entertainment center holds no hidden DVDs, and other than his questionable taste in movies, I get nothing.

His laptop, though? A gold mine of pictures he's taken around town, catching children in all sorts of scenarios: playing, crying, running, fighting, There are bookmarked child porn sites too. Pedophile discussion boards. Saved videos taken right off

YouTube. And the mother lode: recordings of him actually speaking to children. How has this guy skirted by the law? One well-placed search warrant and the cops would have everything they needed. No wonder Judge Penn is so frustrated.

I click on one of the audio files.

"Well, you're awful pretty," Mr. Oily Nose says.

A little girl giggles. "Thank you."

"Is your Mommy here?"

"Yep, just over there."

"Sasha!" A woman's voice yells. "Get over here!"

"Bye!" the little girl says.

"Bye," he whispers.

That whisper makes my lip snarl. This bastard is so going down.

I take his laptop and the magazine clippings and truck it back to my Jeep. Those along with his phone are all I need.

THAT NIGHT, I LAY CROUCHED IN THE BACK OF MR. OILY Nose's Nissan Sentra, waiting. According to his Outlook calendar, he was getting home late from work with just enough time to change and head to dinner with friends. A dinner he won't be making it to.

In his rush to get back out the door, I'm counting on him not noticing the missing laptop and magazine clippings.

In my pocket, my cell buzzes, and quickly I check the display. It's my sister, Daisy. She'll have to wait. Right now I need this more than Daisy and her request to pick her up, or drop her off, or grab something on my way home.

I wonder how many times my mom, the infamous serial killer, crouched in the shadows waiting on her victims. I wonder how many times her cell buzzed with my stepdad, Victor, or one of us kids and she ignored it. But even though I'm here and ignoring my family, I'm nothing like her. I have my priorities. But so did she—her priority being her victims. And now here I am doing the same thing.

What am I doing? Why am I making comparisons? I am nothing like my horrible mother. *Nothing.*

My thoughts are interrupted when the locks release. In my pocket, my cell buzzes again, and without looking at it, I power it down. My needy family will have to wait.

The car shifts as he slides in behind the wheel and shuts the door. All kinds of excited nerves snap across my skin, and beneath my mask, I smile. *Oh, we're going to have fun.*

He cranks the engine and chooses a station with classical music.

I sit up in the back seat and slip the noose end of the animal control pole around his neck. This is the first time I've ever used an animal control pole, and I'm excited to see how it will go. The inspiration hit me as I was taking inventory earlier at Patch and Paw, and I felt like I had just discovered a new invention.

One quick yank and the noose settles tight. He makes a tiny ratchet of panic, and then, that's it.

"All mine," I tell him, and he freezes neat and perfect, already being a good boy. "You're going to do what I say, right?"

He nods, rasping as his neck pinches with the movement. I glance from the side of his face into the rearview mirror, seeing my own masked face and green eyes. I look into his wide, scared ones, and he says nothing, just stares back, waiting. I pull on the noose again, because I can, and his hand flutters up, not sure if he should fight or acquiesce.

"Be good," I warn.

The fluttering hand falls back down, and I loosen the noose. He takes in a breath, the air ripping at his throat, and coughs it right back out. The sound of his panic, his submissiveness, only fuels me. "Drive," I instruct.

Mr. Oily Nose stutters into motion and begins to follow directions. He knows I mean business, and I love that. We drive 236 to 395, going straight into DC. He doesn't object or fight or try to speak, and I find myself wishing he would. This is too easy. He's too nervous. I want him to have hope.

But he keeps both hands on the wheel, his knuckles white, and the rest of his fingers red with blood.

We drive north, the only sounds the soft classical music and the wind whisking by. My eyes drift briefly to the heavy and full moon, and its solemn glow seems to pulse through my veins. Somewhere deep inside of me, a dark rush of excitement dances.

"Exit here," I say, and his eyes fly to mine, panicked. He opens his mouth, wanting to speak, and I cut him off. "Here."

He turns, slumping down. He has no choice. His car rolls over the pavement, and I pull right on the pole, and, like a horse, he follows my lead.

The Sentra exits and then takes a gravel road, barely visible now in the darkness of night. I've never been here before, but my search said half a mile, a few twists, and then nothing but the "seedy underbelly" of DC.

Seedy underbelly. I like that.

But I'm not ready to hand him over to Biker Dudes Against Pedophiles. Not yet at least. His headlights pick up the remnants of a crumbling shack. *Perfect.* "Stop the car," I say.

He lurches to obey in a rigid movement driven by fear. He cuts the engine, and everything falls quiet save for the distant buzz of traffic on 395. Across the street sits a rundown grocery store, closed for the night, with bars on the window.

Next to that lies a park with no grass, two broken swings, a merry-go-round tilted off its axis, and one lump on a bench that

I assume is a person. Weeds and unkempt bushes surround the crumbled shack. A tree lays collapsed through the ceiling. Other than that, darkness engulfs us.

"Get out," I command.

He doesn't move.

I yank hard on the pole, too hard, and he arches off the seat with a gag. I put my window down, reach around and open his door, then shove him out. He flops to the dirt, and I fling open my door and have the control pole back in my grip before he has time to realize I released him.

Darkly, I laugh, tightening my hold again, and I slam my booted foot down onto his chest.

"I thought I told you to be good." Bending over, I stare into his bulging eyes. "You going to listen to me?"

He can't breathe, but he nods his head, and I loosen the noose just a bit. He gasps for air, and tears leak from his eyes, but his gaze holds mine with understanding.

"Now get up," I say.

Slowly, his eyes still on mine, he gets up. His whole body trembles as he waits for me to give him the next instruction.

"Inside," I softly say.

Mr. Oily Nose drops his eyes and doesn't look at me again as he starts for the house with me behind him, holding him at length with the animal control pole. He goes obediently, just like a dog, head down, knowing he's defeated.

At the broken door, he stops, and his trembling body transitions into full-on shaking. I give him a prod, then a shove, and he stumbles through the broken door. A quick glance around shows the place filthy, but empty, the roof open to the night sky, the stars above, and that full and fat moon.

A beautiful night for vigilante justice.

I yank on the noose, and with a strangled scream, he falls to his knees. His fingers grapple at his neck, and then with a whimper, he covers his face with his hands.

"Do you know why you're here?" I ask.

With a sob, he nods. "Please, I promise to be good. I promise to stop."

"Stop what?"

But his only answer is another whimper, or more like a whine. A whine that gets on my nerves. I kick his legs out from under him, hauling hard on the noose, then I slam his face into the nasty floor. A bit of blood splatters.

I come down hard, my knee in his back, and I grab the thinning hair on the back of his head and smash his face down again. More blood splatters.

I get down right in his blubbering face. "You know what I think I'm going to do? I'm going to cut your eyeballs right out so you can't ever look at another child again." I slam his head down even harder. "What do you think about that?"

"No," he cries with his limping tone of voice. "Please. I promise to stop."

"Oh, shut up." I jerk hard on the noose, and he bows off the floor, choking.

"Oh, God," he rasps. "Please."

"That's right, asshole, beg. Beg for mercy."

"Please," he chokes out on a sob. "I only touched them a few times."

What?

He tries to scream, but his throat won't let him. He snivels and cries, snot smearing with the blood and the dirty floor. His bladder lets go, and I climb off him. I've had enough. I pull him up to his feet.

"I couldn't help myself," he blubbers. "You don't understand."

"You're right, I don't," I reply, not even recognizing my own voice. It's deeper, darker, almost as if it isn't even me speaking.

He must recognize it too, because he freezes in place.

I hold the pole steady, staring at his dirty and tear-streaked terrified face. "No, I changed my mind. I do understand. Because I can't help myself either." Simultaneously, I yank the noose and kick his feet, and he lands in another sprawl on the nasty floor. "The difference is, you can't help yourself with children, and I can't help myself with you."

Leaning down, I grab a red brick, and I hold it above him. Does he see me in my mask and dark clothes about to deliver justice, or does he see all those children he's watched, he's touched, he's talked to? I hope he sees the monster in himself and imagines what is about to happen.

I whack the brick into his jaw, sideswiping so his head snaps in the opposite direction. It does the trick, and he blacks out.

I'm not taking this guy to Biker Dudes Against Pedophiles, I'm doing him all on my own. "Let's see how easy it is to touch another kid with ten broken fingers."

Something soft slides through me then, bringing me to a pause and warming me with the realization that I want to make this special.

Carefully, I lay his right phalanges out, spreading them all pretty. Then I take the brick, and I slam those fingers over and over and over again, savoring the release pounding through my body, until they lay at twisted angles with jutting bones and torn muscles.

His left hand comes next, and when I'm done, all of his fingers look exceptionally dead.

"And those eyes," I whisper. "You'll never see another child again."

From my cargo pocket, I take a small knife, and I slide it down into and around the socket. The knife comes into a slight resistance of membrane, and I pop out first his right eye and then his left. Other than a slight squelching, the removal of the eyeball makes no sound.

Consciousness comes back to him in a sudden and quick flash. His mouth opens, trying to form a scream, then just as quickly, he loses consciousness again. Too bad. I was hoping to see his reaction.

Taking the brick, I smash each eyeball, making sure reattachment is not possible. Then I remove the animal pole and noose, leaving him sprawled on the dirty floor, broken and bloody. I'm not tying him up. I want him running out of this place: blind, broken fingers, bloody, and screaming.

If someone were to walk in right now, they would think *I* am the sociopath, the demon, the monster. They would think *I* am the sick and twisted one. But it's not me, it's him.

It's him.

Back outside, I rotate my neck and roll my shoulders, feeling better than I have in a very long time. Relaxed even. Tired. Like my hydraulics have been released. Not a single soul exists out here, only that same body passed out on the bench in the desolate park.

I take everything out of the Nissan that I had planned to give to Biker Dudes Against Pedophiles. I'll mail it to the cops instead in a neat little package so they know exactly what Mr. Oily Nose has been up to.

Taking my mask off, I tuck it down inside the cargo pocket on my left thigh, and carrying the laptop, I make my way down the dark and empty street and several blocks over where I know a Metro stop sits.

I've been through a lot of changes lately, and it's important to take time for oneself. It's healthy to do so, to savor those moments when all feels right in the world. When the universe balances once again. I like knowing I'm part of that balance. I'm part of something bigger than myself.

S. E. Green grew up in Tennessee where she dreaded all things reading and writing. She didn't even read her first book for enjoyment until she was twenty-five. After that she was hooked! When she's not writing, she works as an adjunct math professor and lives on the coast in Florida with her very grouchy dog. Find her online everywhere @segreenauthor.

One last bite from S.E. Green...

I have read pages upon pages of information on killers and violent crimes. A myriad of facts indeed. Some perpetrators came from extremely violent childhoods. Others from seemingly loving homes. Some had psychological issues, while others experienced some sort of trauma. The scariest thing to me is that serial killers blend well. There could be one living right next door to you and you would never know. When I decided to write the KILLER INSTINCT series I made a conscious decision: I want to write exactly what and how I want. I didn't write with anyone else in mind. I wrote for me, and it was liberating! I didn't censor the sex or language or violence. I pushed the envelope and then I pushed some more. Everyone has a dark side, and mine truly comes out when I write Lane. I explore not only nature versus nurture, but what happens when both elements are present in your life. If you have all the makings of a serial killer, do you become one?

WE HAVE BUT LINGERED HERE

LIZ COLEY

"Listen up, all y'all," Marcia, our director, announced. "Break's over. Julianne's here."

"Jelly-anne?"

The guy guffawing over his own completely non-original witticism was, unfortunately, the tallest and most athletic, judging from the neck and arm muscles revealed by his gray tank top.

So was he mocking my name or my girth?

"I go by Jules," I said evenly. "Also, I use they/them/theirs pronouns."

My luck, he was probably Mercutio, or worse, Romeo. If so, as the production fight choreographer, I'd have to work with him a lot. I didn't want bad blood from the get-go.

"Jules. Got it. Listen up, everyone. *They* is her preferred pronoun," Romeo/Mercutio reported to the practice room.

He swept a perfect bow in my direction, doffing an imaginary plumed Renaissance hat all the way to his pointed toe—to all other eyes, charming rather than micro-aggressive. "I'm Josh, he-him-his, in case it isn't obvious."

But as soon as he lifted his face, I met his ice-gray eyes, and my heart skipped a beat. Eyes like cracked glass, eyes just like my Pa's, which could flip from angelic to carnivorous in an instant. The shit-eating grin on Josh's cheek-dimpled face and the sparkle in his gaze could be as much a mask as the comedy/tragedy pair on my thumb ring.

"Shit, dude. Really?" A beautiful twink of a guy gave voice to my thoughts. "You think you're *he* enough for me?"

My new hero. Maybe *he* was playing Romeo. I hoped so. I liked him already, and I appreciated the assist. I couldn't afford to waste my own energy fending off micro-aggressions. They were nothing to the macro-aggressions in my life, which required larger, sharper weaponry than I currently had at my disposal.

Marcia frowned. "Come on, folks. Focus. We've got the practice room for two more hours. Jules has a bunch of fight choreo to teach you."

I did a quick nose count. As per usual, I faced an all-male room tonight, other than Marcia and Elaine. That's the Bard for you. In the original, even Juliet, her mother, and her nurse would have been played in drag, so I guess the theatre has made some progress. One foot in the twenty-first century, the other up to its ankles in superstitions and nonsensical traditions. There were nine guys, all in black spandex leggings and jazz shoes, ready to rumble. Four each of Montagues and Capulets plus Paris. I checked out their musculature, the glimmer of intelligence, or not, in their eyes, judging what I had to work with.

"If I've got Benvolio, Mercutio, Romeo, Tybalt, and their miscellaneous sidekicks, we can do Act Three, Scene One, both fights. About a minute and a half each. That's gonna take the whole of tonight. We'll do Act Five, Scene Three, Paris versus Romeo choreo next time."

Our stage manager, Elaine, pursed her lips. "Okay, Paris.

You're off the hook for tonight. Same time tomorrow. Nine sharp."

"Nine sharp tomorrow, thank you," Josh replied. He grabbed one strap of his backpack. "Later, Jules," he tossed over his shoulder.

"Actually," I said to her, "I need Josh."

"She needs me, Elaine," he repeated. His eyelashes did something weird in my direction.

I rolled my eyes. There was no way he was flirting. No way. Not with me. "We've got to review basic moves and safety before he leaves. I don't want to have to repeat it just for him tomorrow."

"I've done this before, you know," Josh said with unearned confidence.

"Nope. I have no knowledge of your prior experience. You haven't done it with me."

His grin spread.

"I haven't seen you in action," I attempted to clarify.

"What do you want to see?" His tone confused me completely.

I knew from experience that words were tiger traps. Pa's easy questions dug the hole, his teasing camouflaged it with straw, his nudges pushed you over the edge and onto the spears. You only remembered the claw marks on the path after.

Not this time. Not this guy. I pulled myself up to my full five-foot-four, hundred and eighty, and assumed a power pose. "I don't know what you can and can't do. What your good and bad habits are. Are you certified in rapier and dagger?"

A single chestnut curl moving was the only evidence of his head shake.

I pushed on. "Are you SAFD certified in unarmed? Are you certified in knife? Small-sword? Single sword?"

"No," he muttered. "But in high school—"

"Broadsword? Quarterstaff?"

"No." A flush of crimson touched his high cheekbones.

"Well, I am," I said firmly.

"Holy crap," one of the other actors whispered. "You're a beast."

I took that as a compliment in the best possible way. I'd been studying stage combat for six years now, ever since the beginning of high school. I was certified in all the forms, and I was a damn good choreographer. Fake fighting. Where no one gets hurt. That was my calling: to make sure no one got hurt. Here, and here only, I was a fricking pro.

I ARRIVED BACK AT MY APARTMENT AT MIDNIGHT, STINKING of my own sweat and ready for a shower and a Trader Joe's lasagna. I flipped my phone off "do not disturb" and immediately saw I'd missed a call from Mom. She didn't just call out of the blue. Late as it was, I had to call back. Something was off.

My instincts were right. She answered in half a ring. I said, "Sorry it's so late. I just got out of rehearsal. Hope I didn't wake you and Dad."

Probing.

"It's okay, Jules," she said quietly. "He's out."

"Okay," I said.

Out of the house? Or out cold?

"Should we switch to Facetime?"

Testing.

"Oh no, Jules. No, I just wanted to hear your voice. How's the show coming?"

A refusal to show me her face told me all I needed to know. My heart sank. I knew what I would have seen on the small screen. Fresh bruises. Maybe a cut on a high, narrow cheekbone. Evidence of unarmed combat. Thank God, *unarmed*.

"It's going good, Mom," I said, my throat tight. "I just ran the first choreo rehearsal, and it went kind of well." Not that I'd admit this to anyone, but Josh had surprised me. Supple and subtle with his foot- and blade work. He wasn't lying about his high school experience. Must've had a good combat coach. Self-vowing to turn down the volume on my automatic defensive bitch, I rolled eyes at myself. Shook my head in rueful acknowledgement of my only armor—a crusty exterior—and my best weapon, a sharp tongue. Mom, of course, couldn't see me.

"That's super, Jules. I knew you'd do real good. You always do." Her voice sounded smiley. I could imagine the crooked-tooth grin under a button nose and honey-brown eyes, like mine. I tried not to imagine whatever marks she was hiding from me.

I had mixed feelings about showing her my own face too. I knew what she'd be forced to confront. A mixture of her tidy features merged with the fireplug flesh of my father. A beefy fighter and a mean drunk. I shrank from mirrors to avoid the visual comparison. I was nothing like him inside. My fights were plan and story and artistry, not wild fists swinging.

"You okay, Jules?' Mom asked.

I'd been quiet too long. "Sure, Mom. Yeah, of course."

"I can hardly wait to see you home for Thanksgiving," she said.

I knew the subtext. She always counted *down* the days till I came home again. I counted *up* the days I was out from under that terrifying shadow of a force I couldn't fight. And I still had to come home for her, into a house where I felt completely disarmed.

"I wish I could come up and see your show," she offered. "But I don't think your father can—"

"I understand." She'd never drive herself. Long-distance driving was the "the man's job."

"And you know, it's Shakespeare . . ."

"Mom, I know that's not his—"

"But I love that play," she said softly. "*Romeo and Juliet.* Dying for love. It's so romantic."

So fucked, I thought. A pair of randy teenagers making very, very poor choices. Happens.

She followed that review with, "I wonder if that's where the word comes from? Romeo—romantic. I bet that's where it comes from. Wow, I never thought of that before."

"It's—" I bit my tongue. Never mind. Let her think that. "I gotta go. It's so late, it's already tomorrow and tomorrow and tomorrow. I love you, Mom."

I was all her pride and joy, here two years away from finishing college. A self-made person. Paying my own way. Getting my own scholarships and loans and whatnot. I was slaying the ghosts of her very, very poor choices. That was all I could do for her, because I knew she would never leave him. And I wondered whether that was what she had decided to do— die for love of a man with a brutal lack of self-control.

If that's what she got out of Shakespeare, the Bard had taught me another impulse. Whenever I stood between Mom and a fist, I understood the urge to kill for love.

MY TYPICAL CHALLENGE AS FIGHT CHOREOGRAPHER WAS TO design a safe sequence of *cue-reaction-action* over and over to deliver clashing parries, aggressive lunges, quick ripostes, breathtaking glissades and slashes, and then the final thrilling rapier thrust that ends it all. It had to look realistic from every angle in the theater. It had to *be* realistic, up to a point, or the audience would think, "Hey, that's some good choreography," instead of, "Hey, somebody's going to die today. Right in front of us!"

The college theatre department owned eight Veneto rapiers, and while the blades' edges weren't honed, nor the points sharp, you could still do damage with a careless move. I knew someone who needed four stitches to put their left nostril back together. My challenge as fight captain was to keep the boys with sticks under control.

While I plunged all my energies and attention into the work at hand, I could relegate the fear of going home to the dark closet in the back of my head. But when Mom called again and let slip a wistful, "Things are so much better when you're here," I could only wonder how much worse they could be when I wasn't.

Two weeks of rehearsals later, I thought I had their number, these cocky freshmen—Josh (my Paris), Rick (my Tybalt), Stephen with a "ph" who plays Mercutio, and my hero Eli, who was Romeo—and we had three fights to the death pretty well worked out. I made the mistake of complimenting Josh on his footwork. I was being both honest and strategic, thinking of our improved trust and rapport.

"Nice stance," I said. "You've come a long way in two weeks." Something in my guarded tone turned it sarcastic. I regretted the words the moment they left my mouth.

Josh turned his weapon on me. "I bet I can take you, Jules," he said.

Oh, for crap's sake. Really?

I shook my head. I refused to play. Because you never, never play an unchoreographed fight with a weapon, even a stage weapon. This wasn't fencing. It was acting. It was an armed dance and actually dangerous. I turned my back. Second mistake.

"En garde," Josh called.

A gasp from Rick tipped me off.

I spun to avoid the weapon pointed at my spine, danced aside, grabbed Josh's sword arm en passant, and pinned it with a twist. He dropped the prop with a clang.

"Ow," he protested. "I was just goofing."

"They're not toys, Josh," Marcy warned.

That wasn't enough. My heart pounded. My blood boiled. What he'd nearly done! I took him by the elbows and, channeling the darkest, scariest voice of my father, growled, "If you treat me, your weapon, or your fellow actors with anything less than care, respect, and safety, you're going to be dueling with cardboard painted silver from now on and any time in the future you're fortunate enough to have me as your fight director. You got me?"

He nodded tightly, his cheekbones tinged with shame. "Sorry," he mouthed.

My stomach curled. I did that to him. The bitch was back. But this wasn't the time for apologies. It was more important that he get this lesson straight and forever. Humans were fragile. I nodded. "Good. Back to work."

———

Tech weeks were always high stress in any production. The rubber met the road, and the actors got real squirrely. First of all, we were in a new space—the theater, not the practice room—and the unfamiliarity of the setting—the sightlines, the volume, the sound—could throw things off. For these freshmen in their first "big college production," the screwups were pretty predictable. Lines weren't secure enough. Energy levels were flagging from too many late nights. Grades were dropping from missed assignments and/or bad test scores. They'd worked really hard to get into a theatre program, beat out hundreds of other wannabees for their spots, and their egos were on the line. Some met anxiety with humility, weed, and tears, while others reacted with exaggerated swagger to cover the stink of their flop sweat. Guess who? Yes, Josh.

I don't want to think I was responsible for his nerves. In fact, I wanted to talk to him about getting certified. He'd passed my bullshit meter with flying colors. I envied his muscles, his height, his reach, his speed. I envied his bravado. If I had a body like that, instead of standing between Mom and danger like a Smurf version of the doomed Mercutio, I could do something real. What, I don't exactly know. But something to knock my Pa on his ass and keep him there. I imagined Josh and the guys at my back—a phalanx. A phalanx with toy swords.

If the cast had nerves, so did I. I don't think the guys understood how much my rep was on the line too. If this frosh show went well, I could count on two more years of being the go-to fight director for all the studio, black box, and maybe some of the mainstage productions. I mounted my mental surfboard to ride the waves of my own anxiety. If you know how to stay on top, just ahead of the curl, the energy will carry you all the way to shore. The present danger of a complete wipeout makes it all the more exciting, in a sick kind of way. That's the beauty of live theatre.

Ahead of Wednesday's dress rehearsal, I joined Marcy and Elaine for our final production team coffee bonding at Roasters. Marcy's fingers drummed the sticky table—her nervous tic. Elaine kept tucking hair behind her ears with black sparkle fingernails. And I kept scraping my cuticles under the table, hoping I wasn't creating a hangnail that would bleed later.

On our way down College Ave., just as we passed Maple, a black cat scooted across the road in front of us. A car screeched and swerved to avoid hitting it. The bicyclist sneaking past on his right jumped the curb and narrowly missed a lamppost. A pedestrian lurched backward into a shrub to avoid the Schwinn on the sidewalk. He picked himself up and dusted off his dignity. The bicyclist rolled on. The car was a distant pair of taillights. And the cat licked a paw nonchalantly on the opposite side of the street, yellow eyes aglow in the twilight.

"Jesus," Elaine said breathlessly. Her hand gripped my arm. "That was lucky."

Marcy scoffed. "Lucky? Are you kidding me? A black cat on dress rehearsal night? Plus my mom sent flowers! Special delivery. Today! Can you believe it?"

I laughed. "Black cats. Gray cats. Tabby cats. It's just a cat, Marcy, not a harbinger of doom."

Marcy glared at me. "But the flowers."

No one had ever sent me flowers. For anything. "Yeah, so? That's sweet."

Marcy's glower sharpened. "No. No, it's not. You have to get flowers *after* the show. Everyone knows that."

"Seriously?" My theatre world carried a load of superstitions, but I'd never heard this one.

"It's terrible luck to get them before," Elaine explained. "It means the show is going to die."

"I'll take them," I said with a laugh. "I don't believe in luck." Nothing in my life had ever suggested luck was involved. There was hard work, and there were choices, good and bad. I quoted, "The fault, dear Brutus, lies not in our stars but in ourselves."

"Caius Cassius. In Julius Caesar," Elaine said. "He had terrible luck."

I had to correct her. "He committed suicide rather than be captured in battle. Luck didn't enter into it."

"And it's the thirteenth," Marcy added definitively.

Under my breath, I muttered, "Yeah, Wednesday the thirteenth. Famously unlucky day."

Black cats and premature flowers aside, the dress rehearsal was a disaster in so many ways.

We started well. Marcy ran a general warm-up, which was supposed to center everyone and focus their nervous energy. I ran the fight call, to solidify the timing and take any accidental aggression out of the combat. I finished up with, "Looks good. Now, stay loose, boys."

Elaine called, "Curtain in ten."

The troupe echoed, "Thank you, ten." They dispersed for a sip of water, a last pee, a nervous dump.

I strolled across the stage, snapping my fingers, feeling chipper, full of buzzing energy. *Snip, snap, snip, snap.* My brain radio played: *"Boy, boy, crazy, boy. Get cool boy."* Imagination spun me a mashup image of *West Side Story* and our production of *R&J*, which was not a huge leap, since they're the same story. How many million times had I watched it? I whistled a few bars of Bernstein. I may have even sauntered, fancying myself the street-smart Riff, giving the guys (and myself) the best advice I'd ever gotten: *"You wanna live in this lousy world? You gotta get cool."*

A hard hand clamped on my elbow. *Josh.*

"Ow!" I protested.

"Cut it out! You're whistling," he snapped.

"Yeah, so? I'm feeling good," I said, all coolly cool. "You got a problem with that?"

"You're whistling. In the theater." His eyebrows told me he was either scared or pissed off. "What's wrong with you, Jules? You can't do that."

"Because . . .?" I supplied. A teaching moment.

"It's bad luck."

"No, Josh. It's because long before these handy-dandy wireless headsets were invented, the stage crew called rigging cues with a sailors' whistling code. Stray whistles would confuse the men on the lines controlling the scrims, backdrops, and curtains."

"Oh. Okay," he said. "And now I know. But please stop."

"I've stopped," I said, but just to be obnoxious, I piped one more note.

Elaine walked over to us. "Jules. Stop. You don't whistle in a theater. It's bad luck."

"Bad luck." I rolled my eyes. I'd been feeling good a moment ago, and now the knives in my belly were back. Along with my inner chain-mail bitch. "Jeez. And I suppose I don't get to say *Macbeth* either?"

It was like every molecule of air was sucked from the room. A silence so sudden, my ears rang. The hair went up on my arms. The quality of the light changed. The entire cast was staring at me. Glaring, rather.

"It's only dress," Elaine said, making a *calm down everyone* semaphore with her palms.

"We're in production," Marcy said tightly. "We're totally screwed. We're gonna tank."

"Don't be ridiculous." My attempt at soothing words came out completely wrong. We'd worked too hard for weeks for people to be thrown off their game by superstitions. "We're not going to tank because I said the name of the Scot." That's how you don't say Macbeth, as if it makes a dot of difference.

Marcy flinched visibly, as if I'd struck her.

"Of course we're not," Elaine said. "You're right, Jules. Quick. Do the undo."

Eli pointed at my feet. "Spin around three times."

Josh added, "Then spit on the floor."

Marcy said, "And curse. Preferably a Shakespearean one. And repeat."

"Get serious people," I chided. No one smiled. Their disapproval pressed back on me as a tangible force. "Sorry," I squeezed out.

"Jules," Elaine said. "I think you should—"

I cut her short. "Okay, I'm just gonna go watch from the cheap seats."

"Yeah," Elaine continued carefully. "You do that."

"I'll undo it," Josh said. He spun, spat, and said, "Shit. There. I fixed it. Only for you, Jules."

My throat was too tight to thank him, and my chest hurt as I headed toward my favorite seat, row K, right in the middle. When I glanced back through blinked away tears, I caught more than one person spinning, spitting, and mouthing, "Shit."

I flumped into the chair, cheeks red as sunburn. Angry at myself. Embarrassed. I hated confrontations. Why had I stepped right into one? Invited it even? I knew better. We live one whistled note away from disaster. My pulse gradually resumed a steady seventy as the lights dimmed.

The first two stage fights went well. Eli was controlled and damn near perfect as Romeo. I had taught all of them well, and no pretend hexes could undo that. Otherwise, however, the rough spots were rough: fumbled lines, missed entrances, a stage light that kept flickering. None of that was my problem. Or my fault, I told myself. Then Josh stepped on Heather/Juliet's hem in Act Four, Scene One and pulled all the pleats out of her waistline at the back. Her skirt drooped and exposed very non-Elizabethan black thong panties, or rather the parts they didn't cover.

"Oh fark," Heather wailed, out of character. She bunched the fabric up as best she could. "What do I do?"

"Change into the nightgown for now," Marcy ordered.

I stood up. "And give me your dress. I know how to repair it." And because I believe in being prepared for the worst, there was, in a sandwich-sized Ziploc bag in my backpack, a small sewing kit on a card, along with a protein bar, a space blanket, and a plastic rain poncho. I wasn't just trying to make up for what happened earlier. I really did have the costuming skills. That's one way I'd made the money in high school to cover my combat lessons and certifications. I was the unlikeliest go-to person for alterations and beautiful prom dresses. Would my father ever have bought me my weapons set? No. But a sewing machine, of course.

The show went on. I re-pleated and stitched up the skirt by hand. By the final death scene, it was wearable again.

"You're such a lifesaver, Jules," Heather squealed.

I felt redeemed, at least in her eyes.

Finally, rehearsal over, Marcy gave notes. Lots of notes. "Hey everyone, you can be glad we didn't peak tonight, right?"

"Bad dress equals great opening," Josh said.

"Don't jinx it by saying," Elaine scolded. "Now get out of here and get some sleep."

The cast took off, shooting comments back and forth, exhausted and wound up. I suspected they'd all be heading for pizza rather than bed for the next couple hours.

The stagehands took a while resetting all the scenery and props for Act One. I went over the prop tables to make sure all the daggers ended up safely placed and the rapiers stowed in their special stand.

As stage manager, Elaine was the only person left in the theater when I finished. She was dragging forward a caged light bulb on a stem with a long extension cord running all the way to backstage. She stopped and set it perfectly center stage. It stood about four feet high, a single bright bulb on a pedestal.

"Ghost light's all set," she said. "Let's jam."

I was still procrastinating, checking the security of my little stitches in Juliet's gown. There was a new missed message from Mom on my phone, and I knew as soon as I left the theater, I'd have to call her and face—or not face—true demons. Everyone else here had the luxury to worry about pretend problems, and that irked me.

"Ghost light," I repeated.

"To keep the theatre ghosts at bay," she said.

"Yeah. I know the rationale. You know this building's only five years old, right? No one's had time to die here."

Elaine puffed out her cheeks. "You have no respect for tradition, Jules."

"And there's no such thing as ghosts," I added.

"Says you. Come on. Let's get ice cream."

"Okay," I said.

"You need sweetening up," she added. "You're wound way too tight."

"Yeah. Nerves. Sorry." Inner monsters.

She shut off the houselights at the door. Seats and walls vanished into velvety darkness. The ghost light gleamed bravely on the stage, fulfilling its true purpose of illuminating the edge for safety.

"Woooooo," I hooted into the empty house.

"Don't mock them, for Pete's sake," Elaine chided. "Please, Jules. We've got a show in less than forty-eight hours." We walked out the stage door into the frozen November night. The stars sparkled. My breath condensed in swirls. I pulled in a brisk lungful of air and reached for the night sky. I almost howled again, like a lone wolf, calling to his . . . that's when I realized I'd left my pack behind.

"Oh crap. Elaine, can you unlock for a second? I left my stuff inside."

She rolled her eyes and opened the stage door for me. "Go. Hurry. I'm starving."

I scooted back into the theater, foolishly glad for the ghost light I had mocked. Now the dark-defying glow illuminated my path to drop the four feet over the edge of the stage and make my way to row K. I levered on the heavy pack. I stared back at a pretend street in a false Verona. The designer had done a nice job. Theatre magic. Place portrayed by image. Truth revealed through metaphor. Lessons learned by example. Fears faced by proxy.

What did I fear? A violent man, bloodied knuckles, cold as glacier, hard as rock. I couldn't say his true name. Picturing the darkened, twisted face of my Pa in all his rage, I whispered, "Macbeth, Macbeth, Macbeth."

A door slammed.

"I'm coming. Hang on," I called. *Had Elaine heard me?*

I'd made it as far as row D when the crash of metal on metal from stage right told me the unlocked legs of the prop table must have folded and knocked all the Montague weapons onto the floor. A stereophonic crash and jangle from stage left sent the Capulet swords rolling. A single dagger shot onto the stage, spinning in the spot where it landed like a crazed compass needle. It stopped, pointing straight at me.

I shucked off my pack and vaulted onto the proscenium. As my feet touched floorboards, the ghost light pitched forward and, with a final actinic flash, died right in my face. Yellow traces on my retinas blinded me. I blinked hard to recover night vision, keeping my feet completely still at the verge of the stage, my hands clinging for balance. For a moment, a thread of scarlet light turned the fallen dagger blood red; then the source of illumination, the exit signs at the rear of the house, flickered and failed. The entire room was plunged into pitch, molasses-thick darkness.

"Elaine?" I whispered. "Elaine? Are you goofing with me?"

In the answering silence, my heart beat like a battle drum. Maybe it wasn't Elaine. Maybe it was Josh. I never actually saw him leave.

"Josh?" I called with shaky soprano pitch. "Hey. You got me good. Plug the ghost light back in, will you?" In a smaller voice I tried, "Come on. Let's clean up this mess. Hit the lights, will you, please?"

My words disappeared into the black surrounding me. I stood carefully and spun in a circle, tuning my ears to latch onto the smallest something. A breath? A step? A rustle not my own? Senses wide open, I searched for signs of life. Someone had slammed the door. Someone had tipped the tables. Someone had jerked on the electric cord. Silence pressed on my eardrums.

A sudden thunk like a shutter grabbed by the wind knocked me sideways in shock. I lost all sense of which way I was facing, how close I was to the edge. Was it the stage door banging open? A distant door banging closed?

"Elaine? Josh? Marcy?" I shouted to the corners of the room. But I got nothing back. With an electric jolt, the undercut hairs on the back of my neck rose up like quills.

Maybe it was just a weather phenomenon? A sudden change of temperature?

I rationalized like crazy as I dropped to all fours again and reached all around me for the ghost light cage. If I found it, I could track it back to the wall by the extension cord, plug it back in. My fingertips slid over the dirty floor, probing for metal or wrapped cord. This was ridiculous, scrabbling in the dark, using a power cord to establish my position. Daytime me would have a good laugh about this. Right? *Right?*

I touched something wet and recoiled. Warm, thin liquid. Had I peed myself? I scrubbed my fingers dry on my leggings and sniffed them. Not pee. Not coffee. Something sour and coppery. Like blood. I shuddered. My stomach clenched around an acid core.

Next time I put a hesitant hand down, I found the stem of the light. I worked my way to the base and along the cord. This was taking too long. Why was Elaine so patient? Why wasn't she checking on me, bugging me to hurry up? Why didn't I have my phone in my pocket?

The stage floor turned uneven under my knees, rocky and rough, like turf, like blasted heath. And a cold moldy scent filled the air. A basement smell, long neglected. The odor of spider-webs and leeching concrete and rusting pipes. Out of the corners of my eyes, luminescent patches hovered in the dark, vanishing when I turned my gaze on them directly. Pinpoint flashes zigged and zagged. Sparks in the dark enclosed my field of view, narrowing, narrowing. I'd never passed out before, but this was like Mom described it. There was nothing to focus on, and my eyes played tricks in the blackness. There was a wall an inch from my face; there was nothing for miles. I couldn't tell. Couldn't see my nose, my hands. Eyes open or closed—it was the same. Endless, hungry night.

I put my head down, squeezed my eyelids, and concentrated on the cord by feel alone, my umbilical link to normality, my lifeline to restoring light. My head plunged into a pungent fog, a moist remembrance of swamps in the droplets against my cheeks. My eyes flicked open to make out a gray mist generating its own eerie glow. The fog recoiled from my touch, taking shape. And now I could see it still forming, lifting one of the fallen daggers, lit only by the hint of luminescence emanating from the fog itself.

The figure hissed, "Is this a dagger which I see before me? The handle toward my hand? Come let me clutch thee."

I sighed with relief. I knew the line. Macbeth, of course.

And a perfect revenge prank. The voice was unfamiliar, but these were actors. They specialized in illusion. I stood up by the glow of the ghostly figure and laughed tightly. "Josh? Nice one. Now, hand over the weapon. Let's clean up." I reached for the dagger, which clattered to the ground as the fog vanished. *How the hell did he do that?*

The mist coalesced farther away. It took a roughly human form, though the features were blurred.

"Impressive tech," I said. "Let me guess. Glow paint on gauze?"

"Macbeth" looked off stage left, saying, "Never shake thy gory locks at me," and another glowing specter glided soundlessly onstage. Banquo, for sure. I gasped at the sight of large dark holes actively weeping red at neck and chest level. My eyes had adapted just enough to perceive the color.

"Two of you?" I sputtered. "How long did this take to arrange? And does Elaine know you're wasting our stage blood? Who's the other one? Eli? Stephen?"

Another ghost joined Macbeth and Banquo from stage right. "Despair and die," it muttered.

What was going on? What was this? The world's most elaborate joke? I tried to control my breathing, but my voice came out both defiant and small and just a bit worried. "You guys are mixing plays now. First *Macbeth*, then *Richard III*."

Another ghost entered stage left, his glowing toga bleeding from fifteen wounds, and at the same time, someone in translucent Roman garb joined him, the hilt of a sword protruding from his belly, the point out the back, the in-between traversing his gossamer organs. Had to be JC and Brutus. I didn't know the department owned trick swords. In fact, I was pretty sure it didn't. The pulse in my neck doubled speed. My feet filled with the sharp ache of adrenaline. They wanted to run, but wise or not, I stayed. I always chose fight over flight.

"And now you're stirring in *Julius Caesar*. I get it. Okay guys." I breathed deep and tried a dominance stance to reclaim control. I locked my knees against their trembling. "Are there any more of you? Come on. Give me all you've got. Are y'all in on this? Pizza would have been a better use of your time, I think."

My words fell into a vast quiet as, with that encouragement, the haunted host expanded, ghoul by ghost. I recognized the characters by costume, but not who was inside them. I called their names and pointed: "Hamlet . . . Mark Antony." Two spooks with childlike shape and bearing—*were they tech crew?*—traipsed in. "Little princes in the tower?"

Another pair drifted down from the rafters and landed soundlessly. *How?* The theatre program didn't own a flying rig. A shiver ran from my crown to toes. Words of caution entered my head: *"By the pricking in my thumbs, something wicked this way comes."* Something truly *wyrd* was happening.

Ophelia I recognized by the trail of water she left behind, the clinging costume, and the way her hair floated freely around her head. And still I tried to deny the evidence of my senses. "Seriously? The girls are here, too? Nice touch, Ophelia! And you, Cleo." Cleopatra was holding a ghostly snake.

At times I had flirted with cosplay, but, I told myself, this was unbelievable commitment to the art. The stage was getting crowded. The density of wraiths created uncanny radiance. As the glow of each shed more clarity on his or her neighbors, their faces became defined and quite . . . unfamiliar. Not one of them the college kids I knew. Even if I'd changed my philosophy about running, I was trapped. My feet immobile as if they'd been bolted to the stage.

And still they came on. Cordelia, Regan, Desdemona clutching her poor neck, Emilia, tongueless and handless Lavinia, waving her bound and bleeding stumps at me. I realized with failing belief in an elaborate stunt that there were now more "girls" in the theater than were in the entire cast. And guys as well, because in slid Polonius with a belly wound, Mercutio, Tybalt, and Paris bearing the sanguinary signs of fatal combat, plus a host of headless men, walking erect, and to my utter horror, holding their severed heads. So many. Too many.

The breath congealed in my chest. Shakespeare's ghosts. Shakespeare's slain. All of Shakespeare's dead were assembling on the stage before my eyes. I turned to the booth at the back of the house to see if projection equipment could explain it. Of course not. The booth was dark and locked. My knees literally knocked as my thighs quivered, urging me to bolt.

Macbeth extended his arm to a queenly woman wringing her hands as she approached him. "Lady Scot," he said. And then he turned to me. *To me.* The only mortal in the room. "We are assembled. Why have you summoned us?" he asked.

"I . . . I . . . I . . ." Blithering tongue be cursed, I thought.

"Speak, mortal," he said.

"You . . . you . . ." And that didn't help at all. I slapped my own face hard. "You are a mighty host," I said. "How . . ." Again I failed, my mind paralyzed by the undeniable truth of these ghosts. Failing to maintain any semblance of cool.

"How many are we?" he suggested. "Near threescore."

That was sixty, give or take. I ran my finger over the shelf of titles in my head, counting the dead. Ten suicides, at least twenty-seven named characters murdered in cold blood, nine fallen in combat. The calculation grounded me. I had to believe my eyes. They were, in a very real sense, present. Tangible. Corporeal.

"How are you *here*?" I asked. "I mean no disrespect, your Majesties, but you aren't the relics of mortal beings. You're not real in any sense. You're the shades of . . . er . . . fictional characters."

"I beg your pardon," Richard III burst out. "Fictional?"

"Um, historical fiction, some of you, based on . . . Look." I halted to breathe down to my toes. My arms glowed greenish in the cast of the true ghostly light. "Have you heard of William Shakespeare?"

"A cursed name. He killed us all," Macbeth said. "First time with quill and ink. But you mortals have played, portrayed, and slain us more times than man can count. Romeo has died a hundred thousand deaths or more. Enough times dispatched on your stages over the bloody centuries, over the wide globe in a hundred diverse tongues, we have become substantially insubstantial. And you have called upon me thrice. And here we hied."

His pale, wavering face was frightful, but not the worst I had seen. I was emboldened to ask, "Is that the real reason we aren't supposed to say Mac—your name in a theater? Do we . . . did I disturb your rest?"

"It is rude to awaken the shades without purpose. A price will be paid in mischief and mayhem."

And was that the reason for the unexplained "bad luck" that seemed to follow the invocation of his name?

The Scot glowered and cast a glance toward the dagger he had dropped. I gulped and thought fast as he continued, "Here we are, kitted out, swords worn, ready to do battle or else what is your will? Do you wish an argument with us?"

"Not I," I said quickly. The army facing me was rather one I wanted at my back. I recalled my fleeting fantasy of showing up at Thanksgiving with Josh, or with all the Capulets, with all the armed Montagues at my command. Cast myself as Henry V, leading troops at Agincourt against a pugnacious army of one. *Once more unto the breach, dear friends.* But what good would that do? Fantasies aside, I couldn't ask my actor friends to murder the man who had terrorized my childhood and continued to brutalize my mom.

But could I ask the Scot? Might he prove a supernatural ally? I assumed my power pose, legs taut, elbows sharp, chin high. I opened my mouth. To try. "Honored wraiths, I called on you as champions to fight mine enemy."

I felt the press of the ghostly battalion, their energy rising with their curiosity. Called to a purpose.

"We listen," Julius Caesar said.

"Where is thy enemy?" Cleopatra asked.

"Far from here," I admitted. "Can you come wheresoever I call or must I be in a theater?"

"We have strands spanning the Globe entire," Julius Caesar answered. "Call, and we will come." He turned to nod at his former trusted friend. "Et tu, Brute?"

"Let me be resolved," Brutus confirmed.

"Next time I call you," I said, "I will show you the enemy who must be confronted—no, who must be haunted—no, you know, slain would even be fine with me. By whatever means of your choosing." I'd seen the Scot take up a prop dagger. They'd knocked the tables and lamp over. Therefore they could interact with my solid world. Therefore they could interact with my all too solid Pa.

My flair for the dramatic demanded a speech: "Then imitate the action of the tiger; Stiffen the sinews, summon up the blood. . . . Hold hard the breath and bend up every spirit to his full height. On, on, you noblest English."

"Very well," Richard II said heavily. "This we will do. Dismiss us."

"Um, you're dismissed," I said.

"Properly," Lady Macbeth chided.

Feeling somewhat ridiculous, but less so than before, I spun three circles, spat on the stage, and yelped an honest curse as the shades vanished, my foot twisted over the edge, and I tumbled butt over bean into the row A seats down below. Air punched from my lungs as my ribs caught the wooden arm of a seat, my head ricocheted off the back cushion, and my arms blindly reached for the concrete floor to break my fall. For a count of twenty nothing at all happened. I lay there in breathless suspense as my nerves prepared to report the damage. Instinctively I knew the message was going to be bad.

A door slammed. The lights snapped on. "Jules, we're freezing out there. Jules? What the frick is taking you so long ? Where . . . are you?"

I sucked in a scant ounce of oxygen. My ribs burned. My temples throbbed. Numbness radiated down my arm. Shock, I knew from painful experience, was a great—though temporary — protector. I didn't move an inch. "Down here," I croaked at Elaine.

She leaned over the edge of the proscenium. "Oh my God, Jules. What happened?"

Josh peered over her shoulder. "Jules, I'm pretty sure arms aren't supposed to bend at that angle."

I looked into four friendly, concerned eyes and concentrated on breathing steadily. "No. No, they aren't. Tripped over the cord, and yeah, I'm pretty sure my left arm is broken."

Mischief and mayhem indeed. The ghosts had warned me. A price had to be paid.

"Holy hell," Elaine responded. "Told you the thirteenth was unlucky."

Maybe so. But in other ways, the most lucky day of my life. Because Josh knew how to splint an arm. And because I had the chance to tell him on the way to Student Health that I would be proud to work as his combat certification instructor. But mostly because now I possessed the incantation to summon a vengeful army. That alone made me feel safer. And Thanksgiving break was just a breath away.

LIZ COLEY has been publishing fiction for teens and adults since 2011. Her award winning and internationally best-selling psychological thriller Pretty Girl-13 can be read in 12 languages on 5 continents. Liz's other novels include alternate history Out of Xibalba, the Tor Maddox "pink thrillers" series, and The Captain's Kid. Her short fiction has appeared in Cosmos Magazine and numerous print anthologies. Always a fan of the theatre, in 2016 she picked up a quill to attempt playwriting and fell in love. Some of her early work is in development or production in San Diego and Cincinnati.

One last bite from Liz Coley...

I have been fascinated by the "ghost light" tradition ever since I toured the haunted Music Hall in Cincinnati, built on the site of an old Potter's Field. Numerous unidentified skeletons were excavated right along with the foundations in 1876. Since that time, many an employee or visitor has encountered not only eerie sounds and happenings, but also ghostly sightings. Now, each night the ghost light remains lit, hoping to keep the haunts at bay. When Cincinnati Shakespeare Company closed its theatre in one location, the last item left on the stripped stage after the final performance was the ghost light. When the theatre re-opened several blocks away, the shining bulb on a post was the first property returned to the new stage. The ghost light is one of those sacred, unbreakable traditions in the performing world. As a passionate theatre-goer and playwright, I had to find a place for one in my little ghost story.

THE WHISPERS

LINDSEY KLINGELE

The young women of Little Falls were starting to become a problem.

It all began when Hattie Crawford refused a marriage proposal from Ben Livingston, even though by nearly all accounts he was a perfectly amiable young man, one who had a fine height and was expected to inherit his father's printing business one day (and that day would be soon, if Mr. Livingston kept drinking the way he did). Ben Livingston did everything right: he asked for permission from Mr. Crawford to escort his daughter to church, he held his arm out for Hattie when they crossed over muddy roads, and he waited what was considered a *very* appropriate amount of time—two months—before suggesting Hattie leave her parents' home and become his wife.

But Hattie said no.

And to add insult to injury, she didn't give a proper reason for *why* she said no. She wasn't too young nor too old, she wasn't being wooed by another young man in town, and she had no interest in donning a wimple and joining the church (in fact, she hated to have her hair covered, even by a demure but lovely hat, claiming that her head grew too hot in the sun). Hattie's only response to Ben's thoughtful proposal?

"No, thank you."

When, flummoxed, Ben Livingston pressed her for a reason, Hattie declined to give one. At her father's constant questioning, she only added, "I do not care to be a wife."

The Crawfords, it goes without saying, were beside themselves. What could Hattie possibly mean by this? What man would take her now, after she'd made such a scandal of herself? How did she plan on living?

There was something wrong with Hattie, and unfortunately the problem wasn't confined to her alone. It soon took hold of other young women in the town, spreading like a slow but insidious infection. Three weeks after Hattie's abrupt refusal of Ben Livingston, Elizabeth Wicket turned down the proposal of the pastor's own son, Emmett Hamm. Then Clara Franklin told her mother she refused to even *meet* with Jonas Pratt, a potential suitor who'd recently graduated from university. When pressed, none of the girls gave any acceptable excuses.

Then the young women began walking together through the streets of Little Falls, their arms linked, their heads thrown back in laughter over some private joke. Clara's loud, clear voice could sometimes be heard from up to two blocks away, and Hattie's auburn hair shone brazenly in the sun. It was like they didn't even *care* about propriety, let alone what anyone thought of them.

The townspeople began to talk about the girls in earnest, bending their heads together outside of church or in the aisles of the hat shop or the back room of the local pub. Women and men alike wondered what could be the root cause of this unseemly phenomenon: Poor upbringing? Tainted pork? *Books?*

Then things got worse.

It was discovered the girls would be traveling together to attend a women's suffrage meeting in Big Falls, the next town over. Well, *that* partially explained things, then. The so-called "suffragettes," in all of their mad, wicked folly, had been warping the minds of young women across the country for whole generations now, and there were plenty of horror stories, rumors, and legends about the destruction they'd left in their wake. Women abandoning families, women spitting in the face of tradition, women barging into respectable town hall meetings and raising their voices about who even knew what. The towns-people had heard all of these rumors, of course, but the scourge of suffragettes had never affected *them*. But now the threat was here, in their own city, and who knew where all this would lead?

All in all, five young women, aged fifteen to twenty-one, attended the meeting in Big Falls. Hattie, Clara, and Elizabeth recruited Clara's younger sister, Polly, and Hattie's neighbor Frances. Hannah Prescott wanted to attend as well, but her father caught wind of the scheme in time and instead locked her up in the larder for the evening.

For the others, it was too late. If their strange actions and thoughts were signs of an infection, then attending that meeting only set their sickness further aflame. Afterward, they were bois-terous and loud as they walked through the streets, and they refused to sit still to sew or play the piano or quietly pray at their bedsides. Hattie marched right into the office of the Livingston printing press and requested a job as a type setter. Clara made her poor mother cry when she claimed she would never bake a tart again in her life if she could help it, and Frances went shop-ping on the main street and bought herself a pair of men's trousers to wear.

Trousers!

The girls had the town gripped by the throat, and everyone

was equal parts fascinated and horrified as they waited to see what unknown impropriety might be visited on them next. One Saturday in spring, Hattie led a group of ten young women on a march through the dusty streets to the local courthouse, where they demanded they be given the right to vote in the next local election. The judge, Henry Farland, was so frightened that he locked himself in his office to avoid the girls. This only made them speak louder, climbing on top of desks in their long skirts and pitching their voices high so that even the judge, hiding behind his office door with his fingers in his ears, would not be able to ignore them.

The girls had gone a step too far.

Something had to be done.

THE TOWN LEADERS MET IN THE BASEMENT OF THE courthouse on a muggy summer evening, lamenting their town's plight. It appeared—through no fault of their own—that a whole generation of girls in Little Falls had gone bad as curdled milk. But could they really throw out a whole batch of young women? What of the parents who had spent hours raising these girls by hand? What of the young men in town of a marriageable age? What of society, what of order?

No, these girls were not to be discarded but, rather, fixed.

"I may have a solution," said Mayor William Gage, stepping forward into a yellow circle of candlelight. "It is . . . drastic. But so are times such as these."

The town leaders—respectable men, all—leaned forward an inch or two to better hear the mayor speak.

"These women are intent on disrupting our lives," the mayor continued, his mouth pulling down in an impressive, but thoughtful scowl. "The 'why' does not matter. What matters is that our esteemed friend, Judge Farland, cannot work in his own office without his ears being continually assaulted. What matters is our streets turned to bedlam, our dinners gone cold, our morning commutes interrupted."

Of course, the respectable men murmured in assent.

It's the disrespect.

Truly disgusting.

"We may never know the cause of this disruption," the mayor said, "but there is a way to end it. We can cut it out, sure as a surgeon's scalpel cuts out an infected organ or a blackened tumor."

The murmurs grew louder, and the mayor beckoned for a small man in round spectacles to make his way out of the corner and into the light.

"I'd like to introduce you to an old friend of mine. He is an accomplished surgeon and the answer to our prayers. He will bring peace of mind back to our fine town."

The surgeon gave a quick nod of his small, bald head, and clutched his leather surgical bag in one white-knuckled hand.

"How will he manage that?" asked Mr. Crawford, Hattie's father.

The surgeon cleared his throat.

"It's only the matter of a simple procedure," he said. "The girls will hardly feel a thing."

MR. CRAWFORD VOLUNTEERED FOR HIS DAUGHTER TO undergo the procedure first. They came for her in the middle of the night so as not to cause undue fuss. Six men entered her house under the darkness of the new moon, woke her from her bed, and walked her into the street. Hattie Crawford, still in her flowing white nightgown, was alarmed and confused. But her father was there, and she trusted him. It did not occur to her to scream—not until later, not until it was much too late.

The surgeon had set up shop in a small, dark room in the basement of the local pharmacy. When Hattie saw the old metal table and the surgical tools lit by candlelight, her confusion turned to fear. But the men of the town blocked the door. Some took her by the arms, and others spoke in low voices.

Hush now.

It will be over soon.

A cloth went over her mouth and nose, and Hattie's vision began to fade. Everything went dark. When her eyes opened again, she was in a different room. Thick bandages wrapped around her neck. Her body was sore, but she was able to move her limbs. She was able to see. But when she tried to talk, her voice came out as a soft, scratchy croak.

Hattie Crawford was no longer able to speak.

Locked in her recovery room and unable to yell or shout, Hattie had no way of warning the others. One by one, each of the other young women in town was led to the surgeon's room. Some of them fought back, but none of them had the strength to get away—not on their own. All of them were put under, into the darkness. All of them awoke without a voice.

Eleven girls in all had their throats cut open, their voice boxes removed. Eleven girls woke up in recovery rooms around Little Falls, dizzy and disoriented, unable to call for help. The young women were sent back to their lives, but they were sent back changed. No longer could they march through town, laughing and carrying on. No longer could they argue against the merits of needlepoint versus getting an education. No longer could they ask for a right to be heard—no longer could they be heard at all.

The girls were shocked and sullen, their eyes lined red, their spirits low. It was concerning to the townspeople, but Mayor

Gage ensured the folks of Little Falls that things would return to normal soon. The girls' spirits would lift, as was only natural with young women. And in the meantime, quiet and order had returned to the streets. Peace had returned to Little Falls. It seemed everything in their town would once again be well.

Until the day Polly Franklin turned up dead.

POLLY WAS LAST SEEN ALIVE ON SATURDAY MORNING ON her way to go watch the Hasker children. Her body was found later that same evening on a small footpath that ran between the Haskers' dairy farm and the old schoolyard. Her clothes had been torn and her throat neatly slit open, the gash running horizontally across her neck so it made a cross shape with her recently healed scar. Other than that, she looked just like she had in life—small and doll-like, her large eyes open but no longer containing a world within them.

Polly's death shocked the town, but it was more shocking still that she had been killed out in the open, in broad daylight, on a path that had been walked thousands of times by hundreds of townspeople. How could no one have seen this happen? How could no one have heard Polly's last cry?

But of course they couldn't; Polly had undergone the procedure just a few weeks before. If she had cried out for help, her rasping whisper wouldn't have carried but a few feet beyond the sunny spot where she was found. Her voice was cut short before her life ever was.

Little Falls was sent into another panic. But instead of convening to discuss "what to do" about this problem, the townspeople shut themselves away. They couldn't imagine that any one of their beloved neighbors could have hurt little Polly. It had to have been a drifter, a criminal, a madman passing through.

They stuck close together, only leaving their homes in pairs, locking their doors against the night.

It didn't stop the killer from striking again.

Hattie Crawford and Genevieve Peterson were taking a shortcut through a field, their arms linked and their mouths closed. Since undergoing the procedure, both girls were unable to speak above a whisper, and they often chose to remain silent rather than strain their throats. While walking, Hattie realized she'd dropped her purse in the field and left to retrieve it. When she returned not ten minutes later, she saw a man standing over Genevieve, and her silent friend lying still on the ground.

Hattie screamed, but her hoarse, whispery scratch barely left her own throat. So she ran.

By the time Hattie dragged the constable out to the field, Genevieve was dead and the man was gone. Hattie was beside herself, her quiet tears coursing down her face. Even if she'd wanted to explain what she'd seen, she wasn't able to. Her ruined, raspy voice came out in sobs. She made furious motions with her hands, but no one could interpret them. She was hysterical, they said. She'd suffered a fright, finding her friend in the field like that. She needed to rest and recover before she hurt herself.

The townspeople gathered that night to talk about this latest, horrific infliction on their town. They met in the largest building—the church—and their anxious voices carried around the room. Well, most of their voices. A handful of them sat silently in a back pew, their hands clenched tightly together, their eyes brimming with fear and shock and something else the townspeople failed to recognize: a rising anger.

People talked over each other all night. The constable called for calm, the schoolteacher called for vigilance, the reverend called for prayer. The girls in the back row were no longer able to call for anything, and no one looked to them.

Hattie Crawford pushed open the church doors just past nine o'clock, having climbed out her window and run through the moonlit streets to reach the meeting. She couldn't yell to draw attention to herself, so she ran down the aisle and jumped onto the altar, throwing her hands up toward the beamed roof. She held a piece of paper that read, in large, graphite letters: I SAW HIM.

The townspeople gasped.

"Who was it, girl?" asked the reverend.

Hattie Crawford lowered one arm, her finger extended into a hard line. She pointed right into the first pew, at Mayor Gage.

A collective intake of breath, and then, uproar.

Could it be?

She's mad.

She's hysterical.

She never should have gotten out of bed.

Hattie's expression of righteous anger crumpled into disbelief. She tried to yell that she wasn't lying, but her voice, of course, was lost. She stamped her feet. She waved her arms. That only swayed the townspeople against her.

Mayor Gage rose.

"Please, all, leave her be," he said, magnanimous and grave, his hat in his hand. "Poor Hattie has suffered such an ordeal as the rest of us could never imagine. Her mind has never been strong to begin with, and it appears to be straining under a most cruel weight." He turned to face Hattie. "I forgive you, child."

Hattie's face turned redder than her hair. Her eyes went black. Her mouth opened and issued out what would have been an ear-shattering scream; as it was, the noise that came out of her throat was strained and torn. It sounded like a dying thing, half ghost already, issuing its last call of useless rage.

More saddened than shocked at this display, the townspeople slowly surrounded Hattie and led her carefully from the church.

That night, while the town of Little Falls turned fitfully in their beds, the voiceless young women arose and wandered out into the streets. They walked without candles, the moonlight all that guided them. They stuck to the shadows at the sides of the roads. They met in the field where Polly Franklin had been found. They stood in a loose circle, eyes roaming from one face to another.

They could not speak above soft whispers, but they found they did not have to. They looked into each other's eyes and they saw their own thoughts, their own emotions laid bare. They saw their own resolve.

They'd lost their voices.

They'd lost their friends.

They'd lost their right to control their own lives, their own bodies, their own selves.

They would not lose one more thing.

WHILE THE TOWNSPEOPLE OF LITTLE FALLS LAY IN THEIR beds, staring at the ceiling or tossing in fitful rest or locked in nightmares, Mayor Gage slept soundly. His comfortable room was shrouded in darkness, his linen sheets pulled up under his chin. He did not hear the window in his parlor as it slowly slid open. He did not hear the bare feet on the polished wood or the swishing of skirts as they filed into his rooms.

What he did hear, finally, was a whisper.

We see you.

Gage's eyes popped open, the sound of the whisper still resonating in his ear. He could not tell at first if he had truly heard it or only dreamed it. He stared into the darkened corners of his room, but all appeared to be in order—the wardrobe stood heavy and solid against the wall, the comfortable chair rested in the soft, thin moonlight coming in through the single window.

He let his eyes close once more.

We see you.

Gage's eyes opened even wider. This time he knew he had not been asleep or dreaming. And yet the whisper had been so faint it had barely registered above the sound of the wind pushing against the window's glass pane.

His eyes moved around the room quicker this time—not yet panicked, but no longer calm. His heart hammered in his chest. But the room was still and undisturbed. Everything was in its place. He left his eyes open for two minutes, just to make sure, before telling himself he was being ridiculous and letting them fall closed again.

We know what you did.

The whisper was closer this time, as though someone had spoken just a few feet from his ear. As if someone had been hovering over him.

Gage shot up in bed, looking around wildly.

But still, no one was there. No one stood near his bed. No one was in the room at all.

Gage lay back slowly on his pillows, but his eyes remained wide open. A bead of sweat dripped down his forehead. Was he losing his mind? Hearing voices that weren't there? But they'd sounded so *real*.

He was completely still. He strained so hard to hear any little noise in his room that he jumped at the sound of a branch scribbling against the outside of his window. He let out a long exhale, and the noise of it seemed to expand in his room. He considered that maybe he should get up and go to his office, try to get some work done while he was so wide awake. But he could not get himself to swing his feet out of his bed.

The whispers returned.

They were soft and difficult to make out. It sounded as if three or more people might be whispering to each other at once and from all directions. From the wardrobe near his wall. From behind his chair. From under his bed.

Gage shrank back against his pillows, his breaths coming fast and shallow. The whispers grew more insistent. *It's surely nothing*, he told himself.

Wind caught in a draft.

Voices carrying in from down the street.

But he suspected his heart would not stop hammering and his fists would not unclench until he knew, with absolute surety, that he was alone in his room.

Gage slowly counted to ten. Then he sucked in a deep breath, pushed back his linen covers, and lowered his feet onto the cold floor.

The whispers lowered, then rose again. The words were still too indistinct to make out. Where were they coming from?

It sounded like they were everywhere.

He tilted his head, listening. A whisper rose from below him, he was sure of it.

Slowly, his eyes still darting around the room, Gage lowered himself to his knees. He put his palms on the floor and dropped his head to look under the bed—and there he saw a pair of dark eyes, gleaming. They shone out through two holes in a smooth white mask that covered half a pale face. The line of the mask ended at a pair of lips, which slowly moved. Which slowly mouthed.

I see you.

The lips curved into a smile, and Gage yelled out.

He quickly scrambled back, but the masked figure under his bed moved quicker. An arm shot out toward Gage, and through the darkness and the shadows, he saw what came flying for him —the sharpened edge of a silver scalpel.

The scalpel's point just missed Gage's arm, and he yelped again as he jumped to his feet. The movement propelled his body back against his chair, so its wooden arm poked painfully into his side. But even more shocking than that was the way his chair stayed absolutely still when he'd crashed into it, rather than shoving against the wall. Almost as if there were something behind the upholstered back, keeping the chair in place . . .

Gage's eyes fixed on the chair as another figure rose, slowly, from behind its back. This creature wore a long, flowing dress and a mask identical to that of the girl with the scalpel under the bed. The mask was smooth and white, practically shining. When the second girl reached her full height, her head cocked slightly, as if taking stock of Gage. As if finding him lacking. Her eyes behind the mask were shadowy pits, impossible to make out in the darkness. Her cruel lips stretched into a hungry smile.

"What do you want?" Gage barked, barely able to hear his own voice over the sound of his blood pounding in his ears.

In response, the masked girl behind the chair held up her own scalpel and ticked it slowly back and forth.

Gage stumbled backward, keeping his eyes on the girl behind the chair and on the other girl who was now slithering out from under his bed. He missed his doorway and backed into his wardrobe. Its door popped open a crack, and through it Gage saw the white gleam of another mask. Another hand reaching for him . . .

We see you, the girl in the wardrobe whispered. The rest joined in, their voices overlapping and filling the room. Filling every part of Gage's mind.

We know what you are.

We know what you've done.

He screamed.

Gage threw open his bedroom door and bolted down the hallway. In the doorway that led to his study another girl stood stock-still in her long skirts, her masked face cocked to the side, watching Gage as he ran by.

We know you.

Yet another masked figure blocked the entrance to his kitchen. When he passed her, she slashed out quickly, her arm moving in a wide arc. This time Gage didn't see the blade, but he felt it opening a line of skin just below his shoulder. The girl stayed still as Gage ran away. His feet thudded against the wood floor as he reached his front room and pulled roughly on the door. But instead of opening onto the cool night, the door remained steadfastly closed. As if something was jamming it—or pulling on it from the other side.

Gage, panicked, stumbled to the large window of his front room. He took a book from a side table and raised his hand to pitch it through the glass when he saw a figure outside the window. This one was taller than the others, and he could see her reddish hair behind her mask. She didn't smile. She didn't cock her head to the side. She didn't whisper. She walked resolutely forward, moving slowly, getting nearer and nearer to the glass.

Though this new masked girl was outside, she frightened Gage even more than the others had. The book dropped from his hand. His feet moved unconsciously away from the window and the horrifically placid mask moving nearer to him on the other side of the glass. He took one step back, then two. On the third, he bumped into something solid. The red-haired figure on the other side of the window flinched back a moment, as if she'd been bumped, too. And that's when Gage knew, in a split second of terror, that the girl advancing slowly toward him wasn't outside the house at all. She was merely a reflection.

Of someone right behind him.

The whispers intensified as Gage slowly, slowly turned around to see the masked girl standing directly in front of him. The other figures were flowing into the room, their voices barely louder than the swishing of their long, heavy skirts.

We see you.

We know what you did.

We know it all.

He could not see their faces, but he knew them. He knew them by the long, thin scars that ran down their necks in vertical lines. The girl with the red hair was inches from Gage's face. Still, even this close, he could not make out her eyes behind the mask. The two holes looked deep as empty wells.

No more.

Her whisper was so faint, for a moment Gage wondered if he'd heard it at all, or if he'd imagined it. Then the girl's hand shot out, quick as the moonlight that now glinted off the edge of the scalpel she held. The blade punctured the outside of Gage's neck and traced across the skin and meat and tendons there, cutting cleanly through. A little too cleanly through.

Before the blackness creeping at the edges of his eyes could fully overtake his vision, Gage saw the final, stoic masked girl drop her scalpel. Her fist shot out toward his neck, her fingers reaching into the slit as if digging for change in a purse. Her fingertips grasped the pulpy red mass of his throat, and she *pulled.*

No more.

THE BODY OF MAYOR GAGE WAS FOUND THE NEXT DAY. HE lay in his nightclothes on the wooden floor of his empty home, his eyes still open in terror. His neck was a gaping, bloody hole, and the insides of his throat had been shredded. The rips were not made cleanly, as if by an animal's teeth or claws; it was more like his gullet had been forcibly torn to pieces by dozens of furious human fingers. This final murder sent a seismic ripple through the town of Little Falls. Not just because of its brutality, but because the same night the mayor died, the voiceless girls of the township disappeared. They left without a trace, their possessions still in their rooms, their hats still hanging from bedposts, their shoes still tucked neatly by their front doors.

They just . . . vanished.

Some in town claimed to have seen strange things that final, fateful night. Ben Livingston swore up and down that he looked out his window and saw a group of girls moving through a field of fog, silent as ghosts. The reverend's nephew claimed to see a trail of blood down the corner from the mayor's office, but later such trail could never be recovered. And the surgeon, whom Gage had brought to town so recently, vanished in the night as well. He left behind his entire collection of supplies and his surgical bag (which was absent several scalpels) and was never seen or heard from again.

Word began to filter in from other towns. Other wealthy, powerful men found slaughtered in their beds, their throats cut or ripped clean out. Some claimed to see masked figures with bloody hands dancing in the moonlight shortly after the murders were committed. Others swore they saw a pack of girls, dressed like nightmares, standing silent among the trees of the woods. The young women of Little Falls never returned home, and over time, their legend grew. Whenever there was a tale of a woman silenced or abused, the voiceless apparitions would arrive to enact their bloody justice.

Others, of course, dismissed these tales. As time stretched on, the notion of a group of masked murderesses seemed more and more far-fetched. How could a simple group of voiceless girls command so much fear? It was ludicrous to imagine. As one season stretched into the next, the town of Little Falls began, once again, to relax.

Of course it was all hearsay, they said, shaking their heads and huffing. They went about their business of mending socks and plowing land and filling pews. But even still, they sometimes looked to the fields, as if expecting to see a row of girls out there silently cresting the horizon. They simply gave terse nods to young women who laughed too loud or went outside with bare heads, for the argument was not worth the fuss. And just on the cusp of hushing their daughters they'd pause and wonder —for just a moment—and then would still their own tongues instead.

Silly, they said before locking their windows at night.

Rumor run amok, they said while leaving just one candle lit in the dark.

Nothing more than whispers.

LINDSEY KLINGELE is the author of THE TRUTH LIES HERE and THE MARKED GIRL duology. In addition to writing YA novels, she's also worked in the writers' rooms of some of your favorite cancelled teen dramas. Raised in Michigan, she now lives in Los Angeles with her husband and pit bull, and she can be found online at www.lindseyklingele.com.

One last bite from Lindsey Klingele...

When I set out to write a short, feminist horror story, a single image sprang to mind – vengeful suffragettes with scalpels. THE WHISPERS was born from that image, although it quickly came to revolve around something more. I wanted to explore the ques-

tion of what might happen if a repressive society literally took away the voices of women—and those women fought back in bloody style.

My favorite feminist read of the past few years is THE POWER by Naomi Alderman.

SMILE

EMILEE MARTELL

"Hey, sweetheart, smile!"

She stopped walking and turned. An expression of polite puzzlement entered her eyes as she examined the two men twitching like flies at the mouth of the alley.

"Got a pretty face but you're lookin' all mean."

"C'mon, be a good girl, don't be shy!"

For the briefest moment, her eyes narrowed. Then she relaxed. Slowly, sweetly, her lips began to curve until a flawless Cupid's bow of a smile graced her face. The two men whooped.

"That's it, gorgeous, knew you'd look good!"

Most women didn't smile. Those that would usually kept walking, a little faster than before. But this one stood directly in front of them, a tremendous grin on her face as though nothing pleased her more. The men felt triumphant.

Except several moments passed and she was still standing there, smiling wider and wider. One of the men coughed. The other smiled back, weakly.

"You need something else, hon?"

She said nothing. Her smile kept growing. Grotesque now,

her lips stretched as far as they could go, teeth shining in the morning sun.

"Hey, man," one of them said under his breath to the other. "I think something's wrong with this chick."

The corners of her mouth split backward to the hinge of her jaw, and her teeth sprang into points like a cat's claws unsheathing.

"Holy shit—"

She pounced.

EMILEE MARTELL is an aspiring YA author who daydreams of having the power of the woman in this story. Until she unlocks hidden mutations in her genes or receives the blessing of a vengeful goddess, though, she works at a garden-based nonprofit by day and writes otherworldly novels, short stories, and flash fiction by night. This is her first time appearing in print. Visit her at emartellauthor.wordpress.com.

One last bite from Emilee Martell...

Internalized misogyny isn't just for men. Growing up in a sleepy town where no one stood on street corners whistling at you, I thought catcalling was sexy and desirable, just like in the movies. Then I moved to the city and realized it's not flattering; it's frightening. There's nothing quite like the helplessness of being a woman out walking alone, wishing you could pick a fight with the assholes who think shouting at you is great fun but knowing your aim with pepper spray isn't good enough to take the risk. I began to imagine what it would be like to turn the tables, using the smile everyone always wants to see.

POTLUCK
KAMERHE LANE

Potato Salad.

It's the first thing they see when they come down the stairs into the church basement. Anyone could have told Karen the weather's too cold for it. Could have told her not to leave it set out like that either. Must be hours now with the length of that service. But Karen didn't ask, so who is anyone to tell?

The mayo won't spoil, Karen says to no one, to everyone. She used the fat-free kind.

Nods. Smiles. Not a hint of disapproval as the salad's consistency is noted. Cubed. Not shredded. Shredded makes for a creamier dish, but it'll taste just fine. Of course it will.

Karen recently joined Jenny Craig or Nutrisystem or some such program. Now all her cooking is free of something—fat, sugar, gluten, pleasure. The membership was a Christmas gift from her mother-in-law because she knows the Gilchrist men like women with control and it's easier to watch weight than watch him with the office assistant who does yoga.

Iced Tea.

Karen's daughters take the powder and the long-handled spoons from their grandmother. She taught them how to get the color right last summer. They retrieve the serving jugs from the kitchen. They're old enough now to take on the responsibility. They did the same at the last potluck. Was it Melinda's new granddaughter's christening? Who can remember? Melinda would likely rather forget—her husband served her divorce papers soon after, told her with the kids gone he'd like to see more of the world, explore the possibilities. Surely she'd seen this coming. Surely she wasn't happy either. Surely she'd like to explore too.

Everyone likes iced tea. No sugar. This isn't the South. Thank God.

Green Bean Casserole and Creamed Corn.

Melinda's aunt Donna's specialty. But make sure to use French's Fried Onions and RITZ Crackers, nothing store-brand. And make sure the right Donna is asked. The other Donna microwaves hers. No one thought it even possible. But Other Donna managed it.

She's a single mom, has two jobs. That's the only explanation that makes any sense to the older women.

Not to worry this time, though. The right Donna made them. The potholders are a giveaway. Khaki-green-and-yellow-daisy crochet. Mary had a matching set.

Mary.

Paper Plates and Paper Napkins.

Donna's daughter—her name starts with a "D" too, something like Darby or Darcy—brings them because she doesn't cook.

She doesn't cook gets echoed back. A question. A failing. A fluke. A prayer whispered low never to be answered.

Tater Tot Casserole.

Two 15x10 Pyrex dishes full of it. Stacey bought the second one when she took over Thanksgiving dinner from her mother last year. Who else in the family was going to do it? Other Donna—heavens, no.

Stacey always knew it was hard work, but she never appreciated the hardest part was pretending it wasn't hard work, that it was rewarding and fulfilling in the way all hard things are, aren't they?

Both dishes are gloriously hot. Wrapped in newspaper and foil and stained kitchen towels relegated to this purpose alone. The tater tots and cheese are burnt to a crust that will soften with the steam and be served right before any sogginess takes hold.

This is not the work of a novice. Stacey is practiced. Perfect. It's her house that her teenaged son's friends flock to. He'll remember that when he's older. When she does the same for his kids. When she dies. He'll remember his mother made perfect casseroles, and his wife will turn her back to wipe the counter or clear the plates, to deflect the comparison. Accomplishments of one becoming the shortcomings of another.

Butternut Squash and Kale Salad.

It's roasted. No oil. Only ninety-five calories per serving. A recipe from a blog. A gift their grandmothers never had, God rest them.

The brown bits are quinoa. Such a good grain. Burns belly fat. Lowers cholesterol. Makes hair shine and fingernails grow long and feminine.

Keeps demons at bay.

It's a joke. Donna's daughter, Darcy, is joking. But Laura— the one who's not from here, the one whose husband brought her here from somewhere else, the one whom Stacey befriended and suggested a simple Bundt cake or rhubarb kuchen, the one who set her alarm for 4:30 this morning so she could roast the vegetables, soak the quinoa, chop the kale, squeeze in forty minutes on the elliptical, and still be out of the shower before her husband woke—that Laura is not amused.

Scotcheroos.

No one asked Olyve to bring them. No one asked the family to bring anything. Certainly not scotcheroos. At an occasion like this one? This is a church basement, not a backyard. But no one can tell that from the shortness of her hem. Maybe that's what happens when a *y* replaces a perfectly good *i* in a name as simple and old as Olive.

Olyve is Mary's granddaughter, and at nineteen, she's anything but simple or old. They all think of Mary when she walks in.

Oh, Mary. Poor Mary.

Did Mary look like that when she was nineteen? They stare at Olyve. With her jangly anklet, the tattoo snaking up her calf, the ass that every man gawks at when they trample down the stairs and charge to the food tables. The scotcheroos disappear fast, and when Olyve smirks, something on her face catches the light. A tear drop embedded below her eye. It's new. No, it's not a sticker. It's permanent. And she says Mary would love it as much as she loved scotcheroos. And though there was no argument in the first place—not in a church basement, not on a day like this, not in front of all these people—that ends the argument.

Ambrosia Salad.

Too many maraschino cherries. Mary's cousin Pauline catches her grandnephews making nipple jokes, but her husband lays his hand on her arm.

Let it be. No harm. They're just playing.

But play is supposed to be fun. What's fun about this? What's fun about fretting over a nineteen-year-old's hemline?

Deviled Eggs and Ham Rolls.

Their absence is noted early. Empty spaces on the divided relish trays. Bread-and-butter pickles. Black olives from a can. Celery stuffed with peanut butter and cream cheese with plastic-wrap etchings still visible on their tops. All are present and accounted for. Except the items Pauline's daughter told Jennifer to bring.

Someone dares to ask.

A huff in her daughter's breathing, a set in her jaw. Pauline will take care of it. She'll explain. How her granddaughter Jennifer is running late. How Jennifer's picking up her girl-friend. No, wait—fiancée now. How they'll both be here soon. The food too.

Pauline smiles. Her daughter mirrors it. It's fine. Every-thing's fine.

There are side glances. The young, combative ones await the challenge. The old ones say nothing. An honest-to-goodness lesbian. Certainly not their first, but maybe the first to pronounce it so boldly, to thwart the polite nothingness of "friend." They busy hands to seem unfazed, shuffle dishes and point out better placements. Conversations sprout from nowhere as they serve brothers, nephews, neighbor boys. Diversionary topics like state basketball tournaments and work promotions and hair that's so long he couldn't possibly see with it hanging in his eyes like that.

But nothing stops the questions in their heads. Two women together like that. What does Jennifer's mother think? Her father? Who will wear the dress at the wedding? The pants in the marriage? What's sex like without a man? What's love like without . . .

There's a word for it.

They won't say it. Not even in their heads.

But they can't be the only one thinking it. Thinking about what it must be like to love someone, be in love with someone, make love to someone who knows. Who feels this feeling they all feel. This feeling they all know too well but can never remember the word for. What's the word?

Jell-O Mold.

A clatter. A platter breaks. A dome of red Jell-O upends, the pineapple chunks suspended in it frozen like time. Two tiny hands clutch a tablecloth.

They were in their heads. All of them. The men look at the child then look at them.

Whose is he? Which one is in charge of him, of his mess?

Quick. Quick. Put the thoughts away. Focus on the task at hand.

Fix. Wipe. Discard. Replenish.

Smile.

It's fine. Everything's fine.

Dessert Bars.

Lemon bars. Raspberry bars. Butterscotch bars. Bars with chocolate chips and walnuts and marshmallows and blueberries and chunks of candy. The little girls cut them into squares and arrange them on napkins. They serve like it's play—but play is supposed to be fun?—and the men indulge them, digging spare-change tips from pockets, signing homemade receipts scrawled in pencil and crayon. When the girls announce their play restaurant is closed, the men allow themselves to be herded upstairs while the women hang back to clean up.

Sparkling Wine.

Mary's daughter, Olyve's mother, sneaks it in through the back. The bottles clink in her reusable Hy-Vee grocery bags. No one has the heart to tell her it's not champagne. But it's sweet and bubbly and the last thing anyone would think appropriate for the occasion. *Anyone* is not here, though, and they can make an exception for Mary. A private, hidden exception for a woman with a private, hidden love of silly luxuries.

Poor Mary.

There are four bottles, but they only open two. No need to be wasteful. Someone could take the remaining bottles home for a birthday or a special night. No one wants to end up like Melinda.

They gather in a circle. Not planned. It just happens that way. Simple and strong. A shape without a head, without an apex. Old and young mix, no pattern or hierarchy, just shared experience.

They toast.

To Mary.

No words but that. They smile with downcast eyes. Light, wispy ghosts of smiles, seen only in peripheries and vanishing as soon as they're spotted. Shadow dwellers, those smiles.

A laugh bubbles up through lips. Quickly covered. Swallowed.

More sips, sweet and tingly.

The circle doesn't break.

Leftovers.

Their minds should be on other things. There is more day yet. What to do with all this food? Who brought Tupperware? Plastic wrap? So much fussing to do. So much divvying up. Apportioning to. Sharing of leftover recipes from harder times when no food was ever wasted.

But the circle doesn't break.

Someone lifts her eyes first. Her eyes into another's eyes. Their smiles widen. Spread. Soon a contagion. They're big now. Brash. Toothy grins not meant to be concealed, not meant to be buried.

Then comes the laughter that is more than laughter. It's chortling. It's guffawing. It's bigger and bolder than the bodies they inhabit, the spaces they're allowed.

A stair creaks.

The circle goes silent but remains intact.

A little boy in a little boy's suit takes little boy steps in that jerky manner of little boys learning to conquer stairs, learning to conquer worlds. He stares at them. Ten maybe fifteen women, all in black, in a circle. And he knows—it's in his eyes—there's something to fear here among these women. Something to be broken and tamed. These black-clad women with their cackled secrets.

He's too young to have the thought, but still it's there, half-formed. He thinks, Did they kill her? Did they kill poor Mary, cold and dead in that coffin just a floor above? Are they gathered to rejoice at the destruction of their own? Everyone knows that's what women are like. No greater enemy than each other.

The little boy stares.

They could hiss at him. He would startle and run. Run in that jerky, little-boy way that all men do when they're scared of what they don't understand.

The circle holds. It breaths. In. Out. In.

Hold.

The little boy reaches out a hand. A hand that wants. A hand that needs.

The circle is silent. Silent and still.

Just a moment more.

More.

Then there are husbands and sons with cars running on the street above. They won't wait any longer. They don't wait. They move for the table, stacking dishes without care, without lids or covers. Spilling. Jostling. Crushing.

The circle disintegrates. Let me do that, they say. They smile. They put down their glasses, sparkling wine half-drunk, its toast half-said.

Minutes pass. Mindless chatter. A new set of diversionary topics. Plans for the funeral flowers. For the freezer meals. For all the tasks Mary left undone.

Then the moment comes. They're scattered about the room. The circle is not visible, but it's still there. Somehow it's still there.

They stop talking. All of them. Throughout the room. The men mill about them, oblivious.

They lift their glasses again and think about Mary. Not poor Mary, this time—just Mary.

"To Mary," someone says. Or maybe they all say. Hard to tell. "She's free."

KAMERHE LANE is a former international teacher who traveled the world before realizing she just wanted to come back to Iowa and write stories about home. She is represented by Adriann Ranta Zurhellen of Foundry Literary + Media.

One last bite from Kamerhe Lane...

POTLUCK is inspired by every family and community gathering I've ever attended and by the masked complexity of the Midwestern woman.

My favorite feminist reads are Margaret Atwood's short story GERTRUDE TALKS BACK and Sady Doyle's non-fiction TRAINWRECK: THE WOMEN WE LOVE TO HATE, MOCK, AND FEAR ... AND WHY.

THE CHANGE

KATE KARYUS QUINN

They gave us the talk
in fourth grade.
It used to be fifth grade,
but girls are becoming women
earlier and earlier.
The year before it happened to
Susan Bartlett
during summer vacation.
She was only nine years old.

The day they took
the girls aside
we were all clutching stuffed animals.
They were tiny,
the length of a finger,
and softer than a newborn kitten's belly.
We were all rabidly
collecting and trading them.
A pink elephant,
a tiny yellow gemstone glinting

from the tip of its trunk,
exchanged
for a blue camo-print teddy bear,
with two golden suns shimmering in each eye.

They didn't tell us anything we didn't already
     know.
You will become women.
Your bodies will change.
It will be alarming.
There is nothing you can do to stop it.
There is nothing you can do to prepare.
There is only knowing
and waiting
and wondering
when.

By the end of sixth grade
every girl but me
had grown and changed
and fully become
what anyone with eyes could see
was a woman.
I felt both left out
and relieved.

Seventh grade passed without incident.

Then
halfway through eighth grade
I awoke one morning
with a horrible pain
in the depths of my guts.

I could not get out of bed.
My mother came in and knew at once
what was happening.

"At last," she said
not with joy
or relief
but resignation.

We had all known
I could not dodge it forever.

That afternoon I began to bleed.

It was not horrible
and of course
women for centuries
have had to deal with menses
in worse conditions
than my warm bathroom.

The pain that had gripped
me earlier eased,
but I returned to my bed
regardless,
sliding beneath the covers,
pulling an old doll
into my arms.
Knowing worse was yet to come.

Womanhood felt like
a strange land,
one whose border

I'd finally crossed.
But I had not yet
reached its
awful capital,
nor been fully
sworn in
as one of its citizenry.

I fell asleep
and woke retching.
Nothing came up.
My stomach was empty,
readied for this moment.
Mother had come in
while I slept.
She held me and rocked me
while every bone in my body
twisted.

The sun was rising by the time
it was over.

Mother helped me
so that I might stumble toward the bathroom
on uncertain feet.
The aching aftermath of pain
remained,
giving off a strange hum inside me.

I turned off the lights,
afraid of what I might see.

In the shower

I ran my hands over my head
across the tips of my ears
down the length of my back.

All was as it had always been.

I tested my shoulders,
arms,
even the spaces between my toes.

Still I could detect no change.
How could I be twisted apart and put together
    again
with nothing out of place?

I ran my tongue along my teeth.
Nothing here either.

I had come out of it whole.
A girl still.

But even as I thought it,
I knew it was untrue.
No woman goes unchanged.

"What happened?"
my dearest of friends asked,
the next day at school.
"Was it your time?"

She wore a heavy wool coat
though the day was warm.
She had to wear it at all times

while on school grounds
to tame the sharp quills that
marched along the length of her spine.

All the changed girls had to hide who they were.
What they'd become.
Rules and regulations
nearly the whole world over
required special clothing or accessories
to hide and disguise
while at school
or other official government buildings.

Those that grew dangerously curved horns
from the tops of their heads
had wigs or elaborate hairdos.
Those with tails wore skirts,
full and long,
to hide their endlessly twitching bits of flesh—
some soft and slinky,
others corded with a burst of spikes at the end
like an angry star
exploding.

It would, of course, be distracting
to have these uniquely womanly
body parts on display
in a place of learning.
Young men's eyes will wander
while their minds wonder . . .

Girls—
the girls these women had once been

—were not so very different from those boys.

But women
are so clearly
so obviously
strange.
And foreign
And odd.
Almost a different species entirely.

"I changed,
but nothing changed,"
I tell my friend.
She frowned,
not understanding.

My Mother had a similar reaction
when I came out of the bathroom,
wrapped in a towel,
hair wet down my back.
"Whatever it is,
you'll survive it,"
she said,
as she stroked the spikes
that crowned each of her knuckles.
(She has specially made gloves for when she
    wishes to be discreet.)
I shook my head,
not knowing how to explain.

News spreads of my unchanging change.
I am a woman
without armor.

Back in third grade
they told us the change
was a mistake,
an experiment gone wrong
or too far.
Women were under siege,
they needed a way
to balance the scales.
Women were too weak.
They needed a built-in
defense mechanism.

Later, I asked Mom
"Why change the women?
Men being too mean was the real problem . . .
wasn't it?"
Mom sighed.
Then asked if I remembered the story
of Adam and Eve.
I did.
But she retold it anyway.
Emphasizing Adam was
Made by God.
Adam was the original.
Eve lesser,
an imperfect copy.
You don't weaken
that which was made
perfectly by God himself.
Instead you try to bring Eve
up to par.

Except it didn't work.

The change only made women
stranger
odder
less like men
lesser than men,
which made it easy
to justify the hunts.
The thrill of the chase
had never been more
thrilling.
Imagine a women's
horned head
mounted on your wall.
It didn't help that
new weapons laws passed—
a way of evening things out
so they said.
Women were always armed,
so men must be as well.
Fair is fair
they said.

I asked Mom
another question.
What the people
behind the change
had expected to happen.
"Was this it?"
She laughed,
said I asked tough questions.
"Was this it?"
I persisted.
"I don't know,"

she answered at last.
"I don't think so.
I don't think this was what they wanted.
But it happened too fast.
Evolution
is meant to be slow.
But this . . .
In a generation,
maybe two,
everything changed.
Whether we wanted to
or not."

My best friend
has been distant
since I've told her
I didn't change.
I know she hoped
I'd take after my
mother, growing
horns or ridges
of some sort.

Girls post-change
become clannish.
On weekends
groups of them
stroll the long open avenues
with shops on either side
their tails not hidden
like at school
but out and open
twined together.

Men whistle
while older women
cluck and say
they're courting trouble.
Others are more secretive.
You hear of their
sleepover parties
finding new hairstyles
to deceive
or adding waxed sheen
and filing tips.

I now fit in
nowhere.

Doctors insist on
taking my blood.
They perform other tests too,
trying to understand.

And then suddenly
I am news.
Not just at school,
but everywhere.
A hope for the future,
a return to the past.
When women were soft
and simple
and sweet.

I am wanted in a way
all girls know
will come with the change.

But more so.

Mother and I go into hiding
from the men
who wish to make me mother
to their children.
They hope for more like me.
Changed,
but unchanged.

A network of women
protect us.
Transferring us from one place
to the next.
They argue amongst themselves
whether I am worth
saving.
They do not want
to go back.
They think what we have gained
is well worth
what we've lost.

"Don't worry."
The old woman who drives us
from one safe house
to the next
pats my head
from where I'm seated on the floor.
The engine's soft purr
lulls me to sleep
even as my legs cramp
from being curled up

and hidden on the floorboards.

In between naps she tells me stories.
She is old enough to remember the
"good old days"
though she laughs
and says,
"They weren't so good
or so much different than now."

Her mother and
two older sisters
were soft,
which is to say
they didn't change.
"We all figured
our family was safe,
and then at thirteen
I bled for the first time
and later that night
grew fangs."

At first,
her family hid her away.
The change was still
so new,
but also
multiplying quickly.
A girl with a tail
no longer earned a double take,
only old-fashioned
stares.

But no one had heard
of a girl with fangs,
sharp and glistening
with the promise of poison.
Five years later,
fangs were so common
there were plastic caps
you could find in the
modification aisle
of any major store,
easy to fit over the offending teeth.
But by then
hers had already been pulled.
She kept them in an old
jewelry box
with a spinning ballerina,
right beside her baby teeth.
The space where
they had been
never
stopped
aching.

"Do you think
there will be more
like me?"
I asked,
softly.

"Oh, yes, I should
think so,
it seems to be the way of
the change.

There were tails,
then fangs,
quills and ridges
seemed to come pretty quickly together,
the winged girls were later
and still rare,
though less so than we think,
so many stay in hiding—
too many men
think it's cute
to make great gilded cages.
Oh yes, there will be more
like you,
whatever you are."

I thought this would
be comforting,
except I couldn't help
thinking of the winged girls.

What good is it
to fly away
when eventually
you must land?

We ran for years
often hiding in plain sight.
Inspired by my friend
I put caps on my teeth
and pretended to have
fangs beneath.

But we could never

stay anywhere for long.

And though I read
the newsfeeds every day
hoping to hear of another girl
like me
who was changed
but not changed—
there was nothing.

We were on the road once more,
driving into the new drylands.
With every passing mile
more green leached away,
giving way to towns torn apart
by fires
or tornadoes
and then abandoned
rather then rebuilt.
It made me sad almost
or wistful
for something lost forever.
But Mom laughed when
I told her this.
"Most of those people
moved north to the
New South
and rebuilt
their houses and towns
same as it was here—
but nicer."

As another dead town

disappeared behind us
I couldn't help thinking
how we refused to learn
from the past,
but rather used it as a blueprint
for our future.

My defanged friend
was at the wheel
dozing
while the autosteer kept us moving,
and so there was no one
to see or give warning
as they advanced
and surrounded us.

It was Adam's Soldiers.
Obvious at a glance.
All forty or so of them
shirtless and bearing
the same horizontal scar
of puckered flesh
across their right breast.
To be a member
they removed the same rib
given to Eve.

The network of women had laughed at these
      fools,
removing a part of themselves
in response to the change.
But I realized then,
too late,

it was a laugh meant to hide
their fright.

They were all of them armed.
Guns.
Dark and black and deadly
their red laser sights
dotting us red
all over our bodies.

Then our dear driver's head
exploded.
My friend,
they wouldn't have considered her
a casualty.
No, to them she was
nothing
but a handy pincushion
for their bullets.

I screamed
and then they were on
Mother and me
already cheering our capture
while their leader
loudly announced plans
to take and test
Mother's remaining eggs.

Her only value was in making
more of me.

But first:

her hands.

Any women with
Adam's Soldiers
must be as soft
and simple
and sweet
as Eve.

You hear stories
of women who choose
to join them.
They cut their own tails
or burn their own flesh
and come to the camp unclothed
and willing.

But we are not.

I am stunned
unable to believe
this is happening
though the sun beats down
and dust coats my tongue
as Mother's hand is placed upon
the chopping block.

She makes a fist with her shaking hand
and the sharp ridges
at her knuckles
crown.

And then it happens so fast,

I blink away the sweat
a half-second, no more.
But when I look again,
her
      right hand
is gone.

I scream my throat raw
as Mother slumps in the hot sun,
but neither of these developments
concern them.

They cauterize the stump where
Mother's hand had been,
and then they reach
for the other.

This second hand,
limp and unresisting,
is put to the block.
The knife flashes in the sun
and then slices down—
I squeeze my eyes shut
willing it to stop.
To freeze.

Wishing I could
     end
        them
           all.

There is an odd silence as my scream
dies.

My arms had been held behind me,
but now I easily
tug free
and place both my hands
over my face.
I fill them with tears.

It is a long time
until I open my eyes.
It is a long time
until I see
Adam's Soldiers
dead.
And already decorated with flies.

I fall to my knees before Mother.
Her left hand remains intact
the knife frozen above her
never to fall.

I wipe my tears.
I use the men's water
to wet my dry throat.
I get Mother into the car,
while she mumbles
incoherently.
I drive us away
further into the drylands
and then out,
through them,
to the other side.

It may look like we are scared.

Like we are running.
But we are not.
I am not.
Not anymore.

Mother will not understand,
but when she wakes up
I will explain it to her.
At first she will not believe
I stopped them with a thought.
With a wish.
But I will tell her of men
left stiff and frozen
whose hearts ceased to beat
all in the same instant.

And because
we are safe
and alive—
eventually—
she will believe.

From there it will be easy
to understand
how more like me
will come.
Even now
a girl might be bleeding.

"Don't be afraid,"
I will say to Mother,
taking her hand
in both of mine.

"The change is happening.
The change is here."

KATE KARYUS QUINN is an avid reader and menthol chapstick addict with a BFA in theater and an MFA in film and television production. She lives in Buffalo, New York with her husband, three children, and one enormous dog. She has three young adult novels published with HarperTeen: ANOTHER LITTLE PIECE, (DON'T YOU) FORGET ABOUT ME, AND DOWN WITH THE SHINE. She also recently released her first adult novel, THE SHOW MUST GO ON, a romantic comedy.

One last bite from Kate Karyus Quinn...

I have always loved stories about women who kick ass and take names. Wonder Woman. Buffy. Moana. But lately those stories don't feel like enough. The more women advance, the harder the opposing forces push back, determined to hang onto the status quo.

I spent a lot of time trying to figure out the ending to The Change. I knew that I wanted a story that was ultimately hopeful. It's my preference as a writer and a reader to find stories where all is not lost, where no matter how bleak things may get, there is always something better waiting up ahead. I also knew this anthology was called Betty Bites Back, not Betty Gives Up and Takes a Nap.

I ultimately decided on an ending where we finally see a true change. It's an internal change, rather than external - which felt right. And it suggests a future where the power structures are finally re-calibrated. What happens after that, I can't say. But I am hopeful for my main character and the world she plans to remake.

My favorite feminist reads are romance novels. Romance is a perennially disrespected genre, written off as fluffy fantasies with no substance. I don't think it's a coincidence that these are also stories primarily written and read by women. Two all-time faves: BET ME by Jennifer Crusie and LORD OF SCOUNDRELS by Loretta Chase.